THE PHOENIX
OF THE OPERA

THE PHOENIX
OF THE OPERA

A Novel

Sadie Montgomery

iUniverse, Inc.
New York Lincoln Shanghai

The Phoenix of the Opera

iUniverse books may be ordered through booksellers or by contacting:

iUniverse
2021 Pine Lake Road, Suite 100
Lincoln, NE 68512
www.iuniverse.com
1-800-Authors (1-800-288-4677)

This is a work of fiction. All of the characters, names, incidents, organizations, and dialogue in this novel are either the products of the author's imagination or are used fictitiously.

ISBN-13: 978-0-595-42966-0 (pbk)
ISBN-13: 978-0-595-87307-4 (ebk)
ISBN-10: 0-595-42966-1 (pbk)
ISBN-10: 0-595-87307-3 (ebk)

Printed in the United States of America

Acknowledgments

Generations of readers and moviegoers have enjoyed the tale of the Phantom of the Opera. Since Gaston Leroux's novel, the story has been revived time and time again. It has been told as a horror story, and it has been sung as a romance. There is more than a touch of Beauty and the Beast in my version of the tale, which begins where these others have ended.

This beginning owes much to my friends and family. Those who have read my manuscript—Cherie, Charlotte, and Kristi—gave me the confidence to pursue my writing. In particular I'd like to thank Betty, my first reader; Doug, my Angel of English; Zach, my first work of art; and my mother, Joan, who has brought this tale of the Phantom back home to Indiana.

Prologue
The Phantom of the Opera

... I am dying ... of love.... That is how it is ... I loved her so! ... And I love her still ... daroga ... and I am dying of love for her, I ... I tell you! ... If you knew how beautiful she was ... when she let me kiss her ... alive.... It was the first time I ever kissed a woman.... Yes, alive.... I kissed her alive ... and she looked as beautiful as if she had been dead!....

Gaston Leroux, *The Phantom of the Opera*

Should I have left him there?

It was a long, long time ago when I watched the young boy cringe from the slash of the whip, scrambling across the dirty straw on the floor of his cage. The "Devil's Child" was dressed only in ragged, stained pants that barely covered his scabrous knees, a burlap bag covered his features, and he was filthy from his broken toenails to the soft skin of his young chest. He seemed young, so young, younger than I. His arms were skinny, but he appeared to be at the cusp of great changes.

The "Devil's Child" hid his face. The dark man in the cage spoke of horrors of hell and told the crowd pressed against the bars to prepare to look on the hideous visage of the child of Satan himself. Pregnant women and young children were admonished to step back, for to look on the demon's face would surely cause the women to drop their unborn infants from their wombs and the children to be struck mad.

I tried to withdraw—a chill rippled down my frame—but my fellow ballet pupils from the Opera Populaire shoved me mercilessly against the bars in their effort to glimpse the most scandalous exhibit at the gypsy fair. I did not want to see the dark man grab the child who held fast to his burlap sack, a sack with two sad holes ripped from the fabric through which peered dark, haunted orbs. I did not want to watch as the man brought the whip down repeatedly across the boy's skin. Not a sound but the jeers of the crowd, not a whimper or groan, not one word to plead for mercy. I did not want to see the man yank the rough cloth from the child's face. But I did see it. I saw the long, lank hair fall forward over a face that took my breath away. The distorted features of half the child's face shocked us all, and I could feel the crowd take in a sudden, deep swallow of air as we tried to make sense of a child with half the face of an angel and half that of a monster.

For one second, it was as if time had stopped. And in that moment I saw the tear—one sole tear—tremble down a dirty face and in those eyes a jumble of pain and rage that appalled me more than the ugliness of his face. Then the silence gave way to harsh laughter, the coarse words, the jibes and jeers of those bodies around me. I alone made no sound. I looked at that boy, and I felt all the loneliness of the world in those eyes.

They threw coins at him as well as apple cores and bits of paper and pebbled stones and slowly, slowly they drew away. I felt them recede, but I stayed and watched as the dark man turned from the child and gathered the coins greedily. The boy crawled away and reached out for the burlap and slid it over his features.

My heart ached for his pain. The ballet mistress called to me to come follow the others. I slowly went to the opening in the tent. The sound of a strangled cry made me turn back toward the cage. He had risen to his full height, and I saw he was almost as tall as I. He had snuck behind the dark man and had thrown a piece of rough rope around his tormentor's neck and was squeezing tightly. The gypsy was unable to press his fingers between the noose and his neck. His tongue stuck out, swollen, from his blackened face, and I saw him fall. It did not occur to me to call for help. And when the man fell to the dirt, behind him the child looked directly at me. He made not a move; his silence pleaded with me. I rushed to him and bade him come.

He bent and found something lost in the dirty straw, a clumsy doll made from coarse cloth with the face of a monkey and tiny tin cymbals attached to its hands. Then he took my hand, and I dragged him from the tent, down the streets of Paris, through back alleyways, to the Opera Populaire. I pushed him through the grating that shielded one of the low set windows leading to the rooms below the opera house. I told him to wait for me, to hide. Then I joined Mme. Moreau and the others. Later I found him in the little chapel. He sat huddled against the cold stone, his arms wrapped round his knees, his small monkey clutched in his hand. He rose when I came into the small alcove, but he made not a sound. He simply stood and looked at me as he had in that horrid cage that smelled of urine and hay and cruelty and loss.

Down into the underground tunnels I led him. I told him I'd take care of him, that he should hide, and I left him there. I left him there for nearly twenty years.

He grew up in the opera house. I did what I could for him, but he soon learned to fend for himself. Using the complicated corridors and compartments of the opera, as well as the underground tunnels left by the rebels of the Communes, he found his way about the theater and back rooms as a silent shadow of the artists. Through careful observation, he learned music and painting and the basics of architecture and design from our own artisans and musicians. Only late in the night would he come forward and practice his crafts.

I rarely ventured down into his world. Although I pitied him, I was also frightened by him. Even in those first months and years—before I abandoned him for a brief time to make my own family—I could not force myself to descend to the lowest levels to comfort him. The others in the opera house heard him cry at night, and when from time to time something was missing or there were signs that something or someone had rummaged through the props or storage bins, they whispered among themselves, "It's the Opera Ghost, the Phantom." I held my tongue. It kept them from descending to his lair.

After my husband died, I returned with little Meg and took my place as the new mistress of the ballet school. He was still there in the catacombs and tunnels. He was no longer that skinny child, but had become a young man. I would see his shadow flit across the wall or along the backstage curtains and know he was close by. And then, one night when I could not sleep, I came upon him in one of the dressing rooms. A tall, broad shouldered youth dressed in elegant breeches, white ruffled shirt, an embroidered vest I remembered from a production of *Le Marriage de Figaro*, and a long black cape. His back was to me, and when I called his name, Erik, he turned suddenly. I had steeled myself to see that distorted, ungodly face of his, but what met my eyes was a white mask and two deep, dark green eyes. My breath caught in my throat, for he was beautiful and mysterious, the irregular features of his disfigurement hidden by the smooth, stark whiteness of the mask.

That was when we made our plan. I would be his face. I would negotiate on his behalf with the owner. I would bring his supplies and deliver his messages. He demanded a salary and as long as it was paid, he would be the angel of the opera house. But if his demands were not met, like the ghost they all thought him, he'd reek havoc on us all. He didn't cause any damage that couldn't be repaired. The slashed costume just minutes before the performance or the cut ropes that made the scenery shift impossible were enough to make the owner overcome his initial reluctance. From his salary, a minor amount was kept by me for my services as he insisted, another portion was employed for his needs, and yet another was invested in various accounts that I set up here and abroad. For many years, his arrangements at the Opera Populaire seemed to benefit us all and harm no one.

Although he slipped among us like a shadow, I was the only one with whom Erik exchanged a word, and even I did not reach out and touch him. How lonely those years must have been for him! And then he heard little Christine, an orphan I rescued and brought to the ballet dormitories to live and study alongside my own daughter. She grieved for her deceased father, a wonderful musician who had raised her as best he could since her mother's death. She slept in a small bed near the closet, beside that of my own Meg and the others. When Erik heard her cry, he stopped and sang for her, his voice eerily filtered through the hollow wood of the closet behind which ran one of his myriad passageways. He sang her to sleep. Meg heard him, too. Soon Christine slept without tears, but Erik did not completely forget her. Later he would sing to Christine in the chapel, and soon the young woman became his pupil. Even then he did not come out from the shadows, nor did he dare to reach out his hand to touch her.

My poor, poor Devil's Child thought he was her angel, her angel of music. Although he hid behind the mirror in her room, behind the walls and curtains of the opera house, he believed she knew him. He thought she understood and saw him for what he wished to be. And he thought she loved him as he loved her.

But Christine loved a boy she knew from her childhood, Raoul. And when she saw Raoul again—and he saw her—nothing and no one could come between them.

If Erik had revealed himself to her before Raoul came back into her life as the new patron of the Opera Populaire, if he had not hidden behind the mask, if he had not let her think he was her father's spirit or some fantastic angel of music, perhaps she might have loved him. He revealed himself at last—but only partially—on the night of her great success—his great success, too—when she premiered on the stage in place of the diva Carlotta. He took her to his secret rooms far, far below the opera house—a place I had rarely seen—and there he showed her his world, his world of darkness and music, where he hoped she'd join him. She slept, untouched, in his bed and upon waking, curious to know who this strange creature was, she lifted the mask from his face.

He was more horrified than she. He vowed she could never leave now that she knew his secret and had seen his shame. Yet he let her return to the world of light, to the opera. He warned her that she was his and his alone.

But Erik was mistaken to think no one else knew his secret. He found that Joseph Buquet, the company scene shifter, dogged his steps and had discovered some of his secret doors and passageways throughout the opera house. For some time Erik had known that Buquet spied on the artists as they dressed for their performances, but what most sickened him was that Buquet spied on the young girls as they dressed for bed in the ballet dormitories. When the new owners of the opera refused to respect the arrangement Erik had with the previous owner and would not take his demands seriously, he chose to make his point through Buquet. The diva Carlotta was not without influence, and even though Christine's debut had been a tremendous success, the older woman demanded that the young ingénue be given a lesser role in the next opera the company was to stage. Erik was incensed to see his pupil, the better chanteuse, take the humiliating role of the mute. Christine on stage and not to sing? Impossible.

So Erik let Buquet stalk him through the auditorium and backstage until he led the scoundrel to the center of a catwalk suspended far above the stage itself. Below the ballet corps danced. Erik paused only a moment to admire Meg pirouette across the stage, until she was well away from the heart of the dance. And then Buquet found himself face to face with the Phantom he had been seeking all along. Erik gazed maniacally into the pocked face of the man, and when Buquet turned to flee, it was all a matter of seconds. The hapless victim fell to the slats of the catwalk, and Erik wrapped the noose around his neck and yanked it tight. As the last signs of life faded from Buquet's eyes, Erik sent his body toppling from the structure to drop to the stage below. There it hung for a few seconds before Erik released the rope and let Buquet's body crumple to the floor.

Christine could not love a murderer. In the next weeks she sealed her fate and Erik's by accepting Raoul's proposal of marriage. From such hopes Erik spiraled, as surely as Buquet's body had from the catwalk, down into darkness. And when he saw her kiss the young gentleman, he thought the betrayal would surely kill him.

In a final desperate attempt to reclaim his Christine, Erik stole onto the stage during the performance of his opera, *Don Juan Triumphant*, and sang his song of seduction. Before them all Christine went to him and let him take her in his arms, and as he sang to her of his love she ripped the mask from his face for the second time. She pitied him as he stood naked before a horrified audience. The gendarmes who had been brought to trap the Phantom surrounded him on the stage. Perhaps he had expected her betrayal, for Erik had loosened the cables and ropes that held the tremendous chandelier suspended over the auditorium. As the vast gallaxy of light and crystal crashed into the dense crowd of spectators, Erik released the lever to a trap door and plunged to the vaults below with Christine caught in his embrace.

I could not let Erik take Christine, not against her will. And although my heart broke to thwart his plan, I led Raoul, the Count de Chagny, to the underground stairs. But I could not foresee the traps Erik had set, and I could not foretell the horrible choice he'd force Christine to make.

When Raoul fell into the Phantom's trap, Christine was given the choice. If she agreed to stay as Erik's bride, Raoul would go free. But if she refused to stay with Erik, Raoul would die. Her love for Raoul was too great to see him die at Erik's hand. As a sign of her surrender, she went to Erik and placed her hand on his exposed face and in spite of the ugliness of his visage brought her lips to his in a solemn kiss.

I can only imagine what pain, what sublime joy were contained in that kiss. I know she drew back and saw in his face that something had forever changed in him. And then she kissed him yet once more. His lips were warm, his breath ragged, and she saw the tears well and overflow his eyes. Did he think in that moment of keeping her always? Did he wonder how he would ever stand the slow march of time without her? Certainly he knew that he loved her and that he had to let her go.

Above them some battled the fire that had ravaged the belly of the opera house while others gathered with sticks and blades and cried for the monster's blood. Slowly but inexorably they would comb the burned out remains of the opera house and descend to his very lair. Inevitably they would track him down—the Devil's Child—and cut and slash him until he was no more.

When the mob flooded his underground cavern, Meg was with them, her heart in her throat. Christine and Raoul were safely away, and Meg desperately sought Erik in hopes of finding him before those who sought his blood came upon him.

All she found was the mask he had worn, and the music box with the monkey on the barrel organ, a shrine to that ragged doll he had rescued when he fled the cage so long before. That coarsely fashioned doll had been his only possession. Meg searched the grotto, but he was gone.

Should I have left him there in that cage, the Devil's Child? If I had, he would have died there. If I had, he would not have loved Christine. Meg would not have gone in search of him. If I had left him. If I had left him, he would not have become the Phantom of the Opera.

Madeleine Giry
Paris, 1870

CHAPTER 1

The Fire

the fire, the fire ... it's here inside me, inside my mind and the screams of those who were coming torches raised burning away the cobwebs, the rats' nests, the steam rising from the stone walls, the water seeping from the ceilings extinguishing itself in sharp, snake hisses on the flames they emboldened by the riot of destruction I let loose upon the theater the chandelier ripping from its casement and swaying as it fell into their open laps glass ripping across their hands and eyes feet digging into those who had fallen on the brocade flooring younger ones climbing even over the seats to reach the exits the fire that burst the stained glass windows of the temple where we laid our sacrifices to music the fire eating the tapestries the landscapes the parapets upon which they paraded in their moth-eaten vestments the young soldier's cape the virgin's gown held together by constant mending, the blood staining the seams from old women who dreamed of their own masquerades upon the stage shoes that pressed and crippled the non-conforming feet of the dancer there where counterfeit sun and moon shown on pharaoh's slaves and a young goddess entranced us all with her voice but that voice ... the voice mine that voice mine my music my voice my soul through that voice the voice I gave her ... no ... the voice I instilled in her body that body the body that I touch even now as I rub my gloved hands over the hard edge of these stones, her body cold and hard and ungiving to my hands on her body like these stones, these stones, this my prison wall

He won't say her name, he won't, but I know he says it over and over when I'm out of earshot. Surrender I want to tell him, surrender as he had asked of her. As I longed to hear his voice, to catch a glimpse of his black glove as he slid between the walls, dissolving into a doorway invisible, impossible to find, I watched her grow and transform, her songs soaring pure, yet hot with passion and innocence, as if the sounds were not made in her throat but from somewhere deep inside her body, from her breasts and belly or perhaps even from the earth itself surging up through her limbs to her core to stream along her palate until it filled the entire womb of the opera house. She said her tutor visited her in the chapel, where she came to light a candle for her father, and there he would sing unearthly sounds, melodies forged from unknown instruments, that she echoed back again and again until this angel of music, as she called him, sighed contentedly or pressed his shadow over her like a caress. His voice wrapped around her like a velvet blanket blotting out all light and noise except the sounds of coursing blood through her veins and the music of his soul. Little did she understand how I ached to be there in her place. To see him, to have him touch me with his breath, to feel the vibration of his throat as my lips met his.

He clutched his arm around her waist and plummeted down from the scaffold; Christine imprisoned in his embrace fell through the trap door down into the simulated flames of hell to the underground vaults below. Even as she had sung to him, pleading for the passion to begin, there was betrayal in her seduction. His dream of Don Juan Triumphant succumbed to her vengeful Jezebel. There on the stage, the realm of the imagination and artful conceit, she betrayed not only him but art itself and ripped off his mask, revealing his red, twisted deformity to the entire world. The illusion destroyed: Half of his face was raw meat, mangled flesh, seemingly a wound that was never to heal. Yet the other side of his countenance retained that loveliness—the smooth, even skin of a mature man, dark eyebrow and lashes framing an emerald eye—which did not represent, but was Don Juan. And as Don Juan, he carried her off to his hell.

Maman found me in the secret passageway behind Christine's mirror. He must have watched her from the dank corridor, rodents skittering by his boots, spiders tickling at his hands as they braced the inside frame of his window onto her chamber. I blushed to recall afternoons that the two of us stood admiring ourselves in that surface, thinking its reflection its only charm. Christine would remove her chemise and hand it to me as I removed mine. We rarely took off all our clothes, but there were times when we both disrobed before that very mirror unaware that he was perhaps silently observing our bodies. We stood comparing ourselves in the mirrored body of the other, Christine taller and more sinewy, her long neck surpassed in elegance only by her incredible legs. I often envied those legs, her elongated thighs and perfectly shaped calves. In contrast, my body was more compact, more muscular yet still feminine. My breasts were generous for my petite frame. Christine's bust was small, her frame more sharp and angular. Even so, we were able to wear many of the same clothes. Did the Ghost stand before that mirror and watch Christine as she dressed and undressed? Did he watch us, together? What sublime torture it must have been for him, so alone, so passionate, with only that cold glassy surface between him and his desire.

When Maman found me sneaking down the corridor to follow him and Christine, she forbade that I ever go down that path again. I knew that Maman was somehow connected to the Opera Ghost. She defended him when Joseph Buquet told his awful stories of the Phantom snaring hapless victims in his magic lasso, dragging them down to his dungeon to unspeakable torture, slicing off strips of their flesh, even as they lived, to feed on. Maman would clutch at her heart as if someone had struck her own babe in arms. She threatened to have him fired if he didn't stop spreading his malicious gossip. I wondered why she showed such ferocious compassion, why she protected a fiend who constantly sabotaged Signora Carlotta, and who often did horrible things to others if they didn't perform to perfection. Once he killed Pauline's bird, leaving a note pinned to the dead songbird's breast: "You might as well be a raven for your talent at singing. This bird had more right to life than you." She left that very day, refused to continue in the show. These incidents began shortly after Christine and I joined the chorus.

I was afraid, but Maman told me the Ghost would never harm me or Christine and that he was pledged to protect us forever. I thought she was only trying to comfort us. Then I saw that we were immune to the tricks and accidents the Ghost worked, and Christine often benefited. That boy Patrice, who teased her mercilessly, one night when he made Christine cry was beaten with a birch wood cane on his back and legs without ever seeing who wielded the weapon; he said it came out of the walls on all sides of him at once. We also found presents from time to time, such as the morning I woke to find new dancing shoes lying at the foot of my bed, my old tattered ones thrown dismissively into a dark corner of the room. I ran to Maman to thank her for the gift I knew we couldn't afford. She smiled at me as she caressed the slippers' satin finish and told me she hadn't bought them, but that the Ghost must have liked my dancing and given them to me as a sign of his approval.

He sensed someone following him, someone who had found the tapestry over the broken mirror and had stepped through into the labyrinth of underground vaults. He paused and listened to the tapping of the footsteps and judged them to be either far away or belonging to a small person, hardly did they seem to resound on the stone floor, quick and nimble even when irregular. At times the person seemed to skitter gracefully through a passageway and at others tripped and plodded as if playing an elaborate game of hopscotch. He continued forward barely aware that he was counting the turns, two left, three right, one left, one right, two left and so on. Damn the bastard that dared to pursue him! Alone, the intruder was cut off from the search parties that had come to lynch or burn the Phantom. He would soon be lost, the footsteps already seemed to be fading in the distance. Surely the pursuer had taken a wrong turn and was now destined to wander these tunnels hopelessly.

A woman's scream startled him as he turned into another passageway. What if it wasn't one of the posse of men come to drag him to his death? What if Christine had come back?! He turned and retraced his steps. A second scream made him break into a run. Let him find her quickly, for God's sake. She was off the pathway, lost in one of the branches, but he knew them all. He had to find her while her scream still echoed. Otherwise it would be too late. She had returned to him. She loved him. He felt that in the kiss she'd given him. Once she and Raoul emerged from the tunnels, she'd understood her mistake and forced the boy to bring her back into the bowels of his opera house, to return to the Phantom. It was he who needed her, who most loved her, not Raoul. He would rebuild the opera house. Madeleine Giry had faithfully invested his money, the money the previous owner had monthly paid him, except for a modest amount to support his comforts, such as they were. He was a wealthy man who lived among the rats in the sewer; the irony never failed to delight him. Mme. Giry would act as his representative. They would reconstruct the edifice, and Christine would be the star of the New Opera House. Oh, the music he would write for her, the arias she would sing. Everyone in Paris would fall before her feet. As he rounded the corner of the tunnel, the sound of thrashing water hit his ears, and he understood that it was imperative that he find her now for she had fallen into one of the traps that honeycombed the labyrinth. Over the years, he had laid snares and booby traps for those unfortunates who stumbled into his domain as well as those who unwisely hunted him.

A hand emerged out of the black hole and sank down just out of his reach. Without a moment's thought, he threw off his cape and dove into the well. The pitch blackness of the water made it impossible for him to see her. Blindly he swept his arms around in the water, and as he began to despair that she was lost to him he felt a swatch of fabric, and clutching it he pulled her to him. He wrapped his arm around her and trusting his instincts turned his body toward the surface, even though there was no way to orient himself in this blackness.

The water felt thick, and swimming against it was like swimming in oil. Was she dead? He feared she was drowned; he felt no voluntary movement in the body he pressed against him. His lungs painfully gulped the air as they broke the surface of the pool, but he could not waste time. He heaved her limp body out of the water just enough to press her chest against the floor and pray that she would cough, spew out the water, and take in air. At first nothing, and then she convulsed under his arms and expelled water and air in equal measures. Relieved, he heard her throat rasp as it sucked in air, coughed and sucked again. All this time he exhorted her to breathe saying her name over and over again, calling her back to him. He drew her hair away from the side of her face, and in the dimness of the corridor's light he saw that it was not Christine!

Little Meg, Mme. Giry's daughter, turned over onto her back and saw the dark figure retreat until his back pressed against the stone wall. The look of horror on his face was met by an equally horrified response on hers as she saw his disfigured face in the flickering light of a dim torch in the distance. He groped the wall as if injured and receded down the path away from her, but she called to him, pleading with him to wait. She had come to find him. Her mother had told her his story, and she came to help, just as her mother had done so many years ago when she rescued him from the cage at the fairgrounds.

"Please don't leave me here. I can't find my way out. Please. I want to help." But he only heard noises, not words, he only saw Christine in the gondola standing with her hand on Raoul's shoulder, her back to him, the two of them moving like Charon and his charge over the river Styx, for they were both dead to him now. He, too, was dead; this, his crypt.

He staggered forward slowly, and I pulled myself up and followed. My lungs ached from the air they greedily inhaled. The coldness immediately assailed me. The tunnels are naturally cold and damp. My garments soaked, my hair dripping down my back, I felt all my body's warmth abandon me. My teeth chattered like cymbals in the dark. He stopped and without glancing back at me, he handed me the cape he had retrieved by the edge of the pool. I tried, but couldn't keep up with his pace; my foot tripped upon the hem of his cape, and I began to pitch forward with a gasp. In that very moment, he reached for me and took me in his arms to save me from falling onto the stone floor. Inches from his face, I was horrified by the ugliness, the irregular bumps and lesions, the redness and the twisted flesh around the eye and corner of his lip. The disfigurement began along the side of his head, covered part of his scalp and expanded across his forehead and down his right cheek stopping only above the lower part of his face. Where the scar ended the flesh was smooth, a landscape broken only by the evidence of his beard. He lifted me as if I were a leaf, never looked at me. I averted my eyes, looking down the endless corridors with their angles askew, dark recesses on either side, some dark as Hades, others dimly lit by torch light. The coldness began to leave me and a heaviness descended over my eyes and limbs. I turned my head in toward his chest and rested it there. His shirt was damp, but I was too tired to care. There, my ear against his chest, I heard his heart beating deep and strong.

The chamber was one of several that the Phantom had constructed and furnished over time as if he were constructing the mise-en-scene of an operatic piece. The effect evoked a tableau in which the bed occupied center stage. A plush sofa upholstered in a scarlet and gold brocade stood along one side of the room. Perhaps an Italian comedy had been his inspiration, a bedroom farce of infidelities. Wardrobes, closets, and cabinets placed around the alcove suggested hiding places for cuckolds or lovers but in fact served as storage for the mundane necessities of life which rarely made their appearance on the operatic stage: shaving utensils, stocks of food such as butter, cheeses, and wines, dried fruits and nuts, onions and carrots and dried herbs tied and hung in bundles, part of a now stale loaf of bread wrapped in cloth, cutlery, plates and goblets, a tankard of water, several others of wine. Another closet was hidden by a full length mirror which lay slightly ajar. This hidden dressing-room was lined with masks and wigs of varying sizes, styles, and colors. Half masks and full masks affixed to the wall, wigs set upon faceless dummies were perched as if to observe the dressing table where theatrical face paints, brushes and pencils, had been used and left for a promised next performance.

down into the black struggling to reach into the bottom of the pool Christine is there waiting her brown hair floating up toward me her eyes open wide and beseeching me I have to save her to reach her but there's a fire set under the well the walls and depths the surface of a cauldron and we trapped inside the water beginning to boil I can't breathe and her hair is not brown it isn't brown it isn't her hair it's blonde and the hands are too white and small and I drag her up toward the lip of the cauldron before our flesh is cooked off the bone Christine is at the edge of the well smiling at me as I drag the body to lay before her feet as an offering the face of the body is not Christine's the face is a hideous mask of tortured flesh I scream under the water and let loose of the hateful thing it sinks sinks sinks deep to the depths but somehow the darkness does not engulf that face it glows as if lit from behind by the flames Christine wouldn't want to see it I must keep her from seeing it I must go back down to push it down and down and down into the dark

He cries out words I can't understand, groans, sobs and gasping noises. He lies on the sofa, on his side, his back to me, his knees drawn toward his chest. His whole frame shakes with fever and delirium.

He's soaked through; his own sweat replaces the dampness from the pool. I quickly untie his cravat and unfasten the white shirt pulling the tails from his breeches. As I pull it off his shoulders and down his back, tugging at the fabric until it comes loose from under his body and slipping his arms out one by one, I wipe off the sweat from his skin. I sling a blanket from the bed over his exposed chest tucking it around his neck. His body continues to shake from the chills, his jaw clenched, his hands balled into fists. His cummerbund is wrapped several times around his waist and loosens only after much effort. Exhausted from the exertion, I pause, realizing what I'm about to do and blush thinking that I've never seen a man naked much less undressed one. I unbutton his breeches and look for other stays that might impede their removal. As I take the waist of his breeches in my hands, ready to pull them down over his hips, I glance unintentionally at his face. He's lying mostly on his side, his deformity out of my line of vision. In its stead, before my eyes is a beauty that pains me. Sadly, when both sides of his unmasked face are visible, all one sees is the monstrous mimicry of a face, not this dark angelic countenance I now have time to contemplate.

No longer blushing, but rather strangely aroused, I eagerly pull down the wet breeches and uncover him. For one brief selfish moment, I draw back the blanket from him entirely and admire his body. He has stretched out his limbs in response to my tugging and pulling at his clothes, and I see how beautifully sculpted his body is, his muscles sleek and firm, his chest covered by a rich mat of brown curls, his hips narrow. The blood rushes to the surface of my skin as I examine him. The feelings his body arouses in mine are wet and tingling. Although I've only seen the marble statues in the museums and no man in the flesh, I know that I'm seeing true beauty. Unable to regard him further, I wrap the blankets tightly around him and sitting by the couch I stroke his forehead and softly sing to him to calm the shaking of his fevered body.

angels circling in the darkness over and over notes quarter notes eighths and six-teenth notes dancing a wind blows them from the page the paper crinkles and fire devours the staff the lines whole notes half notes words and rests melt and waft away as a red tongue of flame spreads from the center and the paper curls and melts into the heat ash covers my face I can't breathe and the angel's white flutter-ing wing brushes away the cinders and then music freed from the yellow parch-ment plays across the room and Christine sings the scales from major to minor holding that note the one in which her vibrato is best heard, a slightness plagues the arpeggio her voice slighter she needs to push from her diaphragm, deeper, Christine, bring the sound out your throat is not the only part of your body as instrument, it comes from the muscles here I must touch you, show you from where the music comes, not from that final channel before it fills the mouth, not there but here along your body, Christine, below your ribs the depression dips and I swoon in the valley I feel the notes alive and dancing in your abdomen damn the folds and folds of useless cloth between my hand and this womb of sound angels protect me angels sing diaphanous chords a melody I can't recall the melody embraces me wraps me in cotton and lowers me softly to the darkness

"But monsieur I don't know where he is," Mme. Giry protested time and again to the prefect of police. A short man, Chief Inspector Leroux cast his dark eyes in Mme. Giry's direction weighing whether or not it was worth con-tinuing the interrogation. He had already missed his dinner, and had gotten nowhere. He was sure that this woman was complicit with the Phantom. The death toll had risen to eleven people, far more injured. The fire had gratefully not spread beyond the opera house itself, and the damage was mostly within its walls destroying completely the stage and severely damaging the back stage chambers leaving the husk of a building that had been the jewel of the district. All of this talk of a Phantom had repeatedly been disregarded. But this time important people had been killed, and there were witnesses—lords and ladies—not just the riff raff of the theater itself. There was that incident of Joseph Buquet, a scene shifter, who had been hanged in Act I of a performance. The crème de la crème had fled screaming that the Phantom himself had appeared before the spectators, interrupting the opera and warning that his demands had not been met. And now this fire. Leroux was already apprised that the ingénue, a young pretty wisp of a thing, had been swept off the stage by the Phantom masquerading as the old pompous Piangi. Sadly this opera season was now at a close, too many "accidents" and the House itself beyond recovery.

"Madame, do you have any idea where this Ghost might have taken the young woman he kidnapped?" She continued to rub her hands together unconscious of the Inspector's watchful eye. In response she only shook her head. "It's a serious matter to withhold information, you must be aware." Why would this woman hide such a monster? The Inspector knew the rumors that the murderer was a ghost were ridiculous. Most theater people were superstitious. Accidents were common in their profession, and there was a long tradition of ghosts in these overwhelming architectural shrines. Why even the Cathedral was supposedly haunted by some deformed half ape, half man beast that lived in the bell tower. The catastrophe tonight had no doubt been caused by some discontented worker fired for negligence who knowing the legend of the Opera Ghost used it as a mask for his own revenge against the new owners.

Suddenly aware that this course of interrogation wouldn't render the desired information, the Inspector decided to switch methods. He took Mme. Giry's hand and patted it paternally, although they were of an age, and smiling apologized for having detained her so long. "You may go. I can have my officer take you where you will, Madame. If I have more questions, I hope that I may call on you again?" A comely woman, he thought, is always a pleasure to be savored, and perhaps he himself might call on Mme. Giry.

"Thank you, monsieur Inspector. I am always willing to cooperate with the authorities. But I would appreciate it if your man could return me to my apartments near the theater. I'm concerned for my daughter, Meg. We parted just minutes before your men abducted me, and I'm anxious to see that no harm has befallen her." Indeed she was quite concerned. She couldn't avoid thinking Meg had gone in search of the Phantom herself. God protect her if she happened upon him now or fell into one of his traps!

It was inevitable that Meg would become curious, question her mother's behavior, and eventually stumble across the Phantom. Until recently, Mme. Giry had no trouble keeping her daughter innocent of any knowledge of her association with Erik. Meg had no idea that her mother acted on his behalf until everything went out of control. No longer a child, Meg had become more daring and much more independent; on more than one occasion Mme. Giry had found her precocious daughter exploring unused corridors in the opera house, peeking around doorways previously of no interest to her. She was also aware that Meg had asked Christine about her tutor and expressed a desire to be tutored by the same maestro.

The night Mme. Giry found Meg wandering in the corridor behind the full-length mirror in Christine's dressing room, she had to tell her the story. She feared her daughter would be appalled at the secret resident of the opera house, even though she didn't share all the details with Meg. For instance, she failed to mention that the devil's child she had rescued from the cage, the child who had been cruelly beaten and neglected, this child had murdered his keeper, perhaps even his father, that night she helped him escape to the vaults of the opera. Instead she told Meg of the cloth monkey with cymbals attached to its hands that he miserably cradled next to his nearly naked body and how the keeper had taken it from him and beaten him for the public's amusement. It was this last cruelty that she couldn't bear and for this she had helped him escape and had hidden and taken care of him over the years in the vaults.

The opera house had been his refuge, his home, and his school. From the stage hands, the singers, and M. Reyer, the music conductor, he had learned architecture and design, poetry and the art of disguise, and the majesty and power of music. She didn't know how he managed to learn to compose, but he had. Without an instrument, he wrote entire operas. At his insistence, she brought the music to M. Reyer who followed his progress, commented and amended the scores until he came to see that the pupil's genius had far outstripped his ability to correct or advise him.

"Why didn't he choose me as his student, maman?"

"Ma cherie, Christine, too, is an orphan. This brought him closer to her. And, forgive me, ma petite, but I asked him to keep his distance from you."

"But why? Am I not gifted? You know my dedication, my work."

Mme. Giry reassured her, "I never doubted your talent; I questioned his interest and influence. He's a genius, but he lives like a ghost in the bowels of this building. He'll never be able to live outside this opera house in the light of day. I want more for you. I want more for Christine, as well, but he was obstinate once he heard her sing. When she came into her voice, he heard her practicing and wouldn't accept a refusal. He told me in no uncertain terms to bring her to the chapel for he intended to instruct her." Meg sensed the war of intentions and motives in her mother's explanation; she caught the guilt in her voice. Her mother explained how she acted as the Ghost's representative in the outside world, in banking and commerce, in supplying the Ghost with his basic needs, in negotiations with the owners of the opera house, originally her idea, and in the opera house she protected him, guarded his exits and entrances, acted as his eyes and ears when he himself was not spying. For he did spy on all of them, as Meg had come to realize.

"Maman, is he dangerous?"

She did not answer immediately. "I don't believe he would hurt you, me, or Christine, but he is capable of great passion and great violence. For him, the opera house is his home, his shrine, his protection, and music is his life. Without it, he is that devil's child locked in the darkness behind bars, a freak in the carnival, a damned soul in hell. I think he might harm someone if he thought they were trying to take this from him."

"Christine calls him her angel of music; she must be told who he is, Maman," Meg entreated her mother.

"Mais, non. For Christine, he *is* her angel of music." Her pity of the despised child who had grown into a man capable of such sublime art had not been able to conquer her fear and revulsion. She could only give him her protection, her love never growing strong enough to reach out across the chasm to touch him, to accompany him except as a protector and faithful servant. For this lack in herself, she couldn't bear to take from him his connection to Christine. Perhaps Christine could look beyond the ugliness and give him what she and the world had always withheld.

she walks on his arm she's dressed in lavender and white with her dark hair hanging in ringlets down her back the back that I had pressed against me I ran my hands over the brocade of that dress and imagined the sublime it jealously hid from me I feel her warmth in my hands still ... she laughs she laughs and grabs his arm him in his soldier's uniform such mockery of gleaming gold in the buckles and his sword hanging there ready to rip to gash blood on the petticoats of her lavender and white and she laughs and serves tea from a silver teapot service for eight sing, sing to us Christine ... no, Christine, no, Christine will not sing for you she only sings for me she only sings on my stage she stands in the center of the stage and the orchestra plays one two three one two three impossible sixteenth notes and all eyes are trained on Christine but she looks at me with such love such desire the gown turns from lavender to red and the white falls from her shoulders and her voice is straining but I can't hear her sing sing louder Christine sing louder sing for me Christine the music is not coming from the orchestra it's coming from my body it is churning upward and bursting out of my mouth it is painful it's so sublime so rich I am music I am wrapping myself around her body and merging into her pores and traveling up from her breast through her throat and bursting toward the very ceiling of the opera house and down below me I see her she isn't looking up she's looking directly ahead and she's looking at the soldier the soldier and his golden buckles and his sword is drawn and he flings it at my heart and it rains inside the opera house, all the spectators amazed look upward toward my lacerated heart and the rain is blood dripping down onto Christine's face and bosom she's scream-ing she's screaming it isn't the music I wrote it's horror bursting from her throat

He raved consumed by the fires of hell. Each time he kicked the eiderdown to the floor, Meg covered his tortured, fever-wracked body again. It must have been several days. Curses and pleas mixed with incoherent babblings from which Meg only caught bits and snatches. Christine's name spoken in all the possible registers of emotion from exhortation to tenderness, from revulsion to desperation. She tried not to listen when the delirium forced him back to his last encounter with Christine. Raoul had descended to his cavernous world and taken Christine away. He relived her loss again and again. It wasn't from delicacy or courtesy that she withdrew from that corner of the apartment to occupy herself with other tasks as much as her fear of the depths of his anger and despair. She was startled when his fever reached such a level of intensity that he opened his eyes and looked at her without seeing her. He screamed at her to leave him, to go, to forget him. It was Christine with whom he was argu-ing even as Meg replaced the warm damp cloth on his brow with a fresh cool one. She sang to him, and only this seemed to calm him.

I've given him the broth I made from his provisions—dried meat, potatoes, onions, dried parsley, and carrots—spoonful by spoonful unsure how much liquid actually found its way to his stomach. Certainly he didn't swallow much given the dry heaves that seem to shake his joints apart. If only he could recover his senses long enough to tell me how to get to the street above. I could find Maman; we could bring him medical attention, a doctor or at least some medicine to bring down the fever. I dare not venture out into this labyrinth on my own. If I lost my way, we would both die. Better to die here next to him, if that's God's will. Maman would have been here by now if she knew of these rooms. Poor Maman, she must be frantic; I've lost track of time, not knowing whether it's day or night outside this cell. Maman, what do you think has happened to me? That I perished in the fire? That the Ghost struck me down? If only I could find my way to her or she to us! If you should die and leave me alone down here, what will become of me?

"Why are you crying?" His voice was raspy and brittle, the sound of a long abandoned instrument in the attic, the reed dried and cracked.

She looked up at him, focusing on the handsome half-moon side of his face. Was he raving in his delirium? She could see immediately his confusion at finding her leaning across his chest, yet he was conscious and had recovered his wits. "Oh, thanks be to God. I feared you'd never recover." As she raised her hand toward the Phantom's brow, he flinched and tried to draw away. When it paused cool and gentle on his forehead to check for fever, he stiffened momentarily and then brushed her hand away from his face. He tried to sit up, but fell back in exhaustion.

Meg felt only momentarily rebuffed, so relieved was she that he had come through the delirium. "I've made broth for you. You must have it. You've eaten nothing for days." She turned to the chimney and prepared a cup of the clear, fragrant liquid.

"Where are my clothes?" He was naked under the covers. He couldn't imagine how this had happened. Meg put down the cup near the sofa and went to a screen mounted in a corner of the room where his clothes had been hung to dry. Seeing his perplexity, she blushed and stammered that she had removed his clothes because they were drenched. They would have been his death.

His clothes were not the only things missing, he soon realized: gone was his mask. He drew his hand reflexively to his face to screen it from her gaze. When Christine unmasked him on the stage, left him at the mercy of all those spectators, he had vowed he would never again cover his deformity. He resolved to remain in these vaults, unseen and dead to all. There would be no need for a mask. But this young woman, not two feet from him, looked upon his ugliness. Once more he imagined the bars of his cage closing around him, the stares and jeers of the crowd come to see the Devil's Child.

He tried to quell the panic rising in his chest. "Give me a mask, any of them. They're behind that mirror. Quick, bring me whichever one you find first."

"You don't need to put on a mask," she began to console him.

"Don't be stupid, girl! Give me the mask now or do I have to go myself?" Meg hesitated only because she was bewildered by the anger in his request. Although his face was repulsive, it no longer sickened her or frightened her as it first had. With time, she was sure that she would be able to look at him without wanting to turn away.

Thinking she refused, the Phantom wrapped the blanket around his waist and pitched forward in an attempt to stand. His legs shaking from weakness and unable to support his weight gave out immediately sending him forward onto his hands and knees.

"My mask!" he roared at her, a sound somewhere between anger and despair, as she made as if to help him stand. He lowered his face to the ground and reached out with one hand for the desired object.

She hastened to the closet behind the mirror and chose a simple green mask meant to cover all but the lower section of the face, the bottom edge stopping just above the lips. Bending down, she placed it in his outstretched hand. Then she retreated several paces while he arranged the mask on his face. He didn't ask for her help to return to the sofa, nor did she offer any. Instead, she waited until he was settled and brought him his clothes, too. The previous exertions had drained what little strength he had. He lay with his clothes clutched to his chest and remained still.

"I'll bring you the broth. It will help to restore you."

He remained quiet until she sat beside him on the edge of the couch and brought the spoon to his lips. He sipped the broth, his eyes averted from this girl, Mme. Giry's only child, whom he had watched mature side by side with Christine. Strange that as long as he had known her mother, Mme. Giry had never been as intimately close to him as her daughter was at this moment. He found it disconcerting.

"Meg, you must leave," he barely whispered as she brought another spoonful of the broth to his lips.

His crying awoke me again last night. He languishes in his bed. Not a word. He allows me to feed him a few sips of broth, but waves away the crusts of bread I press to his lips. He wears the mask whether asleep or awake, and I begin to forget the face that I saw under its surface. His eyes, though, I'll never forget, although he keeps them averted as if I were the one who should be wearing a mask.

Not knowing whether it's day or night I often wander the hallways. To avoid losing my way, I tie one end of a long rope to the leg of the couch and unravel it as I go along the corridor. This may no longer be necessary since I've found drawings the engineers and architects must have made of this underground world kept in one of several of his chests.

To my surprise I've also come across several letters in my mother's hand, signed with her Christian name, Madeleine, and addressed to Erik. Erik is his name; with these four little letters is dispelled the phantom. Maman had told me part of his story, but she did not reveal how close her contact with him has been. He was perhaps only ten or eleven years old when maman brought him to the opera house. The man who took care of him beat him for the amusement of the crowd. My mother stood by horrified. As the crowd disappeared through the tarp of the exhibit, the boy took a rope and strangled his tormentor. My mother witnessed the murder and helped the child flee from the fairgrounds. She was just sixteen. That was some nineteen years ago. She taught the boy his letters, brought him food and clothes, and when the staff was gone and only the resident pupils like herself remained in the dormitories of the opera house, she would call to him to come from the dungeon.

That first year, she showed him the dressing rooms, the backstage, the properties of the theater, the many workshops where papier maché masks and alabaster statues were molded and cast, the carpenters' workshops, the sewing rooms, the wardrobes, the cafeteria and dining quarters, the stable where he took a tender pleasure in feeding and brushing the horses. In one of her letters, she asks Erik to recall how they put on plays where he was the monster and she the damsel. He became very agile at climbing the ropes and scaffolding and at the moment the monster was about to pounce on the kidnapped princess he would disappear and reappear with a mask of the most beautiful and virile visage and as the prince save her.

Their playful days came to an abrupt end when my mother was betrothed to my father, a prosperous merchant who was a patron of the ballet school. After my mother married, Erik made his permanent abode in the underground cellars. Only there did he feel safe. He chose his clothing from the costumes housed in the theater; in the underground cellars, his rooms were furnished by a fantastic assortment of properties from plays of various epochs and styles, Eighteenth century bedroom farces, mythical pageants, bucolic romances, cloak and dagger melodramas. In the belly of the theater with these pieces from his favorite operas, he constructed the stage whereon he lives.

The legend of the opera ghost was a common superstition among the staff and artists in the theater. It was easy to rekindle the fear of this phantom; objects seemed to move of their own accord, but eventually these harmless pranks gave way to more serious incidents. Still a boy, although he was always tall for his age and unusually strong, he appeared from nowhere and roamed the backstage and party rooms alike, walked along the catwalks, dressed in formal attire, wearing a black and white mask, and deliberately frightened staff and performers. To Erik, it was simply an extension of the play acting that he had enjoyed with Maman and not distinct in kind from the marvelous conceits he watched on the stage itself from hidden shafts among the boxes that lined the amphitheater. So in this way he assured that no one was likely to venture into certain areas known to be the domain of the opera ghost. It was Maman who eventually suggested that he write the owners and demand a salary as resident ghost of the House, and with this money he was able to become independent and self-sustaining.

The letters seemed to date from the time when my mother, just eighteen, was married and had just given birth to me. Erik must have felt entirely abandoned. Maman's letters attempted to console him, repeating in each one that she was still his dear Madeleine, ever his protector. She described my first months, and finally in the last letter reported my father's tragic death at sea and her resolve to return to the ballet school. His answers were, of course, not among the letters I found. Yet, each letter must have been read over and over again; the sheets nearly fell apart when I took them from their envelopes, and all were kept in their original order and lovingly tied with a black ribbon.

"Take it away, I said!" His arm slapped the bowl out of her hands, spilling the contents upon the floor. The bowl shattered into several shards against the cold stones. Even though he barely raised his voice, the words slapped Meg as sharply as if they had been the palm of his hand across her face. He glared for one moment at her through his mask before he fell back on the pillows. "I tire of your useless attentions. Get out. Leave me."

Meg scurried off the edge of the sofa and moved away until she felt the stone wall against her back. Suddenly quite angry herself, she shouted, "Then you want to die?"

"That's not your concern. You're an uninvited guest, and I wish for you to go. NOW!" She couldn't imagine from where the strength of his voice had come. "Tell Mme. Giry that I'm dead. There's a map among my papers in the trunk by the larder; follow the path to the right, and you'll emerge at the Rue des Guards."

"I know that you're sad that Christine ..."

"Don't say that name! Do not!" If he had been able to, he would have risen from the bed and stopped her mouth with his hands, but he was still too weak.

"I'll leave, but I'll come back. Or my maman will come."

"Silly girl. I can live or die without your help. Whatever happens to me in the next days will be of my concern alone."

...

"What are you doing standing there? Go!"

But she didn't go even when I threatened to rise from the bed and strangle her with my bare hands. I abused her, I growled at her as if insane, and in desperation to be rid of her I ripped the mask from my face and scowled at her with my hideous visage. I could tell that I frightened her, frightened her beyond description, and only the fact that she knew I was wasted by the illness from which I hadn't quite recovered kept her from fleeing blindly down the tunnels. She averted her face from mine and wept. Her tears didn't move me; they angered me. For what did she cry? What pain wracked her soul? She wasn't a prisoner under the weight of Paris; she hadn't found and lost her only love. She wasn't abhorred and rejected by all. I had revealed to her the secret passageway by which she could reach the light and return to her world. She was young and beautiful, almost as beautiful as Christine. I couldn't bear her beauty. I didn't want to have her beauty flaunted before me. I had tired of beauty's mockery. If I had the courage, I would have taken the shards of my mirrors and cut my eyes out of my face to better frighten the world and to never see the reflection of my horror in another's face. I only have the courage to lie here and die, to let time and abandonment work their course. And this child has come to thwart even that miserable plan.

"Come. There's blood. Dress. I'll take you to her."

Mme. Giry felt his hand touch her in the darkness of her bedroom. Opening her eyes, she became aware of the denser shadow looming over her as she lay in bed. A dim light from the moon reflected off one silvery eye, and she felt his breath on her face.

"Erik? My daughter, Meg, she's with you? You've taken her deeper into the caverns below the opera house?" The woman grabbed the shadow's arm as she sat up in the bed. What had he done to her?

"Quick. I'll take you to her. I've not harmed her; you mustn't think that I've harmed her." His voice was calm, but intense. He withdrew to the parlor so that Mme. Giry could dress.

Meg hadn't left. Erik began to recover in spite of the fact that he accepted only small amounts of food and water. However, as he regained some strength, Meg grew ill. She was always cold, and one morning she didn't rise from the bed to start the fire for breakfast. From the sofa, Erik watched, and hearing soft whimpering arise from the covers, he called to her. But she didn't answer. He rose from the sofa and went to the side of the bed where she lay wracked by chills.

He knelt beside the bed and pushed the cover away from the young woman's face. Pale and drenched in sweat, she lay as if dead, her breath shallow. Beads of perspiration lined her upper lip. He wiped the sweat from her face with the edge of the coverlet. He brushed her long blonde hair away from her face and neck and continued to wipe away the moisture from her long neck. He didn't dare to loosen the tie of her chemise at the base of her throat, although he thought this might help her breathe.

"There, there, there," he said over and over as if to comfort her. "Meg, you've done a foolish thing. Why did you follow me? You've caught my fever." A note of annoyance edged into his voice as he pondered what to do. He could wrap her in blankets and carry her to the surface, leave her at the crossroads where the night watchman regularly passed and was sure to find her. Or he might hail a cab and pay the man to take Meg to a surgeon. He would have to pay him also for his silence. Neither solution was possible. He was far too weak to carry the girl to the surface. "I'm no nurse. I can do nothing for you, you stupid girl."

Erik dressed, preparing to leave. He would perhaps find Caesar in the stable adjacent to the opera house and with him take Meg to the streets above. Before leaving, he went to change the coverlet for a woolen blanket to keep the young woman warm. Pulling back the coverlet, Erik saw the blood-soaked petticoat. Covering her again, he knew he must bring Madeleine to attend to her daughter.

Mme. Giry reassured Erik that the blood was not from an accident or a wound. At once realizing the origins of the stains, Erik was both mesmerized and embarrassed. How was he to understand these things, kept as he had been in the belly of the earth, away from companionship of all kind, but especially from the domesticating presence of mother, sisters, daughters, wife? These were celestial, strange creatures, beyond his comprehension, even Christine.

She had spent only one night with him; she had slept in his bed. He had kept vigil over her, returning time after time to watch her sleep. He wondered if that night had been a dream. He had sat and played the organ while she slept.

Mme. Giry cleaned her daughter's body, dropping bloody rags into a bucket by the bed; Erik understood that he had been exiled from many pleasures and pains of the flesh. Christine slipped further away from him as he pondered the physical reality of her as a breathing woman, a reality that would forever be withheld from him. Even that night as he watched her sleep, the chasm between them had been impossible to span. He had enjoyed her voice, her beauty had been the food of his eyes, but her body had only fleetingly touched his.

CHAPTER 2

The Singer

Remember thee! remember thee!
Till Lethe quench life's burning stream
Remorse and shame shall cling to thee,
And haunt thee like a feverish dream!

Remember thee! Aye, doubt it not.
Thy husband too shall think of thee:
By neither shalt thou be forgot,
Thou false to him, thou fiend to me!

Lord Byron

he meant for me to sing my voice was God's gift and we do not turn our back on the gifts God gives us he woke me with his violin and played me to sleep at night and my first words were a lullaby he taught me and when he died I thought I wouldn't sing again I forgot my words I was in the tomb with my father and the sounds of the birds faded muted by the stone walls and my father's violins were sold to pay for my education put away for me for my future Madame Giry gave me candies laid me in the same bed with Meg sat me in the theater and let me play with the face paint and gowns and run with Meg around the props visiting India and Ceylon, from Italy to Mongolia, along the Russian steppes but my voice was buried I felt gagged only my body seemed alive my arms and legs bending and swaying to the orchestra keeping step with the dancers one and bend and pirouette and bow my body swaying to the woodwinds tapping to the cymbals but my voice lay there with you, father, in your tomb as dead as you, only returning in prayers and used like a hammer or chisel to ask for bread and jam a needle and thread telling the time and repeating the click clack of other voices leaving and coming and wanting and forbidding and naming ... and so time passed my gift forgotten locked away in a box until he brought the key ... it was in the chapel where he first came to me, I thought he was sent by you, father, I waited and waited for the angel of music and he did come his voice at first soft and hesitant urged me to sing to be the bird to be the wind to be the sunlight bouncing along the stained glass in the chapel to be the nightingale he listened to my prayers and my songs in the chapel where I lit a candle and prayed to my father

The wedding was postponed to let the scandal of the opera house pass. The young man's family managed to quell the interest of the authorities in Christine Daaé's connections to the horrible events of the night of the fire. Raoul refused to allow her to be questioned. To show his cooperation, he led numerous search parties throughout the catacombs of the district, through the sewers, along the vaults immediately under the opera house although these forays had to cease when the city engineers warned that the destruction to the opera house and its great weight made exploration of these subterranean grottoes dangerous. Christine pleaded with him not to lead these search parties, that nothing good could come from persecuting the Phantom. The third time the police called upon Raoul to descend into the underground lake, Christine became hysterical and swore to him that she wouldn't marry him if he persisted in risking his life to find the opera ghost.

"Christine, it's my duty. He's a murderer, and obviously insane."

"Do you forget his bargain?" She took his arm as if to restrain him physically from joining the awaiting party. The intensity of her look inspired him with amazement and foreboding.

"What bargain? What are you raving about, Christine?" Clearly Christine was suffering from nervous exhaustion. Even though several weeks had passed, she might yet suffer a breakdown. She had been so strong in those first days when they found their way out of the Phantom's dungeon to safety. Nevertheless, her opposition to his cooperation with the authorities filled him with doubts. Was it fear for his safety and hers or was it fear for the Phantom?

She had kissed the monster, looked upon him with something akin to pity or was it love? Raoul still recalled the seduction scene in the Phantom's opera, *Don Juan Triumphant*. She was afire, ablaze with a dark light. As she drew closer to the Phantom and allowed him to embrace and caress her body, Raoul couldn't believe that it was an act. He saw Christine, his Christine, not as that innocent playmate nor as his future bride, but as a woman caught in the flames of an illicit passion that was unspeakably horrid.

Perhaps in remembrance of that moment, Raoul adapted a cool tone toward her pleas. "Surely you want him to be found. You don't pretend to protect this monster, do you?"

For the first time since they had pledged their love to one another, Raoul saw anger and coldness in her eyes. She dropped her hand from his sleeve and turned away toward the window before she again spoke, "He gave you your life, and he gave me my freedom. This doesn't seem to you to be a powerful debt we owe him?"

"I owe him nothing." Raoul spat out the words in anger. "If not for his murderous obsession with you, nothing that happened that night would have happened. We wouldn't have been at his mercy in that watery graveyard." He was at the door about to leave when she said the unthinkable.

"If not for him, would you have been satisfied to make me your mistress instead of your wife?"

father assumes like so many in our class that all the artists in the theater are little more than charlatans and whores he allowed me to become patron to the opera populaire thinking I would find a mistress and enjoy some freedom before settling down to married life with one of the young daughters among our friends' families and give him his blue-blooded grandchildren yet he doesn't understand the thrill of that world where women and men laugh and love to excess in the corridors behind the stage rife with lovers taking up every and any dark corner the power and the lust radiate from their bodies and yet the delicacy and refinement of the stories they embody on the stage transport me to a world I had no idea existed and among them Christine, I couldn't believe my eyes when I saw Christine there on the stage among this rabble, this bevy of strutting and capricious bohemians I had thought I might take my pick from the chorus a young, beautiful dancer perhaps who would welcome my attentions I would be kind and gentle with her as long as she promised to give her favors only to me she would have a wonderful adventure no one would be hurt when we tired of one another or when my father decided that it was time to set the date for the marriage with some staid and refined gentlewoman I would tell my darling mistress and we would shed our tears but I would always always remember her and she would be well taken care of there would be no cause for her to regret our affair on the contrary I would find her a good match someone of her class who would be beholden to me for a nice stipend and would treat her well we would only have to be sure there were no children this I wouldn't be able to forgive myself I wouldn't abandon any child of mine even a bastard I would adopt him and bring him to live with my new wife and my wife not wanting to know the truth would accept the waif as a long lost cousin's orphaned child and I would raise him with my own legitimate children although I would never be able to give him the primogenitor's status he would be given a career in the military or I would set him up with a prosperous business what an adventure I imagined when I saw Christine and it was the Christine I had known at the seashore when we were so small and so innocent her father a famous violinist accepted among the homes of many of the gentry for his genius and his little daughter the poor child having lost a mother at childbirth and the father was sojourning at the estate of our friends and each day I found little Lotte as we liked to call her down in the sand talking to herself telling herself the stories her father read to her and I was only somewhat older than she old enough to look at her and blush at her beauty that even then adorned her face and she so young not realizing the flutter she set off in my young breast when she would come and sit on my lap in the sand and take my hands and count my fingers and sing a song for each one I was a young boy of eleven and she only five or six when I fell hopelessly in love with her eyes and her smile and her voice and she was on the stage and a young woman singing the aria because something foul had happened to the diva something unexplained that frightened her or angered her so that she walked out of the rehearsal vowing she would not return and Christine yes it was Christine Daaé on the stage my stage for I was the patron and she was mine my singer my star and I went to her dressing room because of course she is mine and when I saw her and spoke to her I knew that she was the one that I would make my mistress not my wife perhaps I did go to her room that night thinking we would sup and I would explain to her why I wanted to set her up in a small apartment and visit her and how this would be an arrangement that could only make us both happy and would never harm her perhaps I planned to sleep with her and perhaps she is right to wonder when I thought of her as a wife as the legitimate mother of my future children when did I imagine that I could marry a girl from the chorus of the opera instead of one of those women who had been trained to be the mistress of a manor and to be the countess of Chagny a proper wife that would make my mother and father proud how did I imagine that my mother and father would accept this actress, this member of the opera who placed herself on the stage for all to see? was it when he took her from me? is she right that I only knew that I loved her when the Phantom declared his love for her and became my rival? I remember the way he looked at her and it tortured me to see the passion and love in his look and it drove me to distraction to see that she looked at him as if bewitched, this monster this horror had stolen her soul from me and yes it may be true that he woke in me the absolute demand that I knew could only be met if she were my wife so I have the Phantom to thank after all for showing me the value of my little Lotte my childhood love but it pains me to think I might have taken her to bed as a mistress as a woman unworthy of the name of my family and after a year or several years as my concubine would I have been able to walk away from her? my heart whispers that I would have loved her as I do now with or without the Phantom but my mind taunts me that my duty would have kept my heart on a short leash and I would have left her to marry an actor or a merchant or a soldier perhaps I wouldn't have thought her a proper match for me I would have controlled my passion the Phantom would never allow his passion to be controlled by reason or necessity he sees nothing as more important than the passion he feels for her and his passion for her inspired the boundless expression of my own against my family against my honor against all reason

"I can't believe that you said that, Christine."

"Your father and mother have been very courteous to me, Raoul, but I can tell that I wouldn't be their choice for you. I've no family. I was raised as an orphan in the opera world where half of the people living together do so without benefit of clergy. I know how many of the chorus girls obtain the trinkets they wear. Mme. Giry protected me as much as she could from that part of the artists' world, but I'm not stupid."

"I've assured my family that you're innocent and pure."

"Yes, but do you believe it to be so?"

"What are you saying?"

"Do you believe that I'm innocent and pure? When you come to our bed, will you think me your virgin bride?"

Raoul stammered, embarrassed, "I ... I ... I don't understand why you're harping on this. It doesn't matter to me, Christine. I love you, and I don't care what your life was like before us."

Christine could see that he meant this with all his heart and that he thought it a sincere proof of his love for her in spite of everything. It did not occur to him that he also admitted in the same breath that her virginity, her innocence was indeed questionable to him.

"Do you believe I'm a virgin, Raoul?" She asked him very calmly, as if it were simply a matter of fact.

Raoul didn't know what to say. There was no way that he could tell. He wasn't an expert in such matters himself. He had very little experience with women.

"You don't, do you? Oh, my God, Raoul. You think that I ...? How could you?"

"What do you mean, how could I?" The anger that Raoul had been restraining suddenly overwhelmed him and burst to the surface.

"Did I ever give you cause to think ...?"

"Not only did you spend the entire night with him in his lair, but you told me yourself that it was as if he had put you in a trance. You didn't struggle! I was just outside your door. If you had screamed, I would have broken down the door! I never asked you. I tried to be a gentleman. But do you expect me to believe that he had you in his bed and nothing happened?" This was a discussion that Raoul had vowed he'd never broach with Christine. Some things were better left unknown. Such was his opinion regarding the curious affair of Christine's disappearance the night after her début performance at the opera. He'd told himself he didn't want to know what happened in the underground rooms between his betrothed and the madman that had bewitched her. Now he realized that it was because he assumed she had indeed been the Phantom's lover.

Christine looked at Raoul, stunned. It was so unfair. She'd awakened in the Phantom's bed. She'd been at his mercy, and he had treated her with the most gentle courtesy and respect. She remembered how drawn to him she felt. If he had asked to make love to her that night, she would have given herself to him gladly. But nothing had happened.

Curious to see the man behind the mask, she was drawn irresistibly to him the next morning. Standing beside him as he played for her, she caressed his shoulders, his cheeks, and then she lifted the mask from his face. Barely had she glimpsed the disfigurement behind the mask when he sprang away from her in a wild fit of anger. All the self-loathing in the world he heaped upon his own head as he shielded his face from her impertinent eyes.

Instead of answering her fiancé, Christine started for the door. In that moment, Raoul recognized his mistake and ran to grasp her by the arm.

"Christine, forgive me. I was jealous. I didn't want to know, so I never asked you. Please tell me now."

"You need to know, Raoul?" He didn't respond; he just looked at her in expectation. "Very well. You're the only man that will ever touch me that way."

Raoul knew that he should feel relieved, but something still gnawed at him. He didn't know what it was.

I sent her several letters in those first two weeks after we emerged from the depths of the underground cellars; none of them were answered. I paid the coachman dearly to take the missives in secret to the opera district, to find Madame Giry's apartments, and to give the notes directly to Meg. The search parties descended below the streets of Paris every day for more than a week. Raoul took the first groups, retracing our path through the canals of the underground river to the Phantom's secret chamber. There they found the evidence of his residence below the opera house. Of course, I expected that he had gone deeper into the heart of that dungeon to hide from us all. Several galleries branching off from the main quarters were explored without success. I sensed we had nothing more to fear from the poor creature. Even so I feared that Raoul might come upon him, perhaps by accident, and if they did come face to face again, either one or both might die. I couldn't lose Raoul now that we had won the right to live and love. When I remember the screams in the opera house, and recall the reports of those who perished in the fire when the great chandelier came crashing down on them all, I am appalled that the one who led to such death and horror has not been brought to justice.

Yet his was the voice that I heard each night before I went to sleep, and his eyes seemed to hold all the love and sadness in the world. He reminded me that my voice was made for more than reading the list of ingredients for bread, and that the joy of laughter and the peace of prayers are only surpassed by the beauty of song. First I heard his music, then he spoke to me, and my voice awoke, and I sang for him. There were times he frightened me, and there were times he angered me, but whenever I came back to the chapel he was waiting there for me with his music. Nothing gave me more joy; nothing dispelled my loneliness as much as that voice. How could I want his destruction?

But the searchers always returned empty handed. There was no sign of the Phantom. Some said that he was dead. Rumors were heard that he was seen at the Rue des artes, but the descriptions were absurd, bearing no resemblance to my Ghost. Clearly they were the work of the imagination of the mob if not inventions of the press to increase the sales of their daily gazettes.

I had to invent an excuse to go in person in search of Meg. Raoul had expressly demanded that I not approach Madame Giry, nor Meg. For some reason, he acted as if Madame Giry were involved with the crimes of the opera house. He wouldn't explain further when I asked for explanations. So one day I told the servants to say that I had gone to the dressmakers to discuss the design of the bridesmaids' dresses; that I had changed my mind about something or other and would return later in the day. The coachman left me at the shop; I told him to return at a previously agreed upon hour. After he rounded the corner, I hailed another driver and gave him the address in the opera district.

Madame Giry's apartments were on the top floor of a neighboring building. The concierge sent word that I was waiting below. I nervously clutched my purse worrying the beads along its surface as if praying a rosary. Finally the message returned that I was to come up to the apartment.

when she touches my face does she feel for the scars behind his mask? does she want me to hold her more tightly, to be more threatening, to force her to do what I will her to do or is she happy to lie here safe and protected? I still feel the rope scratching against my neck and feel him tugging at it stretching my neck my feet on tiptoe my throat clamping shut unable to breathe the air trapped in my lungs while my eyes blur I see her approach him he stands knee deep in the fetid water of the bowels of Paris and pretends to be a king and he calls her to him with some power of which I have no understanding his face a hideous raw wound and yet she goes to him and places her hand on his scarred cheek and strokes the twisted flesh along her eye and brings her mouth to his foul mouth, a mouth that has condemned her to live in darkness and filth with him or to see me die no way that we can win no way that I can save her and she kisses him and draws back and the look on her face through the blur of my tears is radiant and she kisses him yet again the rope slackens enough for me to breathe I cough and sputter and blink trying to clear my vision I can't believe what I've seen and she's still there close to him from the grate of the iron bars where he has tied me it appears that their bodies touch and she will be the bride of Hell and even if he were to free me now I wouldn't be able to go, to leave her here, he'll have to kill me but the devil's more cunning than we know he drops the rope he lets me go and frees Christine to go with me and in that stroke he towers over us he the one who rescues us both, and I the emasculated pawn even so I'll take my prize, Christine rushes to my side and unties my ropes, if she hadn't stopped me in the graveyard when the madman and I fought it out with swords we wouldn't be here at his mercy now I should have run him through with my sword when I had the chance but Christine begged for his life and I wonder in the dark our bodies pressed close if she imagines my face misshapen and listens for his voice instead of mine

"Forgive me, Christine, for not sending you word. I was frantic. The police inspector continually harasses me demanding that I tell him every and anything I might about the Opera Ghost. He was convinced that I could take him to the Phantom. But I was much more concerned for Meg; she disappeared that same night. I knew that she followed the mob to the caverns below, and no one saw her after they arrived at the ghost's quarters, the room to which he must have taken you that night. After the last of the men emerged from the tunnels and she wasn't among them, I was about to go myself to search for her when the Inspector's men forced me to accompany them to the constabulary." Mme. Giry had embraced Christine with unexpected affection and offered her a seat near the window as she insisted on making tea for them both.

"Oh, Mme. Giry. Is she still missing?" The thought of Meg coming face to face, alone, with the Phantom in the tunnels after she and Raoul managed to escape filled her with dread. God forbid that her friend had to pay her and Raoul's ransom. What revenge might the Phantom take on this innocent young woman if she came upon him unexpectedly?

"No, my dear, don't fret." Mme. Giry patted her hand gently. Smiling sweetly she looked into Christine's eyes and spoke soothingly. "I've found ma petite. She's more remarkable than even a mother's love would have thought. I'll tell her you've come when she returns this afternoon from her errands."

Seeing her former pupil's confusion, the mistress added, "You do him an injustice, Christine, to imagine that he would harm our Meg. You, nor anyone, need fear the Phantom anymore." A dark cloud seemed to cross her face as she turned away from Christine.

"What?" The young woman withdrew her hand from Mme. Giry's and with an urgency she herself didn't completely understand pressed the woman for an explanation. The tremor in her voice betrayed her dread and fear. "Answer me. What say you of him? Has something happened?"

"My dear Christine, I see that you aren't quite as free as I thought. You're concerned for him, no?"

"Please, tell me. Is he well? Does he suffer?" Tears welled up in her eyes as she waited for the answer.

"He's not well. He's retreated even farther into the caverns under the streets of Paris. But he's alive. I see that you're relieved in spite of the harm he's done you and M. Chagny."

"I must be going, Mme. Giry." Abruptly the young woman rose as if remembering that she was about to miss an important appointment. "May I continue to write? Will Meg be able to correspond with me?"

"Mais oui, ma cherie. Shall I tell her to write you immediately when she returns?"

"No, Mme. Giry. No, I mean, yes, please do tell her to write me, but I don't want to distress Raoul. He wants no reminder of this … nightmare. I'll ask my coachman to collect the letters; he's trustworthy and will see that the letters are delivered discreetly."

"Do you have any other message that you might want to leave with us, my dear?"

Christine hesitated at the door as she felt Mme. Giry's hand lightly touch her shoulder. Glancing back, she seemed to consider something but was torn by indecision. "Raoul believes that I shouldn't sing anymore. He fears the music may make it impossible for me to recover from the ordeal that I've experienced."

"Oh, my dear, I'm so sorry. Perhaps it's for the best. But I do hope that you might return some day when you're stronger if you should feel the need."

hold me tightly ever so tightly keep me from sinking into the dark his melodies go round and round in my mind the water licks against the side of the boat and his voice echoes in on every side and yet I know he's here so close that I must be able to see him his voice is just there behind my ear and I feel him leaning against my back his legs press against mine a warmth rises from the depths of my body and I spread my legs but my hands find nothing when I reach behind I grasp only the bedclothes, the sheet warm so warm as if he has just risen from the bed

Dear Christine,

Forgive me that I've not written as promptly as you have wished. Maman told me of your visit. I've had a slight fever and am much, much better now. Maman has taken such good care of me.

Your letter touched me dearly. I'm so happy for you and Raoul. I can't believe that my dearest friend is soon to be married. Of course, I understand why Raoul's family wants to wait. The rumors are so unkind. They've taken your tragic story and made it into a serial novel of the most lurid sort. Forgive me again that I mention O. G., but the rumors are unkind to him as well as to the two of you. Your fiancé is most certainly right to keep you from reminders of that time. However, I can't help but think that it adds to your grief when he forbids you to sing. You have always found comfort in song. Surely He hasn't taken this from you. I know that He would never forgive himself if He thought you had lost that comfort because of Him. I fear that I've already written more than I should; let us forget the matter, my dear friend.

Once you're married you probably won't have the time to attend to old friendships like ours, but I sincerely hope that on occasion we might happen to meet in the Café de l'Opera or in the Bois and chat.
Your attentive and true friend,
Meg

Dearest Meg,

Your kind words have soothed my troubled soul. I wouldn't for the world want to lose our friendship. I'm but a simple girl yet. My good fortune and Raoul's love for me may have raised me above my station, but my heart is still with you and Mme. Giry and all those who were with me as I grew up in the Opera House. I so wish I could visit you without risking Raoul's displeasure. In time I know I'll be able to persuade him that our friendship is no threat.

The rumors have been both unkind and unjust. I must confess that your mention of O. G. startled me and yet filled me with an anxious desire to know more. Raoul believes I must forget it all, but I think he's mistaken somehow.

I've tried to abandon my music. You'll understand by my choice of words that I've not been successful. There's a conservatory in the east wing of this country estate where a piano stands sadly neglected. I asked Raoul's aunt to have it tuned. A music lover herself, she's been taken into my confidence and agrees that Raoul's demand that I not sing is unreasonable and even harmful to me. I play each afternoon before Raoul comes to visit, and it puts me in such a wonderful state that I'm pleasant and the best companion that a husband might want. He attributes this to the country air and the rest, but it's the music.

Yet it brings me a sadness as well. When Raoul departs I think it's his absence—and it is—that makes me gloomy and sad. My dearest Meg, I trust you so that only to you can I say this, but it's more than Raoul's absence, it's His absence or the absence of His voice that makes me ache. Raoul makes me forget this loss; he has such a way of being gay that I must be gay with him. We ride, we bathe in the nearby lake, we read by gaslight on the veranda when the nights are warm. He's begun to take me to card parties with his friends, friends of the family, and last week—in spite of his own injunction against music—we went to Lord and Lady Alexanders' party. I can't tell you how we danced. But that night I lay in bed and incredible as it may seem to you I found myself humming a melody that I knew was His.

If only I knew that he were safe! It worries me. If I am pale, it is for this reason, this uncertainty. When he told me to flee with Raoul, he spoke such terrible words, words that hinted at his own destruction. I imagine him still down there in the damp darkness, and wonder if he's fallen, if he lies suffering somewhere, if indeed he's dead. That time I came to visit, your mother told me he wasn't well. That was only a matter of weeks after we abandoned the opera house. What might have happened to him, poor creature?

Please, my friend, tear this letter and burn it. If it should ever come to Raoul's hands, it would cut him to the quick. He can't understand my concern for O. G. without imagining that I don't love him. This isn't the case. I can't explain it; I only know that it's true.

I've heard that you're taking singing lessons. I hope to hear you sometime soon. Once I'm married, I intend to demand that Raoul bring you to me to live here as the sister that you've always been to me. We'll have such good times! Your ever attentive and loving sister,
Christine

Dear Christine,

I've been very negligent in not responding to your letter for these past weeks. I would like to express my regrets at the death of the countess. This sad event couldn't have come at a worst moment for you. Once orphaned, now you were to have a family again, and you've lost yet again a mother. Please know that my thoughts and prayers are with you.

I understand the marriage will be delayed again. The papers suggest that it will take place next spring. What a glorious time for a wedding, Christine. You shall outshine the spring flowers.

You've heard correctly, my dearest sister. I'm being tutored. Although my teacher is a severe taskmaster, I'm progressing beyond my expectations. My voice is sweet, but not as rich as yours. I fear I'll never attain the mastery that you have. Your voice is not of this world. No teacher will be able to turn my voice into one as lovely as yours. Don't ask who my teacher is, Christine. It's best kept a secret.

My maman told you that I disappeared that same night you and Raoul fled together from O. G.'s chambers. I know you were concerned about me, and perhaps not only about me. You needn't be worried. All is well.

Please don't fail to write even if I answer infrequently. My only excuse is that my tutor is cruel and unbending. I would rather walk across hot coals than displease him.
Your adoring sister,
Meg

Dear Meg,

I've been foolish. Raoul and I expected to wed in a few days. Just before his mother fell gravely ill, we gave in to our impulses. We've been husband and wife in act if not in formal contract. The last month has been agony for me, but thankfully there will be no tragic consequences. I have confessed and been absolved of my indiscretions. I blush that I write this to you, but I want no secrets between us. You're truly the only one to whom I can unburden all my doubts and troubles.

Oh, how horrid that I should write, "the only one," and hence exclude my beloved Raoul. I do share all my secrets with him but one. The one that torments me in spite of your "All is well." I read your letter again and again looking for hidden meanings and turned it over in my hands hoping to find some secret revealed. Perhaps you're a bit cruel with me, as cruel as you say your tutor is with you because you don't make plain if you know anything about the matter that I confessed to you, my dearest Meg.

Perhaps your mother has let slip some fact, some indication as to His welfare? Has he indeed sunk into the bowels of the earth never to be seen or heard again? I hear his voice in my dreams, Meg. And even though it once inspired fear as well as longing, it now holds no fear for me. If you know anything about my Angel of Music, there I've used the phrase for he's still this to me, then I beg you to let me know.

Yours in joy and sadness,

Christine

The wedding was to be celebrated within the fortnight but again was postponed when the countess passed away after a sudden illness. Raoul's father was so despondent that he locked himself away in his apartment for days on end. The wedding must wait until a decent period of mourning had passed. Christine consoled Raoul as much as she could, and their wedding was set for the next spring. With the death of the matriarch of the family and the withdrawal of the count himself from all society, it became prudent to send Christine once again to the country house where she was properly chaperoned by Raoul's aunt.

Unfortunately, the lovers had already been indiscreet. Just before his mother fell ill, Raoul had come to Christine's chamber, and she was not willing to turn him away thinking the wedding imminent. They made love. Quietly before the sun rose the next morning, Raoul slipped back to his own chambers. Confident that they would soon be wed, the two continued to enjoy the rights of husband and wife until the night they awoke to the bustle in the hallway of the servants going to and from the mistress's bed chamber and shortly afterwards the arrival of the doctor. Lying awake naked in each other's embrace, they waited until the doctor retired. Raoul slipped back to his rooms where his father sat in the dim moonlight waiting for him.

Three days after the funeral, Christine was sent to the safety of the country estate. She would remain there through a respectable period of mourning, chaperoned by Raoul's aunt. The wedding would have to wait again. Raoul waited anxiously for word from Christine. Finally, Christine was able to bring his fears to rest. All was well; they had escaped unscathed from their rash behavior. The next spring, nearly two years after the famous fire in the opera house and the disappearance of the Phantom, Christine and Raoul were married in the Cathedral of Notre Dame and departed for a three-month honeymoon in Italy.

The end of summer brought the newlyweds back to Paris; the servants drew the sheets from the furniture in the east wing, aired the bed linens, opened the windows and doors and brought the sunlight streaming into the chambers to welcome the young master and his bride. The last days of summer held their heat clutched against the oncoming winds of October as September slipped away between their fingers. The leaves turned from green to golden buttercup and pumpkin and prepared for their somersaults into the air.

In the exhilaration of their home-coming, Raoul took Christine up into his arms and taking the steps two at a time brought her to the foyer of the mansion. His father greeted the two of them at the bottom of the stairs, gladdened by the happiness he remembered through theirs.

Within a month of their return, Christine told her husband that they were expecting their first child. The count lived to see his first grandchild born on a cool morning in early spring.

CHAPTER 3

The Canary

"Maman, I'm fine. I've had no fever for days now. I want to return to Erik's."

"You say, "Erik's," as if he were a gentleman friend that has come seeking your hand." Mme. Giry regretted saying this as soon as she saw the blush on her daughter's face. How could she erase these past two weeks from her daughter's mind? How could she rescue her from a fantasy that she knew had taken hold in her heart?

Only two days past, they had emerged from the hidden cellars that lay beneath the opera house. The Phantom left Mme. Giry to attend to her feverish daughter and only returned the next evening with Caesar, a beautiful white stallion from the theater stables. Since the fire, the stables had been vacant; the horses had been removed. Mme. Giry couldn't imagine how Erik had found Caesar. Saying not a word, he strode over toward the bed, wrapped the blanket around Meg's body, and lifted her as if she were a feather. He placed her upon the horse and helped Mme. Giry mount behind her. Silently he took the lead of the horse and guided them through the channels towards the surface. As the streetlights became visible announcing the end of the tunnel, Erik gave the horse a gentle pat on his haunch and turned back without a word to the darkness from which they had come.

Mme. Giry sat beside her daughter. "Erik, as you so familiarly call him, has lived a most unnatural life, ma petite."

"I know, Maman, but he's a genius. I want him to teach me."

"Like Christine? You want him to teach you to sing? Don't you remember his obsession with Christine and its consequences? What if he were to demand that you give up all hope of a normal life?"

"Maman, I only want him to be my teacher. What happened between them will not happen between us. He fell in love with Christine."

"Meg, he's a murderer. Have you forgotten that?"

"You chose to forget that when you hid him at the opera house."

"That wasn't the same thing. He was a child. The man he killed treated him worse than an animal. It was an act of desperation."

"Let me go to him, Maman. He's alone. You don't understand. It's like being buried alive down there!"

Mme. Giry saw the same look of pity in her daughter's eyes that she remembered in her own so many years ago. But Meg was her child, and she refused to sacrifice her to the darkness. She had done what she could to protect Erik. He had gone mad. She could no longer turn a blind eye to his violence. Her daughter had been raised to live in the light. She wouldn't have her dragged down to the depths, no matter how much she pitied Erik.

"No, this is my final word, Meg. You'll continue at the ballet school at the Opera National. You'll receive voice lessons from M. Faure. He's a most talented teacher."

"No. I won't. You must go to Erik and discuss my lessons with him. I'm sure you'll see that he's not dangerous. If he refuses to take me as a pupil, or if you still think he's dangerous after speaking with him, then I'll obey you in this. Please. Please, give me this chance. I'll go to him only when you say that I can, Maman, even if it's only one hour a day, one hour a week, whatever the two of you decide. Christine learned so much from him; I know that I can become a great singer if Erik teaches me."

She couldn't withstand her daughter's pleas. Christine always had a lovely voice, but it was nothing compared to the voice she had after Erik took her under his instruction. Mme. Giry had felt troubled as she saw Christine outstrip her daughter, but she hadn't been willing to let Meg pay the price she knew Christine would have to pay.

"I'll speak with him, ma petite. I'll leave a message at the entrance to the tunnels and wait for him to contact me."

"No. You mustn't wait. He may never come out of that cavern again! You must go to him, Maman. If you knew his desperation! He plans to lie there in the darkness and die!"

"Very well, ma cherie. I believe that I know a way to find him."

she has no idea how dangerous he can be, how wounded he is, how he might have taken her in his bare hands and wrung the life from her all the time thinking of what he could not hold in his hands what he could not touch or if touch he could not retain the warmth thereof, the love of a mother didn't teach him the blow from a cane the neglect the derision of those who came to see him how can he even stand that one look at him now he hides in the dark and watches those who had once watched him and she thinks she can negotiate lessons from this raw flesh, this twisted nerve of a man who knows himself to be a man yet lives like an outcast from all society that would recognize him as such he pretends, he acts, he wears his masks and dons his formal dress, his cape ready to wrap around him and swallow him from devouring eyes and struts around his backstage kingdom pulling the strings of his puppets who fear him and she thinks she can control this demigod and teach him to be civil as he teaches her to sing like a goddess but she's more likely to end as a bird with singed feathers and broken wings if she flies too close to this angel in hell a hell that I brought him to meaning to protect him but was it better than the cage? was this burial alive in the belly of the beast an escape? I played our games with him but he knew that I feared him his touch his anger I would pull away if his hand reached out toward me pretending that I hadn't noticed his unspoken plea but I won't give him my child to pay for my cruelty I won't see her wedded to the angel of hell not for all the songs of heaven

Mme. Giry recalled the path the Phantom had used to bring her to Meg, and the same path they had followed to reach the street at ground level. The trick was to follow a sequence, one turn left, two turns right, one turn left, two turns right. The complicated system of vents and chimneys that rose to the surface afforded little light—only he was able to wander these tunnels without torch or lantern—so Mme. Giry had brought a lantern with her. As she approached the last bend, she turned out the light fearing that he would see her approach and perhaps attack before she was able to announce herself. The sight that met her eyes struck her with sadness.

She could see inside the cavernous room he had made his abode. The bed clothes lay twisted and dirty on the floor, a stain of dried menstrual blood still visible on the coverlet that had been wrapped around her daughter. Empty bottles of wine lay abandoned on the stones near the sofa, the remains of several cold meals were scattered across the sideboard and corner table, strewn haphazardly from one end to another of the alcove were masks and costumes as if the inhabitant of the room had been searching for some long lost treasure hidden among the clothes in his wardrobe, but the most bizarre aspect of the scene before her were the sheaf after sheaf of music nailed to the stone wall and the figure of the Phantom moving from one to another as if listening to each sheaf being played simultaneously on various instruments in a mad concert. Gone were his vest and cape leaving him clad only in a simple shirt and breeches. From her position she couldn't tell if he wore his mask.

"No, no, no, no! That isn't right!" The Phantom scratched at the sheet of music on the wall. In his mind, he rehearsed the new motif. Satisfied, he moved on to the next.

As if he heard her breathe, the Phantom stopped before the wall and turned his ear in her direction. He stayed still like this for some time, then searching the floor he seemed to pick something up and bring it to his face. He sensed that someone was in the cellars. When he turned in her direction, she called out to him so that he would know it was she.

He was dirty, his clothes soiled. His hair hadn't been combed and from the looks of the chamber he had done nothing more than eat whatever was at hand, leaving the crumbs wherever they fell, drunk only wine, discarding the empty bottles wherever they fell, and worked on his music. I had no idea whether the music fixed to the stone walls, pinned to the brocade coverings, was music he had written before or whether this might be a new opera or concerto he was now composing. The music was somewhere on the paper or in his head, for the instrument on which he used to compose was nowhere in sight. When he sensed my approach, he hurried to put on his mask, perhaps out of years of habit, and only then turned to face me. He made no effort to flee. Either he understood that it was I or he expected someone else whom he didn't have cause to fear. Or it may be that he was prepared, perhaps even desirous, that it be those who hunted him.

I called out to him in the same instant that he turned toward me, and I saw then, too, the blood covering his chest, the white linen shirt stained. This couldn't be my Meg's blood for it began at the collar of his shirt and dripped down upon his chest. I asked if he was hurt, and he stared at me as if not understanding for a moment. Then bringing his hand to the mask that covered his face, he looked down and saw the blood stains as if for the first time. Instead of answering, he took several strides forward until he was within reach of me. I stood my ground, even though I was somewhat fearful of his reaction to my return. His eyes looked at me and then beyond to see, I surmised, if anyone else accompanied me.

Satisfied that I was alone, he dropped to his knees at my feet and raised his two hands as if to reach out to me and cried, "Why? Why doesn't she remember me?" I hadn't seen him cry since he was very young, and without thinking I reached my hand out to touch him lightly on the shoulder whereupon he seized my hand for only a moment and pressed it to his cheek. Startled by his movement, my first inclination was to withdraw my hand, but his gesture was so sad and childlike that I knew it would be cruel to refuse him this sign of affection. Regaining his composure, Erik rose and turned back toward his room.

"Erik. You will surely die down here in this abandonment. You must let me help you."

"There is no Erik. He's dead, stillborn. There's only the opera ghost."

"But there's no longer an opera, Erik."

At this, he began to laugh, but it was a laugh without joy. "Why have you come, Madeleine? Do you want to play a game? Shall I be the monster and carry you away to my dungeon?" Saying this, he glared at me and ripped off his mask.

I tried to stifle my cry. Now I understood why his shirt was covered in blood. He had lacerated his face as if attempting to cut away the disfigurement. The wounds seemed recent, only now beginning to heal.

"Erik. You mustn't do this to yourself. Haven't you had enough pain? Do you think that this will somehow change your situation?"

"Situation?" He put the mask on again. "Situation? This is not a situation, my dear Madeleine. This is a sentence. I've been found guilty of ugliness, of desire, of inspiration and music. I've been found guilty of murder and revenge. I've been accused of having hoped to be loved. The verdict is guilty, and the sentence is to be condemned to this grave. I only wish to hasten the completion of the punishment. But this, too, is denied me. I'll have to endure, it would seem. I've tried starving myself, but my body won't allow it: It's too strong and forces me to both eat and drink. The time weighs heavy inside the walls of my coffin. My only hope is this." He spread his arms out indicating the music that carpeted the walls.

"I'll make sure that provisions are brought to the gate where you can collect them unseen."

"So, I will live. Rather, I will exist. I will exist. A carcass that breathes, eats, and shits." These words softly spoken hung in the air between us.

Maman has asked Erik to become my tutor. She said that he laughed and ranted that it was impossible. "How can a corpse teach music?" he mocked. I begged her not to take no for an answer, to insist, to flatter or threaten him, whatever it would take to make him relent. She did so, she told me, but to no avail. She thinks that he's made up his mind to die, if he can do so through sheer will. "Does he know that Christine no longer sings? That Raoul forbids her to sing because of her nervous condition?" I asked. Maman dares not mention her name to Erik. He threatened to strike her when she let drop Christine's name in her request that I, too, become his pupil.

She goes nearly everyday to bring provisions to him, and he lets her visit. She cleans some wound that he inflicted upon himself. I know that I'll become a great singer if only he teaches me. I won't disappoint him! The poor man is a danger to himself. If he were to become my tutor, it would give him a purpose again. The next time Maman goes to his chambers, I intend to go with her.

the opera house is a burned out shell, yet I've gone to roam its boxes, the fire burst the stained glass windows and the pit is burned, but the stage remains as does the backstage, the shell is stained black but I can see the gilded statues, there's still music trapped in the recesses of the dome, Christine sings there so I go and listen to her, Madeleine comes unbidden, I have told her not to but she insists and now she brings little Meg who sings although I have told her not to but she insists and asks me if the key is correct, if she should hold this note or that note longer and I tell her I'm not listening even though it's impossible not to hear her voice, a voice thinner than Christine's yet deeper in her throat, a pretty voice if I didn't still hear Christine's ringing in my ears I tell Meg to open her mouth to lift her chest if she wants to sing that note she's trying to wrench from her lungs I don't want to hear her and I don't mean to say those things to her but am unable to restrain myself and she sings and I can hear the smile in her voice which grates even more across my soul for I am not her teacher, am not a teacher, do not teach, cannot teach, teach music teach Christine teach music to Christine who sings who does not sing says Madeleine I have asked her I did not want to ask her but the words came unleashed from my heart my need to know to know if Christine is singing I hear her singing in the opera house above, the ghostly shell of the opera house she's singing there but it's an old song and she must be singing somewhere a new song not our songs but his songs to him to him and not to me and Meg sings but I am not to listen to her songs drown out the song that Christine sings and she sang that song to me, her angel, she sang when she loved me and her love is in that song and the other sounds must not drown out her sound so I tell Meg to do scales which I am able to not listen to and she does them and sometimes I hear a note that blends with Christine's and I'm here and there at the same moment and it's not so painful to listen to Meg until her mother comes for her to lead her back to the light and leave me in the dark to listen to Christine

"Maestro, should I do the aria from the third act?" Meg had performed the warm-up exercises for several minutes, and was expecting Erik to give her some instruction.

The Phantom paced back and forth across the room and waved his hand at the young woman to proceed. He rarely looked at her, hardly sat still as she practiced. Mme. Giry sat in a chair and knitted during the lesson, only the clicking of her needles testifying to her watchfulness.

"No, no, no, no, no. The piece here calls for staccato, not a slur. Do the stops over and over. Watch the phrasing. Start two measures back. You need more command of your breathing. Put your hand on your diaphragm." At this point, he sang the phrase and gestured for Meg to echo it. Again he wasn't happy with the notes, so again he sang it to her.

"Maestro, you sing so beautifully." She no sooner said this than she regretted it. He glared at her, swept the music out of her hands, and directing himself to Mme. Giry told her the lesson was over.

Dearest Christine,

Forgive me that I've not accepted your kind invitations to visit. I do so wish to see your child. Such a blessing must be accepted as a sign that your love for Raoul and his for you are meant to be. I regret that I haven't been there to share even a little of your joy, but I don't know how I would be with you and yet obey the silence imposed on me.

My mother hasn't allowed me to be completely honest with you. She swore me to secrecy. She has the best intentions, and I understand her reservations. But you're like a sister to me. To keep the truth from you is wrong. You mustn't worry about what I'm going to tell you. I'm gloriously happy, and I know myself to be safe.

When you've asked me about my tutor, I have not known what to write. I picked up pen and paper so many times over the last two years only to abandon them in confusion. I owe you my love, but I owe Him my protection and gratitude. I confess to you, Christine, that if circumstances were other than what they are I might even say love. I feel that you've already guessed my secret, indeed our secret for it's held in common among the three of us, my tutor, my mother, and myself. Now I shall break apart that triangle to include you in my trust.

Did you know his name, Christine? I have learned it. He's a man like any man, but wonderful and terrible. His pain nearly killed him in those first months. He saved my life, Christine. Perhaps that may weigh in his favor when God holds him to account for the deaths and destruction he's caused. The night of the disaster, I followed him through a passageway behind a mirror; the searchers didn't see me disappear through the gateway. But not knowing the paths, I became lost and nearly drowned in an underground well if not for the fact that He saved me. As a result of his efforts or from his despair, we'll never know which was more crucial, he fell ill. But it wasn't only his physical body that suffered, he nearly lost his mind in those first months after you left us. Maman and I nursed him back to health.

In his grief, he was so wild, so volatile that for days we feared to approach him. Maman insisted on visiting him, even though he ranted and raved at her. Then one day she confessed to me that she feared he had given up completely and was simply waiting to die down in the underground tunnels.

You know how much I had always wanted to sing like you, my dearest. It came to me that if he were to become my tutor not only would I perhaps attain some of your perfection but that he would have something to occupy his mind. I hoped it would stave off his complete surrender to death.

He refused to teach me at first, but we women are clever and persistent. I came to his chambers with Maman each day and sang. He ignored me completely until on one occasion in particular while attempting a difficult aria he stopped me and instructed me to repeat the last phrase I had sung. I did this, and he said that I needed to work on the dynamics of the phrase. From that moment on, he was my teacher in spite of himself.

How I would love to visit you, Christine, but I don't dare miss even one evening with him. He becomes terribly agitated at the least variation in our schedule. One evening when I came late, he yelled at me cruelly. I won't repeat to you the things he said. Suffice it to say that you will always be the ideal to which he compares me.

Even though I may fall short of his expectations, I've impressed the director of the Opera National. They've asked me to sing this season. Please come and hear me, Christine. Not wishing to boast, but perhaps you might hear some of your O. G. in my voice.

With all the love in my heart owed to a dear friend and sister,

Meg

Each evening the two women come to him. The mother leads her daughter through the tunnels they have come to know quite well. Drawing close to the Phantom's rooms they sometimes hear nothing—a silence so deep it belongs to the graveyard—other times they stop and hear his voice—a voice so beautiful that time itself stops to listen. Before approaching, Mme. Giry rings the bell three times to announce their visit. The singing stops, and a voice says simply, "Come."

Mme. Giry remains vigilant throughout the lesson. She brings provisions, clean linens and clothing. She insists on his maintaining a decent level of care in his hygiene and dress. At first he had fallen into such despair that he had forsaken all semblance of manners and proper behavior. He was living like an animal, but Mme. Giry has slowly managed to return him to his former habits. Although he does not wear the formal dress attire that he once wore, he dresses with more care now, and he has begun again to pay close attention to the disguise that masks his deformity. Soon she is tranquil enough that she leaves her Meg with him and does her errands in the streets above only to return when she knows the time is drawing near. The first time that Meg was left alone with him, the Phantom was puzzled and ill at ease but now he pays no heed to Mme. Giry's comings and goings, so concentrated is he on his pupil's progress.

Meg's improvement is undeniable. Erik no longer paces back in forth in his cell. He stands behind her, peers over her shoulder at the music, and marks the notes that are problematic. "Again," he says. "Louder.... softer ... enunciate ... round your lips."

he is pleased with me I hear it in his voice and I see it in those eyes those eyes that are warm and soft and then sharp and dark that change as swiftly as the notes on the sheets I love to watch his eyes as he looks at some point beyond the walls and I sing and with my song I see his eyes respond with passion, with joy, with sorrow, with all the shades and colors of the monochrome notes on the yellow parchment paper he gives me his music not the music I've always known the music the lords and ladies listen to in their box seats now at the Opera National it's a strange music that surprises and violates my expectations even the expectations of the ear and he has explained that music is learned the ear learns to listen and the ear that is complacent comes to forget to listen and only hears what it always heard before and is trapped in a past a repetition of sounds and forgets how to listen and needs to be struck by the distinct, the transgression, the new sounds that he hears and marks down on the papers he puts before me challenging me to rise from the low-

est of notes to notes that fly higher than the hawk, bouncing off the moon beams and I swoon from those eyes in which I see his music his music reflects back at me from those eyes that touch me I feel them like hands upon my body it's the most exquisite touch

In the middle of the piece, she turned a ghastly white and swooned. Her eyes rolled back into her head, and she listed to the side, and I caught her in my arms before she hit the ground. The music was dancing round the room, reverberating off the stones, funneling down the passageways. Little Meg was singing with the angels, and her soul must have fled her body with those sounds for she fainted into my arms.

I held her close, the first time that I had held anyone since I buried myself in this lost corner of my kingdom, since I held Christine against her will. I felt myself aroused by the solidity of her flesh; her body fragile like a bird's, even so, lay heavy against my arm and warm against my body.

She awoke, and her eyes looked into mine. Irresistibly I felt my lips descend upon hers. They lightly touched, and my body screamed out to me the illusory sensations of a lost limb, Christine's body, Christine's kiss upon my lips, my first kiss, my only kiss.

I brought Meg to the sofa and laid her on the cushions and left her there. I heard her call to me as I hurried away, down the tunnels, even deeper into the bowels of this hell. I ache with remembered desire and pain. I will leave Mme. Giry a note. The lessons are over. She can't learn anything more from me, and I can't bear to have her here again.

Dear Mme. Giry,

Your daughter has completed her course of instruction. Her voice is quite adequate for the dull ears of any of the opera buffs in Paris. Indeed, it's quite exquisite, and the public will never appreciate the fineness of it. You mustn't be surprised that she has done so well at the auditions. I regret that I missed her début at the Opera National. If our Opera House were still in service, Little Meg would be given the role appropriate for the prima donna that she has become. They will soon recognize her superiority at the Opera National.

She should also continue her ballet training. Her true talents, I've always felt, are in the music of the body. She can't surpass my former pupil in voice, but she has always done so in the dance.

I'm grateful for your continued attentions. I wish to retain your services according to the arrangements included in this letter and for which you will receive an appropriate stipend. Please be sure that the solicitor receive these instructions and that he carry them out exactly as stated.

I think that I will perhaps hear our little Meg at the Opera in the not so distant future. I've been buried long enough. I begin to tire of my surroundings.

The Count de Chagny is wrong to forbid his wife the use of her voice. He mustn't insist on this.

Your humble servant and friend,

O. G.

CHAPTER 4

The Lover

"It's for your own good, Christine," Raoul insisted yet again.

Christine turned away from him in exasperation. Raoul went to her and gently embraced her. Whispering into her ear, he said, "You dream at night, my love. I sometimes wake and hear you. It's there in your mind. The music is all tangled in your mind with all that happened to us that night."

She turned in his arms and buried her face in his chest. "I didn't know, Raoul. Yet I can't lose the music. I think that the only way to untangle all this, as you put it, is to win back my father's music and make it my own. How can I hear anything but the Phantom's music if I've nothing to replace it."

She didn't mean that her love for Raoul and his for her were nothing. But she saw that this was how her husband understood her words. He was hurt that their love was not sufficient to make her happy and to bring her peace. She tried to explain, but his cold expression stopped the words in her mouth.

Raoul informed her he was late for an engagement in town. Clouds passed over blotting out the sunshine that had filled the sunroom, and Christine felt a chill run down her back as her husband abruptly turned and left.

In the graveyard, at my father's crypt, I feel a peace that I don't fully comprehend. It was here that Raoul nearly killed the Phantom. Had he done so, we might have been free. I wouldn't have been forced that night to betray the man who had been my constant companion. I might not have had to rip his mask off before all to see. I wouldn't have had to inflict such pain. I'll never forget his eyes. He was singing to me his opera. Father, all the passion in the world seemed trapped in those notes.

I don't know how I had the strength to resist him. Oh, forgive me, Father, I know he was a monster. Only our love, Raoul's and mine, was able to save me. But wasn't that proof, Father, of something noble, something pure in his soul, something that the night had not yet destroyed? He had dragged me to his rooms, he had demanded that I put on a wedding dress and veil, and he had forced on my hand the ring that Raoul had given to me as a pledge of his love. He intended to make me his bride that very night, unwitnessed by man or God. How can I pity him? Oh Father, since the days you told me the dark tales of the north there were many stories of monsters, demons, and yet I couldn't think this man a monster. I still can't think him evil. Can love be evil? Can music be evil? Listen while I sing this to you, one of his melodies. Can anything that touches me so deeply be monstrous, Father, unless I too am monstrous?

"What are you saying, Roger? That my wife visits the cemetery to meet someone? She speaks with someone at her father's grave?"

"Forgive me, sir. I shouldn't have said anything; I didn't mean any harm. Mme. Montre and I were just talking in the kitchen when you came in. Just idle talk, that's all."

"Yes, I know. I want an explanation of what you were implying when you said she was talking with someone in the graveyard. Who did you see with her? Tell me, man."

"No one, sir. No, you misunderstood what I was saying. She talks to no one. That is to say, no one is there except the stone angels on the gravestones. I fancy she's praying, my lord. She kneels down in front of the Daaé crypt and talks or prays. Then she sings at times. That's what drew me over, sir. I didn't mean to pry. I heard this voice, and it was so lovely, you see, that I just wanted to hear it more. So I walked over, real quiet, so as not to startle her. She always has me wait outside the gate, you know. She used to spend about a half of an hour, but lately she stays longer and longer. Well, a man gets a little jittery, and so I thought I should check up on her to make sure she was okay."

"So she sings to her father at the crypt. And you see no one there? It's very important, Roger, that you're sure of this."

"No, sir, I see no one, ever." Seeing the relief on his master's face, Roger thought to continue, "Didn't see anyone, but the last couple of times I swore I heard an echo or something answer her singing."

"What?"

"It must be some effect of the stones. Her voice is so beautiful, my lord. Forgive me for being so forward, sir, but it's a gift she has. A shame not to use it."

"Never mind that, Roger. What did you hear? What other sound did you hear besides my wife's voice? Was it a man's? Answer me."

"Well, yes, it was very, very soft but low so I suppose it might have been a man's. It was as if someone were singing along with her so to speak. But I couldn't see a soul there, my lord." Raoul didn't hear the rest for he was already down the hall.

"Darling. It's only because of your condition. The child. You must rest more. The doctor advises against riding out along the country lanes; they're usually in a lamentable condition, especially after a rain, and the jostling around might be bad for the baby. You must think about your health now that your confinement's drawing near."

"But I simply wish to visit my father's grave. I'll go less frequently if you insist, perhaps once a week."

"No."

"But Raoul, why are you so adamant?"

"I told you. I don't want you to put yourself or our baby in danger."

Christine was distressed. Her husband's concern meant that he might have guessed the nature of her visits to her father's grave.

It had happened only recently. She thought it might all be in her mind. But Raoul's reaction filled her with dread; it must be real, or Raoul would not be worried. Why would he forbid that she go to her father's grave now? And how did he know that when she sang, she sometimes heard the Phantom. She had thought it a trick of the wind at first, a low warm note sustained against which her song wafted along as on the waves of the sea. Then she began to hear her words echoed in his voice; it was undeniably her teacher's voice. Still she thought she might have invented it herself as she sometimes imagined her father's voice in her head answering her, consoling, praising, and warning her. Raoul had made her realize that it was real. The Phantom had been there at the graveyard; he had sung with her! But he had remained hidden and had not spoken to her.

"Perhaps you're right, my love. Perhaps it's best that I remain close to home. I'll pray to my father in the chapel here. I'll light a candle for him there."

Raoul kissed her on her forehead, relieved that she was finally listening to reason.

"But I ask you one favor. I want to visit this Thursday as I always have. Just this last time."

He didn't want to agree, but realized that she wouldn't relent in this request. He would let her go, but she wouldn't be alone. He would follow close behind and wait to hear the Phantom himself.

He glances around the corner of the crypt and sees Christine's carriage approach. She didn't come yesterday, nor the day before that. *I wait here for her, knowing that she will come. I spent too long in the darkness trying not to forget her face. These moments in the graveyard are my only peace.* He feels his blood rush to his heart as he sees her descend from the carriage; the driver assists her. She's delicate. She must take care of herself and the child she's carrying.

Out of the corner of his eye something attracts his attention. He retreats farther behind the gray limestone of the mausoleum to get a better view of the opposite side of this avenue in the graveyard. A shadow by a small tomb catches his eye. It's the shoulder of a man concealed. What might he be doing here? Is he here waiting in ambush for Christine? She's coming this way, when the Phantom sees that the intruder, the other shadow in the graveyard, is Raoul. *No, this is not yours! This is all that you've left me of her, and you cannot take it from me! Isn't it enough that you have her all the other waking and sleeping moments? You cannot take this from me!*

Christine has now approached her father's grave and places the flowers on the steps leading to the crypt. There she kneels and then sits upon the lower step. Erik glances over to the spot where Raoul hides. He wants so to whisper Christine's name, but he knows Raoul will hear it also. Every muscle in his body tenses as he holds himself back. She's saying her prayers now. Raoul leans close to the tomb to listen. *He's waiting for me to speak, to sing to Christine. What would he do if I came down to her now?* But sadly the thought comes to him, What would she do if he were to come down to her? Would she stay and smile at him, offer him her hand or would she freeze in terror or scream and flee to her coachman? Seeing Raoul emerge from his hiding place, would she encourage her husband to run this poor soul through with his sword? If he were to lie there bleeding in the dirt, would she cry for him? Or would she throw herself relieved into Raoul's arms?

I cannot bear to know.

So Erik withdraws to the shadows of the mausoleum just out of sight, close enough only to hear Christine's voice as she begins to sing. It's so long since he has felt the sting of tears; now they run freely down his face. "No more," he says barely in a whisper, a sob.

I heard him, I know. A sound of pain, of sorrow. A word indiscernible to my ears, yet the sadness all too easily understood by my soul. I knew that he was here. Sweet monster, my monster, he wouldn't come out, wouldn't show himself to me. I've banished you, my Angel, and you obey. Didn't you like the song that I sang to you, or is it possible that you somehow know that this is the last time that I come to the graveyard to sing for you and for Father? Raoul loves me so much, but he's sometimes a little cruel. He won't let me give you even this one kindness. No, my poor creature of darkness, not even a song. Oh, it almost breaks my heart. I don't know why. I should be hardened to you. I should punish you, but I can't.

Although I searched the whole graveyard before Christine's coach arrived and found nothing, not one sign of his presence, I know that he's here. I can sense him out there waiting behind one of those stone-cold angels or crouched behind one of the many mausoleums that stand in this cemetery.

My beloved prays at her father's tomb and sings the songs I forbid her to sing in the safety of our home. I had forgotten the intoxication of that voice. It's no wonder that the Phantom loved her. Who could listen to her and not love her?

A sound. I heard him. I heard his voice coming out from the graves around us. But now it's gone. I wait for him to speak again so that I can find him and drag him out from his hiding place. As long as he lives, we'll know no peace.

She stopped her song; she heard him, too. She must be frightened. But, no, she doesn't move, she stays and looks about her, not in fear. She seems calm, even desirous of hearing that voice again. She looks about, trying to find the source of the sound. I wait and watch. Christine waits and watches too, for only a moment. Then she's crying. Oh, my God, she's crying for him!

Erik withdraws at a distance and waits for Christine to rise and turn away from the crypt. He follows from tomb to angel to cross as she follows the avenue to the gate. He sees Raoul similarly tracing a parallel path to Christine's until the two men stop and watch their beloved get into the carriage and depart. Erik in despair sees Raoul hesitate just long enough for the carriage to disappear down the lane. Once the carriage is out of view, he sees Raoul double back to a section of the cemetery where his horse is tethered.

Erik considers attacking his rival now, here alone in the graveyard where no one can come to his assistance. He could kill Raoul, drive his sword through him and leave him to bleed on the stones. He would go to Christine and steal her away to his lair and force her to stay with him. There would be music all around them. She would forget Raoul.

With these bloody thoughts in his mind, he draws near. Unaware that the Phantom approaches within striking distance, Raoul stands next to his horse. He hasn't mounted. Instead, he presses his face against the horse's mane. The horse nervously neighs and swings its head toward his master to see what the matter is. Erik stops in his tracks, unable to strike, as he sees his rival's shoulders shake with grief. Instead, he watches from behind a granite angel; his hands curl into fists in an effort to hold back his own misery.

Dearest Christine,

Maman and I send you the booties and dress for your lovely little boy. You're a mother, Christine! How wonderful you must feel. Is Raoul proud? What a stupid question, for all fathers are proud! You'll be quite busy now, I expect, with the chores of motherhood.

I'm so pleased that you finally came to hear me sing at the Opera National. The manager treats me with such care and respect. Maman is pleased with my success as is my former tutor. Oh that he were still my tutor! The night you and Raoul were here my tutor was also present. He has found a way to be quite discreet. I'm sure that you weren't aware of his presence, although I know that he was aware of yours. He left me a kind note in my dressing room applauding my success. He seems well.

I have asked Maman to arrange with him more lessons, but she says that he has retired from tutoring for the present.

Please let me know when you plan to attend the opera again, and I'll arrange a special dinner in my dressing room for the three of us—you, me, and Raoul.

My warmest thoughts are with you, your most faithful friend,
Meg

Little Raoul is sleeping; he has found his thumb. I sing to him the songs my father sang to me and pat his hands together. Unbidden the memory steals across my mind of the little Persian monkey on the barrel shaped music box. I woke in the Phantom's bed to its melody, a melody that I hear now in the back of my mind. It drowns out my father's lullaby.

That night did he stand over me as I slept in his bed and watch me the way I watch my beloved child? He sang, I know, for there was always music.

Raoul doesn't understand how important music is to me. How can he move about the world without the sounds of it? I've encouraged him to support the ballet, and we're subscribers to the Opera National. He resisted for weeks and only when we discovered that Meg was to open as lead soprano did he change his mind. On my insistence, he agreed to be Meg's patron. Evidently she already has one patron, but our contributions to Meg's career were eagerly accepted. After all, the opera takes a percentage of any allowance set for its performers.

My confinement and recuperation have finally come to an end, and my husband can return to my bed. I've missed his touch, his arms holding me tight, his breathing in the night. Some wives, I know, complain that their husbands annoy them and disturb their sleep with their large bodies and loud snoring in the night. Raoul's body is a comfort to me; the sounds he makes only lull me further into peaceful sleep. His presence anchors me to the here and now, and I forget everything else. I reach out in the night and touch his body and know that I'm safe.

We speak for hours of our plans for little Raoul. The best tutors shall be brought, he shall have ponies and we will spend the summers, just as Raoul and I did as children, near the sea. And we must give him brothers and sisters. I don't want him to be alone, like me or like ... Tonight we can begin again, my love and I. We will fill the rooms with children, and, yes, with music. I will insist. Raoul has to stop this vendetta against music. I'll make the sunroom a conservatory of music, fill it with musical instruments, and our children will become an orchestra, each learning his own instrument as well as the instruments of his siblings. We'll hold concerts for Raoul, invite his friends and play for them all, and I will sing and teach my darlings to sing.

Tonight I start. I'll insist on singing an aria after dinner. I won't ask permission; I'll just do it. Let Raoul make a fuss in front of our guests, if he dare. I think he won't. It may be naughty of me to put him in such a position, but only he and I will know how naughty I am.

CHAPTER 5

The Garden

"Raoul! Oh, for pity's sake tell me you're all right?" The men carried the Count de Chagny through the foyer and into a side room where they laid him on a couch. The surgeon followed and gave swift orders to the chambermaid. Christine had been reading in the library, waiting for Raoul to return from his card party when she heard the carriage approach and the urgent voices of several men. The sight that greeted her in the foyer nearly made her swoon. Raoul covered in blood groaned softly. If not for this and the urgency with which the men settled him on the couch, Christine would have assumed he was dead. "What's happened? Is he all right?"

The surgeon did not reply immediately but attended to the injured man. The chambermaid brought the requested items and set them beside the couch.

"Please, will he live? Will he be all right?" Christine could see Raoul's face in the lamplight; it was ghastly white in its paleness. She was hovering over the surgeon to see the wound when he barked at her to give him room.

"He'll live. I've managed to stop the bleeding. But stay out of my way."

One of the grooms cleared his throat and approached the lady. Drawing her back from the couch with a gentle touch on her arm, he whispered so as not to distract the surgeon, "My lady, the count was attacked by several thieves as he left the establishment. He barely had time to draw his sword and dispatch one of the brigands when he himself was wounded. There were two others who would have done him in for sure except that this man came out of nowhere and fought them back. The count lay there in the street while this man ran one of the thieves through with his sword and strangled the other with a rope.

They say it was the Opera Ghost; he was dressed like a gentleman all in black and wore a white mask like a skull's face."

"How do you know all this?"

"Well, the men lay there dead so it's no trick to see how they were killed. Then there was a witness that ran into the inn yelling about this masked demon that flew past her. It's not the first time someone's seen the ghost. You must have heard the stories about him, my lady, the one they say haunts the district." He sputtered an apology when he saw the effect his words were having on the young mistress. She had gone nearly as pale as her husband. "Forgive me, my lady, but she probably wasn't in her right mind."

"Where is he now? The one who saved my husband's life?"

"Ah, that's the funny thing. He ran off. You would think he might stay to account to the police officers if he were a regular man, that is. As these came running around the corner, they caught just a last sight of someone disappearing."

"Countess, I think your husband stirs." The surgeon was washing his hands in a basin of warm, soapy water. Raoul was coming out of his swoon. Christine rushed to his side. She took his hand in hers and softly kissed his pale cheek. He opened his eyes and looked at her. She placed her hand on his chest to keep him from trying to rise.

"You must lie quite still, my love. You've been wounded. We don't want you to start bleeding again."

The surgeon gathered his materials and told the groom that he would return the next day to check on his patient.

"Christine." Raoul began, but she would not let him speak.

"Rest. You were attacked. You're home now, and you'll be fine after you rest. The doctor has given you something to help you rest."

"Madame, little Raoul is awake. Will you go to him?" The nurse stood in the doorway, reluctant to bother her mistress at such a moment.

"No, Lucille."

She began to instruct the nurse to go to the baby, but Raoul interrupted her. "I'll be good. You go on now. He's hungry." He chided her with the little strength he still had. As he did so, his head turned gradually toward the cushions, and he dropped off to sleep.

Later Christine returned to the room and sat beside the couch watching her husband sleep. She watched his chest move in and out with each breath. The dressing seemed to be holding; the blood was drying to a dark brownish stain and only a hint of fresh blood lay in the center of the bandage. He might have died this night. She imagined he would never again laugh at her or stroke her hair or make love to her or chide her for leaving her books all over the floor of the study. She would not sit by his side and read to him. They would not argue about the benefits of grains versus fruits in their diet or make fun of the latest lecture at the Royal Academy of Science. He would not hold her and soothe her when she had nightmares and called out for her dead father. They would not go berry picking in the late afternoon or ride the fields or strip to their underclothes and bathe in the stream out of the view of the manor house and servants.

Raoul was such a good swimmer. He had tried to teach her to swim under the water like him, but she couldn't do it. He would disappear under the surface and catch her legs as they dangled or grab her by the waist, startling her into laughter.

So many memories! She cried silently as she remembered the day little Raoul was born. Her husband came into the room, and the midwife placed the child in his arms. Tears came to his eyes, and he burst into a smile as he touched each of the tiny fingers of his son. Then he stooped towards the bed, and embracing her in one arm and the child in the other told her he loved her again and again. He was so relieved the child and mother were safe and healthy he didn't even know that he had a son until Christine asked him if they were going to call him Raoul as they had planned.

She wanted so to wake him now and make him talk to her, smile at her, laugh. Only then would she believe that he was not going to die. But she knew that she must not. He must rest. So she sat and watched him breathe as if her watching were the force that made this happen.

It was nearly dawn when she woke and realized that at some point in her watch she had drifted off to sleep. As she yawned and stretched in the straight-backed chair, she saw Raoul looking up at her, smiling. "Oh, my love. I thought you might die." She couldn't stop crying. Whether from worry or relief she did not know.

"There, there, my love. I feel like Ajax dragged me through the streets last night. I'm quite weak, but I think I'll be well soon."

"Ajax would never treat his master with so much disrespect. He's more a friend to you than a horse," she laughed. "Let me call Mme. Montre for some broth or tea for us both."

As she gave him spoonfuls of the sweet milky tea, she was pleased that he had an appetite which seemed to improve with each sip. "Raoul, do you remember anything from last night?"

"I only remember that I had a bit too much to drink. I lost only modestly at the games, and I was on my way home when I was hit from behind with something blunt. There were several of them; I can't remember how many. I think I wounded one. I can't remember much else. It's all fuzzy, like a bad dream." Raoul could tell that Christine knew more. "How is it that they didn't kill me? Did the police come upon them?"

"The important thing is you're alive. Now let me try to get the rest of these clothes off you and dress you properly for your convalescence." She helped him out of his shirt and pants and called to the maid to remove them and bring a fresh night shirt. "I don't think these will mend easily. We should throw them out."

Inspector Leroux gently pushed his officer aside and placed his hand on the young woman's arm, pressing his fingers into her flesh. He had always found the gesture to either distract or comfort, especially in the case of women. Women seemed so easily governed by physical contact. Of course with this sort of young woman, it was even more effective. He controlled a fleeting surge of revulsion. Her clothes were soiled, and the smell of her body palpable in the closed space of the office. But on his face there was no sign of disgust. The poor girl after all was no doubt doomed to this life of prostitution from the time of her birth. More and more of these unfortunates found their way to the seedier parts of the Left Bank. As the city nourished some, it ground others under its unmerciful heel.

"There now, tell us again what you saw. Patrice, bring her a glass of water and some of that bread. You are probably ready for a bit of breakfast, no doubt? Or would it be supper, my dear?" He smiled at the girl, who quieted immediately and simply nodded her head at the Inspector of Police.

"Go on," Leroux encouraged her to sit down at the corner of the desk. He drew up a nearby stool and sat as close to the girl as he could stomach.

"Monsieur, I didn't do anything wrong. I was just frightened. I was trying to get away, and the officer he grabbed me by the arm and dragged me off. I was so relieved at first that it was the officer. Then he didn't let me go; he brought me here. I didn't do anything wrong, Monsieur."

"Why were you screaming in the street? What frightened you?" The inspector knew that he had to be calm and to repeat the questions simply. Eventually the young woman would circle back to the information he wanted.

"I was going home, Monsieur." Suddenly aware that she was speaking to the officer in command, she searched for some plausible explanation for her presence in the middle of the night on the Rue du Lac. "I was visiting a sick friend, Monsieur, and I was on my way home."

The inspector knew well that there was no sick friend, only a satisfied customer who spent time with her in one of the cubicles over the café or in a dark recess of the alley and left her with a few coins before heading home. But this was irrelevant. There had been a street fight, an important gentleman had narrowly escaped with his life, and this was perhaps the only witness. In the street were three ruffians, all dead. So he played along with the prostitute's fanciful excuse. "Yes, I hope your friend is better soon. Please tell us what you saw in the street. What frightened you?"

"It was a giant of a man, all black; he had wings. He ran toward me, and all I saw in the black was this white face and eyes that glowed. It was the Phantom, your honor. It was him, and he nearly knocked me down before he vanished into the street." She looked at the officer with eyes wide with wonder and panic as if she could still see the apparition.

"A giant? Wings? The Phantom, you say?" This was not going to get him anywhere. The ignorant were like children. It was impossible to get anything of use from them. It had been more than two years since the murders at the Opera House. Even though everything that had happened had a rational explanation, the public was unwilling to give up the fantastic version the newspapers had published. Since the murderer was never apprehended, the papers felt free to publish superstitious nonsense. The articles described in lurid detail the crimes of a Phantom who haunted the Opera House. It was the Phantom who brought the chandelier crashing down on the audience. No matter how often such drivel was corrected by reports from his office, the common man preferred his drama to the truth. Now anything that happened at night in the streets of Paris of any mysterious nature whatsoever was attributed to the Phantom.

"Yes. But I felt him as he ran past me. He was a man."

Well, this was progress at least. The girl was not such an imbecile after all.

"Good. Mademoiselle …? What is your name, my dear?" Perhaps he would yet extract some solid information from this witness.

"Call me Sophie, Monsieur." Feeling more at ease, she smiled and drew even closer to the inspector who resisted the temptation to draw his stool farther away. "I was coming around the corner when I heard scuffling and cries in the street. I can recognize the sounds of a fight, I can tell you. I've been at enough of them." Realizing the possible effect of such a statement, she seemed to hesitate before continuing. "At least, I thought this sounded like fighting. I peeked around the corner, and there they were. There were two men on the ground. I couldn't tell if they were only hurt or dead, but one seemed to be lying in a very awkward position, his legs all twisted round at weird angles, so I daresay he was dead or an acrobat. The others were still fighting. Two of them were up against the other. The two kept lunging forward; I think they must have had knives the way they were jabbing with their arms. The other man was the Phantom. He kept dodging out of the way as if it were nothing. He swirled this big, black cape around and around like wings. One of the men just fell forward holding his stomach. The other one got scared and turned to go, but the Phantom threw this rope and caught him around the neck from behind and jerked him back. The poor soul fell to the ground. It looked like the Phantom stuck his foot on the man's chest and then pulled up on the rope with all his might. All I could see was the man's hands fall back to the ground. Then I heard the police whistle. Then the Phantom did the strangest thing. I thought he'd run right off, but he stopped."

"What did he do?"

"He went to one of the other two men who had been lying there in the street and did something. I couldn't tell what. And he waited until the officers came round the corner instead of hiding right away. It was almost as if he wanted them to see him." She paused dramatically to be sure she had the Inspector's complete attention. "That's when he flew past me. I turned, and he just disappeared into the street."

"Down the street, you mean. Which direction?" The inspector nodded to the officer who was taking notes.

"No, your lordship. Not down the street. Into the street. He didn't go nowhere except perhaps into the ground itself. I swear."

The officer taking notes stopped, his hand pausing over the note pad, as he waited for the inspector to give him a sign. The inspector nodded, even as he cast him a skeptical look.

"Very well, Sophie. You are to let this officer know where your rooms are. Where we can contact you if we need to talk to you again. You are not in any trouble, and you are not to talk about this to anyone. Do you understand? He'll escort you home." The young woman was immediately relieved and smiled gratefully at the inspector as he rose and bowed ever so gallantly.

He was about to leave the room when something caught his eye among the pleats of the woman's skirt. "Here, what is this? Blood?"

"Oh my stars!" The young woman examined the bloody stain across the green and gold design on her skirts. "Yes, it does seem to be, your honor."

"But you never approached the count, nor the thieves?"

"No, I can tell you. There was nothing that would make me go over there! I don't care to look on dead people."

"You were at the alleyway; they were well out of distance for this to be their blood. Is there any other way you might have come into contact with blood? Is it anywhere else on your clothing?"

"No, sir. It seems just to be this one spot. No, look here, on the side of my sleeve there's some more."

"As if you had rubbed up against someone bloody."

something else I can't quite see it something else in the corner of my eye is flashing by my side and I do remember hearing the cries of others the men who attacked me one is on the street near me I see my sword has fallen from my hand but the man does not rise the other men are there why don't they run me through with their daggers why aren't they rummaging through my clothes as I lie here I am completely incapable of protecting myself I feel paralyzed or absent as if I am not here I am up above it all and looking down and see three men fighting in the light of the street lamp one man is huge he seems to be everywhere towering over the other two like a bat he has wings, no, it is a cape and oh my god it is him he has come to kill me and I see his mask it's white and stands out luminous in the darkness and he comes near me and draws back and the two men are fighting him but they are not here to protect me they are common thieves and they hold knives in their hands and thrust and parry and they are attacking him, the Phantom who uses his cape to deflect their slashing knives and one of them gasps and falls and the other clutches at his throat and falls and the cape stands over him and I cannot see because the cape covers everything and there is silence except I hear someone breathing hard and I think it might be me but it might be him, too, he turns and comes toward me I wait for him to throttle the life out of me as well or to pierce me with his sword but I see a mask on one side of a face, a face that is comely in the part that is not covered and I remember the ugliness of that other side the side under the white luminescent mask the moon shines from his face and then I am falling into the night sky and there is nothing else to remember

Meg placed the gas lamp on the side table and shut the door behind her. The admirers outside her dressing room had finally been whisked aside by the backstage manager allowing Meg to retire. She was elated, yet tired. She was also disappointed, and her disappointment had prevented her from enjoying the praise of these opera buffs who nightly escorted her to her dressing room.

He had not come tonight. This was his usual night. On the stage, she had sought out his face in the secret spot he had shown her, between the gallery and the box. He had found secret passageways even here in this new, modern palace of the arts. No one would be able to pick him out among the Rococo bas relief. He would appear to be only a glint of light across the purple cloth that hung next to the column. When he first visited the opera house, he would startle her on her way to the dressing room. As she rushed through the passageway to change costumes, a gloved hand would suddenly come from the wall and lightly graze her arm. After the performance, she would sometimes only hear him remark on this or that aspect of her singing, sometimes praise but often advice or criticism. When she had done especially well, he would be waiting for her in the dressing room. He would step out from the shadows and smile. He promised that he had not forgotten her and that he would come regularly every other Tuesday to hear her perform.

She looked forward to these visits hoping that they would eventually lead to greater intimacy between them. Here in her dressing room was the man she desired. Yet he never did more than lightly touch her arm with his gloved hand. If she approached him, he drew back beyond her reach. If she began to remove her make-up or even her wig, he would bow slightly and bid her adieu. In order to keep him longer with her, she would sit on the sofa in full costume and make-up until he himself seeing the lateness of the hour would instruct her to change and get her rest. No sooner would he say this than he would disappear into the shadowed recesses of the room. So she tried to content herself with these encounters.

The opera buffs, in particular the old barons and dukes that buzzed around the performers, sent flattering notes and expensive gifts. But she understood their intentions were not honorable. Knowing that Erik looked after her gave her the confidence to keep these men at bay.

But tonight he had not been among the public.

When she turned from the door, she sensed him. Yes, he was in the chamber itself. Why had he not come to listen as he always did? Why was he here now, and why did he not reveal himself? There was heavy breathing in the room, and for a moment she feared that perhaps one of her many suitors had bribed a stagehand to let him slip inside to lie in wait for her. She turned the lamp up, and the shadows were gradually dispelled. Lying on the sofa, breathing with some difficulty, was a man. It was Erik, and he was bleeding from his side.

In the moment that she discovered him, Erik drew himself up into a sitting position on the couch. He held his gloved hand to his side. Blood oozed between the fingers and dripped to the carpet below.

"You're injured. I'll call for a doctor."

"No, my canary. Don't call for anyone. I have pricked myself on a needle while sewing. It will soon stop; I cannot have that much more inside." He tried to laugh, but the pain made his voice catch.

Meg brought several clean rags to his side and knelt before him. She forced his hand away and pressed the cloth to the wound. He was too weak to protest. She needed to see how serious it was, so she began to tug the material of his shirt away from his side. He started to protest, but his head fell back upon the cushion, and he remained still. It was a knife wound, more a slash than a piercing. The depth was irregular, varying from a superficial cut to a gash of some seriousness. The blood oozed but did not spurt, a sign she felt that the wound was beginning to close. She maintained pressure on it until she felt the bleeding diminish.

When Erik came to, he was bandaged and lying stretched out on the sofa. Meg was not in the room. He forced himself into a sitting position and found his bloodied shirt on the floor. When he stood, he nearly swooned but kept from falling by clutching the edge of the vanity. He had to wait several minutes for the dizziness to pass. He left by the secret door before Meg returned.

"My lady Christine, I found this in the count's breast pocket of his vest, the one he had on the night they attacked him. I forgot till now to give it to you. I hope it's not urgent."

Christine took the folded paper from her maid and examined it. Stained by blood, it was folded several times and had no distinguishing marks to suggest the sender. Perhaps it was simply an I. O. U. from one of Raoul's gambling friends. She placed it in her pocket and decided to give it to her husband later after he napped and had supper.

However, she forgot about the note. After supper they sat in the sitting room where Christine read. Tonight Raoul could not take his eyes off her as she sat in the glow of the gas light. And when she put the book aside and rubbed at her eyes, he took her hands in his and kissed them fervently.

The gesture was so intense that Christine asked, "Raoul, what is this? You seem distressed."

He still held her hands tightly and brought them again to his lips. She moved closer to him, and he gently drew her into an embrace. Careful not to touch his wound, she rested her head against his chest. There she listened to the rhythm of his heart until he brought her chin up to meet his face. He kissed her warmly and deeply with the stirrings of a passion that for now they both must resist. As their lips parted, Raoul whispered, "Christine, will you sing for me?"

Never had she felt so happy as in that moment. "Of course, my love. I will sing for you every night and every day if only you will ask."

She sang songs that they remembered from their youth, and when she didn't remember the words she hummed the melodies. When she had finished, she took his face in her hands and kissed his eyes, his cheeks, and his lips. They remained in each other's arms until the moon rose above the clouds in the sky and shone into the sitting room, at which point they turned out the lights and retired to bed.

Count de Chagny,

I have spared your life on two occasions, and you are in my debt. You have kept Christine away from me and from her music. It is small repayment for my mercy that you allow her to visit her father's grave unescorted. I am aware that you know that I, too, visit the graveside of M. Daaé, and that my sole purpose in doing so is to be present when she comes. What you may not know is that I could easily have ended your life when you came to spy on Christine the last time she was there.

I have given up everything for Christine's happiness. I wish only to see her and to hear her sing. I give you my word that I will not approach her unless she were to call upon me to do so. She has made her decision, and I abide by it. In all honor, I cannot see how you would not grant this one request since it is her fondest desire to visit at her father's graveside and to sing in the only place that your command that she not do so carries no weight. To withhold this one request of me will confirm that we are enemies, and the consequences will be on your head alone.

O. G.

"How did you get this, Christine?" Raoul tore the letter up into several scraps and threw them on the tea tray.

Christine was surprised by his tone. She had assumed the note of no particular importance. She only now had remembered it and taken it from the bureau where she had placed it several days ago. "Why, the chambermaid found it in your breast pocket, in the vest, I believe, that you wore the night of the assault. She passed it to me."

Raoul seemed lost in thought as if working out a difficult problem.

"Why, Raoul? What is it?"

"Nothing," he responded and waved his hand as if to chase off a bothersome fly. Christine's look of concern reminded him of his duty to be forthright and truthful. Yet he couldn't speak of the letter without revealing that he had spied on her at the graveyard. Nor did he wish to reveal to his wife the Phantom's request. He wasn't sure what her reaction would be, and this displeased and disquieted him even more. What if she was touched by the Phantom's continued desire to be near her, to hear her sing? The man was insane to think that Raoul would allow his wife to sing anywhere within any distance of him. Had not that been the binding force of her enslavement to him? He remembered the look in Christine's eyes when the Phantom sang his song of seduction to her in his dark opera. And he had been maddened by the obvious passion that she evoked in the Phantom.

"Tell the coachman that I wish to send a letter. Have my writing materials brought to the smoking room." Curtly, he rose from the couch and with only the slightest sign of a limp left Christine, puzzled, in the sunroom.

M. Phantom,

Your presence in our lives is unwarranted and unacceptable. I seem to owe you some debt only from the incident outside the gaming rooms. For your other intrusions into our lives, I owe you nothing. My memory of the night in question is vague and fragmented, but there is cause to believe that you were the unknown gentleman who intervened in the assault and prevented the scoundrels from killing me. For this, I am grateful. You must ask some other boon from me as recompense, for my wife, dear sir, is not a trifle that I use to pay debts. I will protect Christine from you at whatever cost. If I had known that you planned to exact as payment for your good deed access of any sort to my wife, I would have asked you not to come to my assistance.

Indeed on one thing and one thing alone we agree. Christine has made her choice. We are happy. I will ask you to remove yourself from our lives. It is beyond all the bounds of mercy that you are allowed to exist at all. If I come across you, I will surely remedy this error.

Sincerely,

Count de Chagny

Raoul reread the letter several times, rose, and paced the room. He wanted to make it clear that he would not allow his wife to be alone in the cemetery with the Phantom looking on. How could he trust this man? The monster had killed in cold blood. This was not a rational human being but some twisted soul that had lived an unnatural life. He might take Christine at any moment and drag her to the depths of his underground lair never to be heard of again.

On the other hand, and for this reason Raoul held the letter clutched in his fist as he paced back and forth, could he afford to declare war on this same monster? How had he survived the catastrophe in the opera house? How had he evaded and continued to evade the authorities?

Then, too, the Phantom had allowed them both to live and to escape that night knowing that Raoul meant to marry Christine. He had freed them to establish their lives together. Even the visits at the cemetery were perhaps not made with any intention to do them harm. In addition, there was the inspector's report. It confirmed Raoul's own fuzzy intuition that it had indeed been the Phantom who defended him that night outside the club from certain death. Had he just been there by coincidence? Or was he also following Raoul? And, if so, for what purpose? Obviously he could have killed him at any time or he could easily have allowed the thieves to do it for him. But he had not.

Raoul sat to draft another version of his reply.

M. Phantom,

I ask you to remove yourself from our lives. We are happy. Your presence is undesirable. It appears that you may have saved my life recently when I was accosted by thieves outside the gaming rooms. My memory of the night is vague and fragmented, but there is cause to believe that you were the unknown gentleman who intervened in the assault and prevented the scoundrels from killing me. For this, I am grateful. I acknowledge that I am in your debt. However, you must ask some other boon from me as recompense, for I cannot treat my wife as a trifle, dear sir, to be used as payment of my debts.

You are dangerous; you have killed in cold blood. I will protect Christine from you at whatever cost. If I had known that you would ask to have access to my wife as payment for my life, I would gladly have given my life instead.
Sincerely,
Count de Chagny

Satisfied with the second version, Raoul placed the letter in an envelope and sealed it with his crest. Passing the envelope to the coachman, he instructed,

"Give this to Mme. Giry in the Rue des artistes and ask that she deliver it with all speed to the person there named."

He wouldn't tell Christine of the note. She must not know that he had stalked her even to her father's grave, and he didn't want her to know that the Phantom had intruded yet again upon their lives.

She comes to the garden with her child and sits in the grove by the park of elms and spruce trees. The trellis that shelters her from the afternoon sun is wreathed with verdant clinging vines; grapes hang heavy on the branches. A nurse accompanies mother and child. I watch from the stand of elms near enough to hear her coo to her babe, a rosy fat cheeked boy. Today I watch as Christine unbuttons the lace at her bodice and brings the baby to her breast. I catch only a glimpse of the smooth, white flesh of her breast against the blue satin and chantilly lace of the garment before the child latches on and brings his fingers to grab at a strand of her hair that hangs at the base of her throat. The sight is too much for me and I have to turn away. The heat is too harsh for the baby to remain long after nursing. Soon the slumbering child is returned to the nurse who gently lays him in the pram. She wheels him down the pathway toward the manor house, leaving her mistress unattended.

The garden is awash with wild flowers where the sun is not blocked by the copse of trees where I hide. The trellis knotted with vines gives her shade and relief from the summer heat. Christine is seated inside the enclosure. Alone now, she opens the buttons of the bodice of her dress and fans her neck and the edge of her bosom. Pregnancy and childbirth have molded her body. She is voluptuous, soft and ripe, like fruit dripping heavy on the branches. She per-spires in the heat. She gathers her hair and pins it high upon her head exposing the alabaster column of her neck as it descends toward her spine. A few stray hairs tease her collarbone, and I can almost taste the salt on her skin. I try to wipe these thoughts from my mind. I come to see her, to be near her, and hope to hear her voice, even the mindless cooing to her babe fills me with excite-ment.

I try to look away from those full red lips. I have tasted those lips. I have held that body in my arms, felt its weight, know how the garments caress its shape. I had once thought she would be mine forever. I had thought that she might come to love me. We would lie together in my bed. She touched me here and here, and I still feel her hand.

She looked upon me once with devotion, with trust, and even with desire. She came with me of her own free will; she came to my chambers and slept in my bed while I wrote her music and watched over her dreams. It was only one night, one night that she might have loved me. Then she stole my mask from me, and she no longer looked at me in the same way. She saw the face behind the mask, and she could no longer see the heart of the man behind the horror. She shrank from me. I felt it in her eyes, in the touch of her hand as I led her to the boat to return her to the opera house above. I felt it in the cold, limp fingers of her hand as I hopelessly clasped it in mine.

Why could my love not blind her to my ugliness? How was it that she turned so quickly indifferent to me and ran to his arms? I who had sung to her and been her companion? I whom she sought every night and welcomed every day? Oh Christine, how I trusted you to be kind, to love me, to be constant, and to find beauty in spite of the deformity of my face.

Please look this way and see me, my love. See me for what I really might have been if the world had not rejected me. I come like a viper into your garden only to catch a glimpse of you. I forgot what heaven looked like, so long did I exist in exile from your beauty.

Christine sat knitting, glad to be in the open air. She hummed as she worked the needles. Unaware of those eyes observing her from the glade of trees, she sang one of her father's folk songs. Then she shifted to an aria from her début at the opera house. At first she sang softly, but emboldened by her solitude in the silence of the garden, she lifted her voice and sang as if she were on the stage still. Remembering that night of her triumph, the public held in sway by her song, Christine closed her eyes enjoying the crescendo of the final notes of the piece, oblivious to all around her.

As the last note drifted away on the breeze, she opened her eyes. Before her among the elms, as if merely across the span of a room, he stood. She had not seen him for over two years, but she remembered his tall muscular frame, the taut power of his limbs, his proud stance. He stood, both arms at his side, his right leg set slightly forward allowing the angle of his torso to shift his masked side toward her. Behind that white molded mask, his eye gazed at her unblinking. He wore, as he always had, the same long dark cloak, a vest and high starched white collar, dark trousers as if he were indeed at her premier performance in the opera house instead of standing among the thistles and acorns of the manor's park. Neither spoke. He remained transfixed before her.

Christine made an effort to rise. Seeing her move, the Phantom feared she would run from him. He put his arm out as if to stop her and spoke, "Please. Don't be afraid, Christine."

"What do you want? You told us we were free. Why have you come here?" She was on her feet and was gathering the pleats of her skirt so as not to trip when she fled.

Before she could dash away, Erik begged her to wait. Slowly and carefully, as if it gave him some pain, Erik knelt on one knee.

"Christine, it is I who am not free."

She backed away and prepared to call for help.

He, too, rose but saw that this only frightened her more. "Wait. Hear me out." He raised both hands, palms out toward her as if she were a wild mare he sought to calm. She froze, but still clutched at her skirts. Both stood silent measuring each other's reaction. Erik fearing she would bolt at any moment, retreated several paces and again knelt before her, as a supplicant, on bended knee.

When he spoke again, she heard the trembling he could not control. "You said that I would not be alone, Christine."

She drew her hand to her lips recalling the kiss she had given him. In that kiss, she had meant to comfort him, to touch the humanity buried deep in his soul. Moved by his gaze, a look that held pain and despair, she waited for him to speak again.

Yet Erik did not speak but rather sighed and gazed at her. Unable to bear not knowing the Phantom's intentions and overwhelmed by anxiety and confusion, Christine pleaded, "Do not harm my child or my husband. I beg of you." She collapsed onto the ground in tears. Without thinking, he rushed to her side. Her fear cut him like a knife.

"Don't cry, Christine. I promise you I intend no harm. I wanted to feel the light of your eyes once more on my face. Forgive me for coming out of the darkness. If you so wish, I'll go back to it. But for pity's sake, Christine, do not ask me to go back there. I have tried to bury myself; I have tried to die, but I can't. The only thing that makes my existence tolerable are the times I glimpse your face at the graveside or now in your garden."

"You have been spying on me at my father's grave and now you come here and watch us?" She had never imagined that he would follow her to her own home.

"Yes, but I never made my presence known to you. At the cemetery, I listened to your prayers and your voice. You sing as well or better than you ever did at the opera. Forgive me. I was drawn to the graveyard. In my unending purgatory, I took to wandering through the underground tunnels until one evening, just before sunset, I found myself at the cemetery. I found the silence peaceful there, the only time silence is ever peaceful to me. This one evening, though, I expected no one to be there as usual given the lateness of the hour. I was walking, as I often did, among the tombs reading the epitaphs of mothers, daughters, husbands, sons. All that love, all that despair and hope. I sat for a while and spoke to a stone angel as if it were you. And suddenly I was beside myself with wonder when the angel began to sing in your voice. I soon realized that it was not the cold, unfeeling statue that I had before me. Your voice carried over the tombs of the dead, and I followed it until I came upon you sitting at your father's mausoleum, singing.

"For the first time since those days when you still loved me, I felt the heaviness in my heart lift and the pain lessen. I stayed long after you left, long after nightfall, still listening to the memory of your song. I came back again and again but didn't find you until a week or so later. You did not always come on the same day or at the same time."

Christine was touched by his story and confided to him, "I sometimes sensed you were there, my angel of darkness."

A look of pain stole across his face. She had not meant to be cruel.

"So, that is what I am to you, your angel of darkness?" Erik pulled himself away from the young woman. Her words had frozen his soul. "No longer your angel of music?" He walked away toward the copse of trees. With his back turned to her, he spoke again. "Your husband is correct: I am nothing but a man. I have a man's name, Christine. If I cannot be your angel of music, then I would prefer that you knew me by the name of a man, Erik." He did not wait for her answer, but slipped quickly into the gathering shadows of the park until she saw his shape no more.

"Erik," she barely whispered, but there was no one there to hear her.

she comes not

"Let us have tea in the park by the elms."

"No," Christine responded sharply. Raoul looked up from the gazette that he was reading, startled by her abruptness.

"I see no reason why we shouldn't enjoy this late summer. You used to take little Raoul out there almost every afternoon to get away from the heat. You have barely set foot in the park in months."

Christine stammered something about snakes in the garden and excused herself. She needed to speak with the nurse about Raoul's nap times.

Before Christine could leave the parlor, Raoul suggested, "Well, I suppose we could set up the tent down by the stream. Would that please you?"

Turning, she smiled and said that it would suit her fine, and left the room.

each afternoon I come and wait and she does not come, she drives the knife deeper and deeper into the wound, I seem drawn to the pain, why do I come why do I slip in among the trees to wait for a meeting that will not take place? I see her stroll along the stream, she walks holding the tottering child by the hand and I cannot take my eyes from her, she glances furtively over her shoulder toward the stand of elms I imagine to see if I will swoop down on her even there in the glen where the sun drenches her, out in the light she feels safe from my shadow, she avoids this garden, a garden no longer, a crypt, a prison, a lair, a dungeon, the rack, antechamber to hell, oh, Christine I thought you might ...

Erik waited until the sun's rays dipped below the horizon painting the clouds with broad brushstrokes of blues, violets, and brilliant bloody pinks. He had lost track of time sitting with his back to the grand elm he now called friend. He had waited to catch sight of Christine in the glen, by the river, or in the distance on the patio outside the manor house. All he had seen were the comings and goings of gardeners and house staff. For nearly an hour he watched the child running round a fountain in the middle of the English garden next to the house. The nurse sat watching; at times Erik could see her come to the child's side to kiss a scrape when he fell on the stone or to help him retrieve the brown leaf he set sail in the fountain. He found himself laughing in wonder to watch the child. There was a childhood wrapped in the protection of the love of many. This was a spark from Christine's soul. The thought struck him unexpectedly, and he found himself warmed by the child's play.

Sitting among the thistles, lost in the contemplation of the child, he heard her approach only when she was within several feet of him. The thistles and dried leaves crunched under her footfall and Erik, startled, looked up to see it was Christine. He rose quickly to his feet to go to her, but stopped when he saw the sudden look of apprehension cross her face.

Overcome by sheer joy at her presence, he could not speak but only stood and gazed at her. He had not seen the features of her face since the day she became aware of his presence in the garden. Nor did she speak, for she had only then realized that he had been watching her child all this time. Fear gripped her, but she dared not let him see it. Then Erik, as before, knelt on bended knee thinking to reassure her that she had nothing to fear from him and recited verses he had once memorized from Shelley:

Art thou pale for weariness
Of climbing heaven and gazing on the earth,
Wandering companionless
Among the stars that have a different birth,
And ever changing, like a joyless eye
That finds no object worth its constancy?

"I have spent the days waiting for you to tire of coming. What of your weariness?" She didn't offer any excuse for her long absence from the glade, nor did he ask her for one.

"I neither climb to heaven nor lack for an object of constancy. My gaze is constantly on you, Christine, even when I cannot see you, you are emblazoned on my eyes."

"But I find that you have other objects of your gaze." Saying this, she indicated the garden in the distance where little Raoul now chased the nurse around the shrubs.

"I watch and wait for you. Your child has some part of you that, in your absence, calms me." Erik could sense her disquiet and rushed to dispel it. "I would give my life to protect your child, Christine. I swear to you that in this as in all else I am your angel."

She could see the truth of this in his eyes, and a warm, safe certainty poured over her heart. "Come, sit by me."

Erik could not believe he had heard correctly and waited until Christine sat on the bench under the trellis and gathered her skirts close around her so as to make room for him to sit beside her. He stood and approached hesitantly, waiting and watching to see her reaction. But instead of fear, he saw her smile sadly up at him and beckon once more for him to sit. They sat there silent, together, watching little Raoul in the distance, watching the colors of the sunset. Soon she would have to return for it would grow dark.

Christine turned ever so slightly toward him and recited:

Swiftly walk o'er the western wave,
Spirit of Night!
Out of the misty eastern cave,
Where, all the long and lone daylight,

Thou wovest dreams of joy and fear,
Which make thee terrible and dear,—
Swift be thy flight!

Wrap thy form in a mantle gray,
Star-inwrought!
Blind with thine hair the eyes of Day;
Kiss her until she be wearied out,
Then wander o'er city, and sea, and land,
Touching all with thine opiate wand—
Come, long-sought!

"Long-sought," he whispered back to her. His eyes cast down toward the ground, he dared to recite the next strophe of the poem:

When I arose and saw the dawn,
I sighed for thee;
When light rode high, and the dew was gone,
And noon lay heavy on flower and tree,
And the weary Day turned to his rest,
Lingering like an unloved guest.
I sighed for thee.

The poet's words hung suspended between them. Christine was the first to rise. "I must be getting back. It will soon be too dark to see the path. Raoul will be worried and send someone for me."

She offered him her hand, and he took it gently in his. He wanted to bring it to his lips to kiss the palm, but feared she would withdraw it. So he held it until she pulled it free. Before she turned to leave, she said to him softly, yet earnestly, "If I come, you must not talk of love. Promise me. And you must not come any closer than you are now to me or to mine. Promise me."

And although the words caught in his throat, he said, "I promise."

CHAPTER 6

The Mask

The figure was tall and gaunt, and shrouded from head to foot in the habiliments of the grave. The mask which concealed the visage was made so nearly to resemble the countenance of a stiffened corpse that the closest scrutiny must have had difficulty in detecting the cheat. And yet all this might have been endured, if not approved, by the mad revellers around. But the mummer had gone so far as to assume the type of the Red Death. His vesture was dabbled in blood—and his broad brow, with all the features of the face, was besprinkled with the scarlet horror. "The Masque of the Red Death," Edgar Allan Poe

mardi gras, carnival, masked revelers pour out into the streets, noise makers and streamers and hand-held tapers swirl in the darkness, poor slaves shrieking against the grasp of mortality, the death skull and crossbones click clack behind each fool, king, and harlequin, all the phantoms are out tonight, one more among them will not be noticed, I select my mask, one that covers all but the lower half of my face, my lower jaw and my mouth, white, chalk-white it evokes a death mask, I paint black around my eyes and they seem hollow, eye-less, I change my usual dark attire for the red of Poe's walking death in his story of plague, I walk among the crowd tonight and touch their bodies with my contagion, I stand within a breath's distance of men and women who look at me as if I were one of them, at last accepted, at last, and I smell them and watch them laugh and shout and dance with their heads thrown back, tonight the chaos of the mob in the streets will find its refined version in the salons and ballrooms of the gentry, masked balls with ladies and lords dancing waltzes and drinking champagne in pristine palaces of glass, marble, and brocade, I hail a carriage and instruct them to take me to the Count and Countess de Chagny's mansion where I know such a ball even now has begun by invitation only, I come alone, I come uninvited, but they will not be able to keep me from the masquerade, for what is a masquerade without one authentic phantom, one real ghost, one walking mask among the charade? The doorman asks for my name, I merely look at him unblinking, my eyes two coals that sear him, he haughtily demands, again I give no answer, he hesitates, his shoulders bend, I walk past into the foyer and scan the room that I have never seen, only imagined, the guests mill about talking too loudly, the voices rise too shrill, the laughter too gay, the flood of color blinds me, I look for her knowing that she will be looking for me, perhaps dreading to find me among her guests, each one a mystery to her, behind their borrowed visages, the Count is obvious, dressed as Louis XVI, he presides over the guests in a position of honor, many eyes drawn to him, hanging on him as their host, and next to him, on his right the Queen Marie Antoinette, the frivolous and tragic, her powdered wig satirically decorated with miniature guillotines, I make my way toward her, but must wait for her to drift from her husband's side, suddenly I feel as if my mask has dropped from my face, knowing that the Count will recognize me as will my beloved Christine, they will see me coming through the masqueraders as if unmasked, the mask I wear but one version of my face, my face a mask, my mask a face, I draw to the side, I make my way through the crowds of young men as they mutter their obscene comments on the flesh of the young women paraded before them on the dance floor, through the club of lords discussing the latest political fiasco of the mayor of the city, a charming and young woman dressed as a clown bumps unexpectedly into me as her partner lets go of her hand in a pirouette and she laughs gaily and looks up at me, I see in her eyes a look I do not at first understand and surprisingly realize is admiration, she places her hand gently on my chest as if to regain her balance, but I can tell that it is only a pose, a pretext to touch me, and stirrings that often torture me when I dream or think of Christine assault me, stirrings that I dampen only after arduous concentration, stirrings that I turn into my music or eliminate only through self-inflicted pain, now I allow those stirrings to spread unhindered through my body, I take the young woman's hand, it is soft and warm, the fingers long and thin, fingers that might play the violin except that they are too soft, they have no calluses, I take her naked hand and bring it to my mouth, my lips slightly parted, slightly moistened, press into her flesh, I imagine her in my embrace, I see the effect as her breast heaves, her pulse quickens, she is comely, her partner, a bantam rooster complete with cockscomb pecks his way to us and takes her arm leading her back to the dance, I enjoy his discomfort as she glances back toward me, I smile a half smile, pleased with the devilry that I have wrought, the couple will fight tonight, she will lay her head on a pillow and dream of me, of me as a handsome man who comes and makes love to her … Christine glides down the ballroom toward the terrace, she fans herself, she wishes to feel the breeze from the garden on her throat, I see the Count engaged with the old men smoking their cigars talking business, rents, the economic significance of import and export taxes in Marseilles, I laugh to think of his boredom as I draw near to my prize, Christine stands, her back to me and to the room, I step forward so that my breath touches the back of her neck, she stiffens and turns to me, before she can speak, before she can step back, I take her in my arms and turn us into the circle of dancers and we glide across the room, I, awkwardly at first, given that my feet are not used to dancing, Madeleine having taught me so long ago but the body must remember just as my hands recall the recesses of Christine's back and press it knowing that in this one spot I control her steps, I remember the steps, I follow the music as if it were the very floor upon which we turn, she looks at me as if indecisive, I smile and keep my eyes on hers, willing her to follow me, she will not cry for help, she will not let the others know that she is dancing in the arms of the Phantom of the Opera, the murderer, the Opera Ghost, the Devil's Child, she dances with the commanding figure of a young lord in the guise of the Red Death, and like the prey of that Plague, she has no will other than mine, the music stops and I must release her, she stands and waits until the music begins again and my heart beats like a trapped animal in my breast because she does not leave me, she waits until the music begins and we dance and dance and I see out of the corner of my eye, the King advances, he has not seen me but comes for his ill-fated queen, I turn from her and walk among the other guests before the Count can see me, a swatch of red is all I must be

"There you are. You can't fool me more than once." Raoul took Christine in his arms. "I danced three times with Meg before I realized that she was not you! When did the two of you decide to wear the same costume?" He peeked under her mask to assure himself she was indeed his wife and not Meg. The two friends had planned the trick all week. "Why, you're pale, my love. Have you become overheated with the dance? I saw you dancing quite gaily with one of our guests. Who was he?" Raoul looked across the ballroom, trying to catch sight of the man dressed in red that he had seen dancing with Christine just moments ago.

Christine did not answer, and in that silent moment a chill ran along Raoul's spine as he realized with whom she had been dancing. "Where is he?" he asked tensely, unconsciously tightening his grip on Christine's arm until she winced from the pain.

"Wait, Raoul. Not here. He won't do anything here," she begged, restraining him from hunting Erik down among the crowd. "Promise me you won't throw our guests into a panic."

"He's dangerous, Christine. How do you know he won't do something horrible?"

"He told me," she lied. "He promised that he only wanted to dance with me and to know that I was well. It's mardi gras, a special night of madness, the only one in which he can walk among us all, as one of us."

"He's a fugitive from justice, Christine. He's a fiend."

"It's been three years, Raoul. You yourself have often said that we must bury the past. Let him have his one night. What can a confrontation solve tonight, here with all our guests? He saw you approach; that's why he left. You see, he wasn't here for a confrontation. He's probably long gone by now."

"If you insist, I will not raise the alarm. But you are to withdraw to the upstairs library and lock yourself in. I'll send my valet to be with you. I'll find Meg and send her, too. Until I know he's gone, you must stay where I know you are safe."

"As you wish. But promise me you won't confront him, Raoul, even if you were to come face to face with him here."

Raoul did not answer, but escorted her to the stairs. He left her in his man's care and returned to the ballroom to search for Meg and the Phantom. Christine, too, scanned the crowd to see if she could find him, but he was not there.

I slip among the dancers, weave my way round through several adjacent rooms, catching snatches of inane conversation, admiring many of the figures of young women who shamelessly flirt with their young beaux, I stop and drain two glasses of champagne, the wine burns its way down my throat and sends a fire surging from my stomach to my limbs, only then the anger softens, the frustration, the disappointment of having left my Christine on the dance floor when he intruded, I stand gnashing my teeth considering whether I should leave now or stay and watch him make love to my Christine, his wife, the word cuts into my mind like a razor, and I turn and look at all these fools, walking carcasses amass with waiting, dormant worms, walking corpses that cannot see that death stands among them, the bile rises in my throat and I consider drawing my rapier and slicing into the mass of bodies when I see her, she comes to me, she comes around the corner, my Antoinette, my Queen, she glances round the room and when her gaze lights on me, she stops, I push aside those in my path and walk to her, frozen in her spot she looks at me, I say only her name, and taking her hand I lead her out of the side room toward the terrace into the dark, there in a dark corner of the terrace amid the vine covered colonnades we see two lovers kissing, their bodies pressed against the column, her petticoats lifted to her waist, her legs wrapped around his hips, we turn away from their furtive, shameless lovemaking and then my Queen pulls me by the hand, leading me, walking purposefully toward one of the small rooms off the ballroom, past the lovers' nook, and we enter a room lit by candlelight, unoc-cupied, yet she does not stop there but presses her hands against the panel by the mantelpiece, a secret compartment opens and she takes a candle and guides me, never releasing my hand, into this secret alcove, Christine, I whisper again and she places her fingers on my lips to silence me, she leads me to the divan and places the candle on the side table, she lies back on the cushions, she takes my gloves from my hands and pulls me down to her, she guides my lips to hers, her mouth is parted, and the taste of her lips burns like champagne, I bring my fingers to lift her mask from her face, but she stops my hand, we are both to be masked, moistening her finger tips she puts out the one light in the room and wraps her arms around me bringing me closer to her, my body sinks down upon hers, I caress her, my hands wander down her throat to the bodice of her gown, I draw her skirt and petticoats up to her waist as the young lover in the garden had done with his maiden, I fum-ble with buttons, her fingers are there to help me, I shudder as our bodies touch in the darkness of the room, my angel Christine, my lips press against hers, her flesh against mine without revulsion, without horror, without sorrow, I lie spent by her side, I caress her, her skin is smooth except for a tiny mole I find and tease at the base of her throat, I lower my lips to it, she embraces me and draws me to her again, this time more slowly, more gently we make love, the pleasure is unbear-able, and with my last strength I say her name again, Christine, she sobs, I take her face and kiss the tears that wet her cheeks, we hold each other until the dark-ness begins to fade in the chamber, she pushes me gently from her and rises, I, too, rise from the divan and she leads me out onto the terrace where we kiss one last time

Christine slipped out from under Raoul's arm. Her husband turned over and fell back into a deep sleep. The darkness was chalky, and she knew that sunrise was not far off. Silently, she tiptoed to the guest room and tapped lightly on the door. Hearing no answer, she slipped into the room. The bed covers had been turned down by the chambermaid, but no one had slept there; the curtains were wide open. Christine saw no sign of Meg's costume. Her day clothes were still strewn across the screen, make-up lay in disarray as if she had just applied her blush and powders and left the room. A stab of anxiety grabbed at Christine's heart. Where could Meg be?

Shortly after he had sent his wife to the library, Raoul had found Meg among the party guests. He had told her the Phantom was on the grounds, perhaps even in the ballroom. Meg complained of a headache and assured him she was on her way to her room anyway. Why had she not returned to her room as she said she would? Had Erik seen her at the ball? Had he mistaken her for Christine? And if he thought she were Christine, what then? She could not imagine Erik harming Meg. Where would Meg be at this hour? The guests had left hours ago.

Christine sat in a chair near the balcony doors to wait.

The sky lightened perceptibly in the next several minutes. As she looked out the window, she saw a streak of red stealing across the grounds. The Red Death had just left the east wing of the terrace just below Meg's chamber. Christine stood and pressed her hands against the door panes watching Erik as he reached the grove of elms. Only then did he hesitate and turn, his hand on the hilt of his sword. He had been in the house all this time. But why? What could he be thinking? Then he melted into the darkness of the copse of trees.

Shortly thereafter, Christine heard someone approaching. Still dressed as Antoinette, Meg stepped into the room, closing the door behind her quietly.

"Where have you been?" Christine's question startled Meg who wheeled around to see her friend's silhouette against the first light of dawn. Christine asked the question yet again, but her friend stood speechless. Then Christine noticed the disarray of her friend's costume, the bodice had been hastily and badly closed, the skirts were wrinkled and lay askew as they fell from the waist, Meg's powder and rouge had been all but rubbed away. "What? Has he …?" She did not know how to continue.

Meg pulled the wig from her head, and fell crumpled to the ground with her hands before her face to contain her sobs.

"Oh despicable monster. Oh, how could he?" Christine came to her friend and grabbed her in her arms.

"No!" Meg pushed herself free from Christine's hold. "No, no, no. You don't understand, Christine."

"What don't I understand? I saw him just now leaving the house. He raped you, here in my own house, he raped you. And to think that I let him roam freely among us. Raoul was right: he's an animal, a demon. I should have treated him without pity."

She was overcome with anger, but when she looked into Meg's face she sensed that something else was wrong, something that she was missing. Silently Meg cried, and reached out to take Christine's hand in her own. "No, Christine. You've got it all wrong. I sought him out. I let him think I was you. I led him to the secret alcove you showed me. We made love, but he thought he was making love to you." With this last confession, Meg dissolved yet again into tears.

"Why?"

"How can you understand? I've wanted him since the first time I saw him in the opera house. One night you were ill, and I couldn't sleep. I went for water, and when I came back to our room, I saw a shadow hovering over your bed. It was him. He knelt beside you and brushed your hair from your forehead with such gentleness. From that moment on, I watched for him. I saw him in the flies of the opera house many times. I followed him, once, to a secret panel near the chapel and heard him sing with you. Another time, I saw him in the costume rooms looking through the masks. He examined each one, turning it over in his hands and putting it up before his face in the mirror. Then he removed the mask he was already wearing, but he did not look at himself in the mirror; he kept his head bent as if in shame. Even so, I could see his face in the mirror; it was indeed horrible, but so sad. Only when he placed the other mask over his deformity could he look at himself. I wanted to cry for him. Except for the disfigurement that he hides behind that mask, he is handsome and well formed. The night of the disaster, after you and Raoul escaped, I was with the search party when they found his lair. There was a broken mirror behind a heavy curtain; it was the entrance to other tunnels under the opera house and streets. No one else saw it. I alone went through it to look for him.

"And last night Raoul told me he was here and told me to go to my room. Instead, I went looking for him. Christine, when he saw me, it was as if time had stopped. He stood and looked at me the way he must always look at you! With never a glance to one side or another, he came to me parting the crowd in his wake. I was riveted. I meant to reveal myself to him, but when he drew near, he took my hand and said your name." Meg broke off in sobs. After a moment, she continued, "I knew how much he loved you. Oh, Christine, the look in his eyes when he thought I was you, when I did not turn and flee! I let him lead me to the terrace, and there in the shadows were two lovers embracing. That was when I knew what I wanted to do. I did it for me; I did it for Erik. I led him to the secret room, and I lay on the divan and pulled him to me. You cannot imagine the look of hope and gratitude in his eyes when he realized what I was offering. I will never forget his tenderness. I couldn't tell him it was me. I couldn't let him know that I was not you, Christine."

Christine drew back in horror. "What have you done, Meg? To me? To him?"

Meg begged her forgiveness, but Christine ran from the room.

He flung his cape upon the conch shell bed and ran his hands along the silken netting that cascaded from the ceiling. Every surface had a soul of its own as if it breathed and purred under the caress of his fingertips. He listened for sighs and closed his eyes to feel the walls of his chamber shudder, knowing that it was his body that trembled and his voice that moaned from the memory of his recent passion. Even now his pulse raced, and his blood pounded warm and deep in his veins. What magic is this that everything around him glowed? The whole universe seemed trapped in a gauze web tied to his limbs.

Erik was aware of every fiber of his body and knew for the first time in his life that it was whole and sound and strong and vibrant. It was sensible to a pleasure that he thought forbidden to him forever, and it was gloriously capable of giving pleasure to another human being. He approached one of his many mirrors that lined the walls of his abode, lifted the curtain, and examined himself as he stood there. What had she seen? He still wore the costume of the red death. His mask, the visage of a death's head.

Had Christine transformed him? She knew the ugliness that the mask covered, yet she yearned to touch him. For so many years he had shunned his reflection except as he prepared himself to walk among them. As he applied his make-up and arranged his wig, he lost himself in his craft, envisioning only the role that he intended to create by these counterfeits. As his true visage disappeared under the theatrical illusions, he would gradually become what he wanted the world to see. The Phantom was more than a man; he was power and mystery. The mask and costume gave him this power, but behind the mask of the Phantom cowered the devil's child in the cage. But last night Christine had made love to him! She placed her hands next to the warm naked skin of his unprotected body and made him whole! Surely she had worked some magic on him?

Erik tremulously lifted the mask away from his face and studied himself in the mirror. Foolish illusion! Foolish hope! He laughed at the distorted face that sneered at him in the mirror. It was as ugly as ever, the bulbous projections, the weeping sores, the twisted lines of flesh, the tortured eye. Yet she had desired him. This truth was unassailable, and it had transformed him. Damned the ugliness; she did not see it! He pulled back his shoulders and faced his reflection like an old enemy on a field of battle. "I am a man, not a monster!" he challenged.

he made love to her here in this room, on that divan, he lay with my friend and he took her in his arms and kissed her and she let him make love to her, she who has always been my friend, she wore the same disguise as I did and she led him to this secret room to be alone with him, he did not force her, he did not abduct her, he followed, he let himself be brought here, and she let him touch her, and she touched him, I imagine his hands, always in his gloves, no, one time he took them off, he did not wear them the night he carried me off to his lair, he took them off in the opera and they were warm and broad and powerful, he could hold both my hands in one of his, he caressed me with those hands and I was frightened and excited at the same time, but he would have kept me in his lair, he would have ravished me, he would have taken me by force, but here Meg gave herself to him, she insisted on telling me, I ran from her room, why? I did not want her to see that I was crying, and I don't know why I should cry, I am shocked, I am repulsed that she would surrender herself to him, that disfigured, horrid creature, he could not have given her any pleasure, it's impossible, it's so frightful to imagine the Phantom touching her, kissing her, saying her name ... no, he did not say her name, she at least was honest with me, he had gone with her to the secret chamber anticipating an encounter with me, he kissed her lips thinking they were mine, he touched, he took her thinking that it was I who was making love to him, he loves me, not Meg, he wants me, I can feel his desire in his eyes, in his voice, I see it in the way his body bends toward me when he's near me, oh my God, it's not horror that I feel, nor am I frightened, I am not repulsed, I am jealous, I smell them on the divan, I feel the warmth from their bodies, I see the impression their combined weight made on the brocade cushions, and it is my body that should have lain under his

Raoul was surprised by Meg's decision to end her visit a week earlier than they had all planned. She had complained of a headache; perhaps she was indisposed. Christine was upset that Meg was leaving and had not come out to say her farewells. The events of the past two nights had put everyone's nerves on edge. Raoul could not put out of his mind the threat from the Phantom's letter. He had declared war on Raoul and his family. The women had been in danger with the Phantom present at the masquerade, no matter how Christine protested otherwise. From now on, he would double his vigilance. He would insist on accompanying Christine to the graveyard whenever she wished to visit her father's grave.

Erik waited impatiently in the garden for Christine, but Christine did not come that day, nor the next, nor the next....

CHAPTER 7

The Viper

He paced back and forth like a wild animal. Mme. Giry had not seen him this angry in some time and although she resisted the emotion, she was quite frightened. Had he ever struck her or threatened her, she would have thought her life in peril. No, she was sure he would not lash out at her, but surely someone would have to pay the price for this frenzy. He mumbled and shouted alternately words that sliced and bore into the silence of the cavern creating sinister echoes against the stone walls. She waited, there was no other choice, until he spent his energy and eventually crumpled onto the couch. He turned away from her, anger giving way to despair. The silence was more oppressive, more ominous than his ravings had been, but Mme. Giry sat patiently and waited.

"What have I done?" Only sounds of anguish were audible as Erik collapsed into himself, folding his arms about his head and sinking his face into his chest.

A chill of dread washed over Mme. Giry. What could have been so monstrous that Erik would cry out in such regret and hopelessness? He had committed barbarous acts without regret, with not so much as a thought given to his own culpability. He was directly responsible for the deaths of eleven souls on the night he abducted Christine. What crime might he have committed now that touched him with repentance? She wasn't sure that she wanted to know.

She waited still and hearing no more from the creature whose very existence owed much to her, she knew she must ask, "What have you done, Erik?"

I waited day after day for Christine to join me in the garden. Each day I antici-
pated renewing our bond of love. I longed for her more than ever. What had been
a dream was now a reality, and I could not go back to the solitude I had endured
for so long. She had made love to me; we had been in each other's arms as man
and woman. She and I were wedded by that tryst, I could not continue without
her. I was willing to accept her love in secrecy if it had to be so; I'd be with her
when I could, when she was free to come to me, but I would not do without her. I
was patient. Yet she didn't come. I waited every day in the garden for her; she must
have known that I'd be there. She knew my desire. Until that night, I had thought
myself incapable of making love to her or any woman. I thought this a joy forever
forbidden to me. My life as a man was not to be, as my life in society had been
denied. I thought that music was my only solace. I learned from my earliest con-
sciousness that embraces and kisses were not for me. I was cast out of that paradise
by a mother who couldn't bear to hold me, to touch me. Christine gave me back
my body. I felt sensations that I had never allowed myself to feel. And I gave her
pleasure, too. My touch, my body didn't repulse her; it pleased her. I waited for her
to come to me again in the garden. I would lay her in the leaves and caress her; her
every desire would be my pleasure. She spoke not a word that night, but I could tell
from her touch, from her sighs that she loved me. Yet now I see her in the distance,
I thrill to think she will turn this way, come down this path, and run into my
arms, but she hurries away, she glances over her shoulder as if afraid someone is
sneaking up behind her and she leaves me here, my heart breaks every time I see
her and she doesn't come. Does Raoul keep her from me? Perhaps he's discovered
that we were together and now keeps her prisoner on the estate? Perhaps she fears
the child will be taken from her? She does not come. My despair burns inside me
and turns to anger. I seethe with it. I curse her that she opened the gates of heaven
only to cast me down into this pit. I can't leave; I can't forget; I can't forgive. I must
hear some explanation from her lips. I wait here day after day, and she doesn't
come! She does not wish to come! There are opportunities; she could steal away in
the afternoon to come to me here. She knows I wait. We met before in this garden.
Several times she trod down this path and glancing into the wood bid me
approach, let her monster come and kneel at her feet, let her dog lick her shoes as
she threw him crumbs from her dinner table. She dared to read poems of love to
me! She must have laughed to see me, a monkey imitating a man, an ape dressed
like a lover. I didn't ask her if I could come to the masked ball. I feared she'd forbid
it. I put on my mask, my disguise, and paraded for her entertainment as if I were
a man, not a monster. And she took me by the hand, and she gave me her body,

not once but twice only to see me destroyed now with her mockery, her rejection annihilating my very soul. I won't wait for her in the garden; I'll come to her at night when she doesn't expect me. I'll steal into her room and take her by force. She'll know the cost of her injury to me. She shall not treat me as her plaything; she will know me as the monster that I am.

"What did you do, Erik? Tell me," Mme. Giry demanded.

"I can't. I can't. Please don't ask." He sighed one last time, his emotions spent, before he rose from the couch and retreated farther down the tunnels away from Mme. Giry's questioning look. She couldn't assuage the sinking feeling in her stomach as she thought of Christine.

I mustn't avoid him any longer. I can tell that he waits for me in the garden. I sense him there, his eyes bore into my body whenever I am on the terrace. I don't know what to do. How could Meg do what she did? How could she let him believe that he was with me that night, not her? He waits now for his lover to come to the garden, for me to come. I have to tell him the truth, and it will destroy him and maybe the two of us. He promised me he wouldn't talk of love. How can I stop him now from holding me to a debt I don't owe him? Surely he understands that something is wrong. I haven't gone to meet him for several weeks. He'll be angry, hurt, but surely the break between us has already begun. He must be somewhat prepared by my daily evasions.

I wait for Raoul to depart for town; he has business that will detain him the rest of the afternoon. The nurse has taken little Raoul to play. This is the best moment for me to face Erik.

I walk toward the garden, but well before I approach our usual spot, he steps out of the shadows into the sunlight and stands in my path. I am so startled that I gasp and bring my hand to my mouth. He has a dark and wild look in his eye, and his clothes are crumpled and dusty as if he has slept in the woods. He doesn't speak but walks quickly toward me and grabs my arm. His grasp hurts me. Suddenly terrified of this man, I beg him to let me go. I stumble and fall, but he drags me off the path, and I see he means to take me into the woods. I am stunned, and my arm aches as if it were being wrenched from its socket. I think to scream but he has pulled me to my feet and clamped his hand across my mouth. We are so close that I feel his breath on my face, and his eyes glare into mine. I cannot breathe for his hand is locked over my mouth. He removes it only to force his mouth on mine in a savage, cruel mockery of a kiss. All the tenderness and love I thought I had seen in him have disappeared. In their place is madness! I feel myself grow limp in his arms from panic, and I whimper deep in my throat like an animal. I can't believe his strength; it feels as if he were crushing me. He lowers me to the ground, still trapped in his embrace, my arms pinned to my sides. I close my eyes, I can't bear to look him in the face, his mouth is distorted in a grimace. His body is heavy and lies upon mine. I feel his knee wedge between my legs, parting them, and his hand is pulling at my skirts. I know what he means to do! I open my eyes wide in panic and have the strength to shout at him. "No," I gasp. I can't think of any other words to say to him. My arms momentarily freed from his grasp flail against him uselessly. His fury seems to increase, and I feel him now between my legs, his hand covers my breasts, and he again presses his lips brutally against mine. I know that I can do nothing to stop him. I sob deep inside my throat for his mouth stops my voice. I can see no other recourse than to give in to his violent demand. I wait for him to penetrate me, but he does not. He is looking at my breasts, my throat. He is breathing hard; he looms over me like a giant. His hand goes to my throat, and for one moment I fear he means to strangle me. But he passes it gently over my skin down my throat to my collar bone as if he were looking for something.

I wait for the next assault, but it doesn't come. He glances into my eyes and then looks away as if in shame. In the next moment, he lifts his weight from my body and moves away from me. I cover myself and double over in fear and revulsion, bringing my knees to my chest, as he releases me. He mutters something inaudible over and over to himself, something wild that makes no sense to me, something about a dream. He turns toward me as if to touch me, and I scream at him to stay away. He retreats as if stung. I don't know what he's saying. I tremble all over, my heart is pounding so hard that the blood stops my ears, I see him turn and run into the woods. I lie on the ground on a rough carpet of turned sod, mushrooms, twigs, and twisted leaves, and cry. No one hears me. The servants are too far away. I fear he'll come back. I crawl across gnarled roots to the trunk of the elm, press my back against it, and draw my knees up to my chest as if I could in this way disappear inside myself. When I can cry no longer, I wipe away my tears with the back of my hand. My hands are dirty. I brush the leaves from my petticoats, straighten my skirts. The fasteners on my bodice are torn so I hold the fabric together by hand.

It takes me several moments to rise, my legs are trembling so. Then I hear the crunch of breaking twigs. I see the monster standing among the trees. I scream with all my strength. He doesn't move. I scream again, and he turns and vanishes into the thicket.

Dearest Christine,

I have sat to write you several times and despaired that I would be able to make you understand. I beg your forgiveness, Christine. You are my truest and only friend, my sister, and I cannot bear to have hurt you the way I did. I was selfish and stupid. I did not think of the consequences of that night for you. I didn't care what might happen to me, but it was shameful for me to put you in this situation. If I can make amends for it, please ask me whatever you think I should do and I will do it.

I have not had the courage to tell Maman, nor have I had the opportunity to confess my horrid deed to the one that most needs to know. He has not come to the opera house for these several weeks. I have asked Maman to go to him, to see if he is ill. She has returned, and with such a frightful look on her face that I can't tell what must have happened. She wouldn't tell me anything; she only told me that he was not ill. He simply doesn't choose to visit me. I had at least his friendship. Now I seem to have lost even that. When I tell him that it was I that lured him into the alcove, I am sure that he will hate me.

Christine, please do not abandon me, too. I'm punished enough by my own stupidity. I now know what I am never to have again, and it breaks my heart. I only wish that I hadn't done what I've done. I am willing to live with the consequences, but I am pained to know how you suffer and how he will suffer as a result of my selfishness.

If you can forgive me, I will be so thankful. I will face Erik even if I have to disobey Maman and go to his chambers alone and tell him there. He may kill me on the spot. It will be what I deserve.

Your sorrowful sister,

Meg

"Raoul, please stop. It hurts, please." Christine pushed her husband away and drew the covers to her chin. Raoul lay back panting hard in exasperation. He had made love to her as gently as if it were the first time, stroking her and whispering that he loved her. He had held her until she softened in his arms. He kissed her over and over, yet once again at the last minute she'd stiffened against him and wedged her arms between their bodies to separate them. She lay there crying, and he did not understand what had changed between them. He had vowed to be patient with her. Sometimes after the birth of a child, he had been told, the woman was reluctant to resume marital relations, but that had not been the case with Christine. She was as passionate as ever once she physically recovered. Little Raoul was walking now and talking; this sudden aversion to making love with him was bewildering.

He turned to Christine, controlling his annoyance and frustration, and stroked her long dark tresses. Gently he nuzzled close behind her, but almost immediately felt aroused. She, too, was aware of his body pressed against hers and edged away from him even more. This was intolerable. She acted as if he were diseased! Raoul brusquely threw the covers back and left the bed.

"Christine, I've tried to be understanding, but this can't go on. You have to explain this to me. You flinch when I touch you. It's unbearable." His voice became more and more agitated as he spoke. No longer able or willing to hide his frustration, he demanded an explanation.

"I don't know what the matter is. I know that it makes no sense. Please, please, Raoul, come back to bed. It will be all right. I love you, and I want you to make love to me." She was desperate to prove to him that there was no problem. His anger melted, replaced by concern. He sat beside her on the bed and took her into his arms again. He rocked her back and forth and told her that it was all right, that he loved her, and that he could be patient. Nevertheless, he needed to know why she was suffering in this way. What had changed?

"Please, Christine. If you ever loved me, tell me what I have done to make you uncomfortable or fearful? Is it that you no longer find me desirable? Is there something that I do that causes you discomfort when we make love? I know that it might be difficult to tell me, but you must. I know that I can find a way to make it better if you only tell me what it is." He drew her face to his and kissed her eyes, her nose, her lips. She was stuffy and had to breathe heavily through her mouth. He brought a handkerchief from the bureau and told her to blow her nose and wipe her tears.

Raoul nudged her over in the bed, and climbed in beside her leaning against the headboard. He held her until she calmed.

After a while, she began to stroke his chest lightly with her hand. Hesitant she brought her face up to his and kissed him long and sweet. Afraid that she would again draw away, Raoul remained still and waited for Christine to let him know what she wanted. Slowly they kissed each time more deeply, more passionately, until Christine drew back ever so slightly. Pushing him down against the bed, Christine sat across his hips. Raoul held his breath lest she bolt away. Slowly and awkwardly at first she brought herself down upon him. He lay beneath her, overwhelmed by the pleasure, yet alert to any sign on her part of distress. When they were both satisfied and exhausted, Christine lay beside him and sighed with pleasure. Relieved that so many nights of frustration had finally come to a close, Raoul hugged Christine close.

"Raoul, we must leave here for a while. I want us to go to the country. Your aunt would be happy to see us. Please, can we spend several months in the country away from the city?" He did not understand why she would so much like to leave the Paris estate, but after this night, he was happy to grant her any request she might make of him.

They would close the mansion and move to the country for the season. The change in air would do all of them good.

Caesar whinnied nervously outside the gate of the cemetery. He was winded and sweating profusely from the mad race his master had led him through the country lanes. The white horse pawed at the dry ground as the Phantom ran along the rows of marble and granite tombstones.

Erik's hands wouldn't stop shaking. His shirt stuck to his skin from the sweat. He whipped off his cape and dropped it as he continued to run amid the statues and shrines. The silence of the graveyard was what he sought. Near the Daaé mausoleum stood a beautifully carved Virgin Mary over the grave of a child; the dates indicated the unfortunate death at the young age of nine. Erik didn't know the child, but he was always drawn to this monument of the Holy Mother standing vigil over the mortal remains of this boy. Her head was inclined toward the grave, and a gentle smile was carved across her face; her arms were open as if inviting the child to come into her embrace. Erik reached out toward Mary and placed his trembling hand in her stone cold palm and bowed his head in torment. The cold stone cooled his fevered brow as he rested against her skirts.

He had gone mad! What good was pretending to be a man? What good the fine clothes, the gentlemanly carriage, his fine behavior, his haughtiness? He had tranformed into a wild animal. With teeth bared and claws extended, he had thrown the woman he loved onto the ground, eager and ready to rape her. All those years of restraint, of self-denial, of control and he had abused her in that filthy way. He had used his strength to harm her, to shame her, to treat her like a common whore. And in this madness he had defiled the only pure and noble thing in his life, his love for Christine!

"Oh, Mary, merciful Mother …," he began, but he couldn't remember the prayers he may have known as a young child. Some phrases swam to the surface of his memory. Surely his mother had pitied him enough to have him baptized? Even animals were brought to church for blessings, he was told. Lambs, goats, dogs, cats. But not wolves or jackels, nor vipers or scorpions!

Mad! It had been a wonderful, glorious delusion! He had made love to a ghost, an incubus, and it had stolen his heart and soul and led him to damnation!

Dearest Christine,

I understand your silence. I only hope you will eventually forgive me. Perhaps you would feel some pity for me if you knew of my suffering.

Maman has coaxed Erik back to the opera house. He's changed. He's morose. He shows little interest in me or my singing; even the music seems to have lost its appeal for him.

I was surprised that you have closed the mansion and gone to the country. I can't help wondering if the move is your way of avoiding us, me and of course Erik. Did Erik come to visit you after that night? I fear that this may be at the heart of your silence, your evident coldness towards me. Have you told him of my deception? I can't believe that you have, for surely Erik would despise me if he knew. Yet he comes to the opera house, seemingly unaware of my betrayal of you both.

When he comes, he sits in my dressing room, and we hardly exchange a word. He comments absently on my performance, nothing really pleases him, and leaves each time earlier than the last. Oh, Christine, I have tried to tell him, please believe me, but the words freeze on my tongue when I think of what he might do and what he might think of me.

I would like to know why he's become so dejected. When we parted that morning after the ball, he was truly happy. This is why I sense that something must have occurred between the two of you. Of course, if he came to you, you must have had to rebuke him. Is this why he seems to die inch by inch, day after day?

What have I done, Christine?

Please forgive me and free me from these fancies.

Your repentant sister,

Meg

Dear Meg,

Raoul insists that I write you. He has seen your letters arrive and watched me destroy them without response. He assumes it is some silly disagreement that rankles me, and he chides me for being unforgiving. I had no intention of writing you ever again. But as I write this, I remember the love we've shared as sisters and feel my heart melt ever so slightly. You have done a horrid, horrid evil to me and to him.

You shall know the consequences of your deception. In part I fear that if you don't know them, you may be in danger.

I've no doubt that you may have believed that your actions were a charity to him. You've no idea how much you've actually injured the man you profess to love. Having spent the night with you, all previous restraints on his lust and desire have been lost. He could not and would not be satisfied with your one night. He came each day to wait for me. In his mind, I cruelly withdrew what I'd already given, my body and my soul. He stood, "my impatient lover," in the woods and waited. I ignored him, avoided going to the grove of trees where he hid, week after week, but I realized I couldn't continue to do so. Gathering my courage, I went to tell him the truth. Little did I understand the extent to which his passions tormented him.

Your Erik attacked me in the woods. He was like an animal. I couldn't fight him off. I lay there beneath him, humiliated and in fear for my very life. Then just as suddenly as he had attacked me, he stopped. I don't know why he restrained himself when he did.

Although he did not succeed in raping me, the effect of his assault on me was so terrible that until recently I couldn't bear for Raoul to touch me. I only now feel that I'll recover.

I will never forgive the Phantom. I will never forget how he grabbed me and touched me. He was monstrous. I was terrified! There can be no forgiveness between him and me. I blame you for awakening that animal skulking within him. Needless to say, it must have always been there inside him. Perhaps it was inevitable that I would be victim of it at some point.

I will try to forgive you. It won't be easy, and it will take much time. But you must promise me that you'll save yourself from him. He is capable of great violence even to those he says he loves. What love is that which attacks and tears what it loves?

He must be told the truth. I was unable to defend myself to him. He wouldn't let me speak. I had hoped that you would tell him, but after this encounter I fear for your life should he ever find out that you deceived him. I believe your only hope is to distance yourself from him and only when you are safe send him a letter explaining what you've done.

Please don't write me as often as you have. Give me time to let this wound heal. I'll write you when I can again call you my dearest sister.
Christine

CHAPTER 8

Revelation

"Monsieur Baron, you are too kind, really." Meg accepted the bouquet of roses and gardenias and placed them on her dressing table. The Baron, a large imposing man, glided in behind her and shut the dressing room door. As one of the major patrons of the arts in Paris, the Baron had taken a particular liking to the new diva at the Opera National. He liked the turn of her leg, the petite figure she struck on the stage, her ethereal voice. He had tired of his mistress, the lady Monpart, and was excited by the appearance of this new young woman.

"The managers have spoken so highly of your talent, Mademoiselle Giry, that I have ached to see you. Indeed their praise falls quite short of your gifts." The Baron edged closer to Meg as she covered her chemise with the silk dressing gown Erik had left for her once as a reward for a particularly taxing performance. As he approached, she stepped back until she found herself next to the dressing table itself and could retreat no farther.

Most of the men who visited her backstage were admiring yet timid. They sometimes sent her gifts, many times slipping a note among flowers or jewels that they bribed the backstage manager into delivering. She was always kind to them, but firm. She had made it clear, as had her mother, that she was a decent girl and would not be wooed by these gentlemen who, no matter how entranced by her beauty and talent, offered her no promise of a respectable future. Her mother had told her she must be cautious and aim her sights appropriately or she would be hurt, perhaps ruined. There had been a few gallants that she found hard to resist, but she was able to do so because Erik was always present.

Knowing that Erik protected her gave Meg the strength to resist the onslaught of these admiring predators. In a recent incident, a particularly persistent young gentleman much given to boasting and drinking had become tiresome in his attentions. One night when this ardent admirer finally left the theater after beating repeatedly on Meg's door and calling her a tease because she would not have supper with him, Erik was waiting for him. Later, her protector assured her that the young man had decided he didn't like opera that much after all and planned to switch his attentions to natural science. At first she worried that he had done something violent to the young man, but when she searched the gazettes and found no mention of any assaults that night she was relieved to believe he had simply "reasoned" with the importunate suitor.

But lately Erik came only seldom, and Meg felt more and more abandoned. The Baron was a powerful man, influential, and not easily discouraged. She was sorry that he had focused his attentions on her, for it would be difficult to refuse him. All she could think of was getting out of her costume, washing off the lurid face paint, and preparing in case Erik should come to visit. She desperately wanted to be rid of the Baron's foul smell of cologne and cigar smoke.

"M. Baron," she began.

"Call me Jean Claude, my diva." He bowed low, then proceeded to remove his hat and gloves. He threw them on a chair as if he had always visited Meg after her performances. Then he took off his long coat and threw that, too, upon the chair in a careless fashion.

Meg was beginning to worry. It was late. Her other admirers had already left. Unfortunately, her mother had also departed just minutes before Meg retired to her dressing room. There were few hands still working at this hour in the theater.

"Now, my pretty Meg. You don't mind if I call you Meg, do you?" He grabbed her arm firmly and pulled her into a tight embrace. She smelled the cognac barely masked under the smell of a cigar on his breath as he forced his mouth on hers. She felt smothered in cloth. He yanked at her clothing until he managed to open her bodice and pushed her back onto the divan. He landed heavily on top of her, and she realized in a panic that she wasn't strong enough to fight him off. His mouth stopped her cries.

She began to feel faint when suddenly the Baron's weight lifted from her body. On the Baron's fat-cheeked face was a startled expression as he flew backwards toward the dressing room door, struck his back against the jam, and fell forward unconscious onto the carpet. Only then did she discern a dark shape towering over the collapsed figure of the Baron. Opening the doors, the Phantom secured Meg's suitor by the back of his shirt collar and dragged him effortlessly away down the hall. Meg lay waiting, listening to the sounds of scuffling along the wooden floor recede in the distance.

Shortly thereafter, her teacher and patron stood in the doorway silently looking at her. Pierced by his gaze, she suddenly became aware of the disarray of her clothes. She drew her arms across her exposed breasts in an instintive gesture of modesty. But his preternatural silence and stillness were not evidently a sign of either prudery or lust! Something had drawn his attention so strongly that he seemed frozen to the spot, unable to look away.

"Erik," she began, but he interrupted her with his outstretched hand. Drawing near, he peered down at her. With his finger, he traced the line of her neck from her chin down toward the rise of her bosom. Meg's pulse began to beat wildly as she felt his hand touch her. Then, just at her collar bone, he stopped and gently examined a dark brown mole, the one spot floating in a sea of cream. She saw it in his eyes, behind the mask, the recognition.

she lay beneath me small and fragile, I remember now feeling large and heavy on her worried that she might not take my weight, she was smaller than Christine, she wore the disguise of Marie Antoinette, a mask covered her face, a wig disguised her blond tresses, did she speak to me? she must have told me to follow? no, she did not speak because I would have recognized that voice, but I called her Christine, she heard me say Christine, she knew that I thought I was with Christine and she didn't say a word, I didn't want to see that she was petite, smaller than Christine, I was bewitched by her presence, by her seduction, by the dream of possessing Christine, in the dim light from the moon I could see only the vague outline of her body, I traced her figure with my hand, as I lay with her in the moonlight, my hand came across a mole at the base of her throat and I bent to kiss it, I would have died happy in that moment, Christine had given herself to me, and I let nothing awake me from this dream, because I wanted it, I needed it to be true, and where was her husband as she lay with me? did I not think for one moment of how strange it was that the mistress of the house slept by my side until the first rays of dawn filtered through the glass? did I not wonder why her husband had not raised the alarm and gone from room to room until he found us? did I think that Raoul hadn't noticed that his wife didn't occupy his bed that night? I, the fool, I let the illusion overwhelm me because it was my most ardent desire, the masquerade of my passion, the mask of my love played her scene for me and like an eager admirer

I said yes, yes, this is my love, this is Christine, so little Meg has gotten her way at last, she's stolen her friend's part, she came to me in the grotto, she became my pupil, she opened the season as the prima donna at the new opera due to my instruction, she occupies the stage that I wanted for Christine, sings the songs that Christine should sing, she has lain in the bed I intended for Christine, but her most ambitious role she played that night at the ball, she usurped Christine's body and tricked me into lying with her, into making love to her, my only desire was for Christine, she's taken my soul from me … all I had was my desire for Christine and she's stolen it from me and dirtied it, she's taken away any hope that I might be with Christine, she's tricked me, deceived me, she's given me to believe that Christine was willingly my lover, and now I've earned Christine's eternal curse, I've been a fool, and I've done such terrible things to the only woman I've ever loved, I can never be forgiven, I have unknowingly committed such an outrage that I deserve Christine's hatred because Meg made me believe that Christine loved me and now the truth crushes me, the truth is that Christine never loved me, the truth is that she loves Raoul and that she now despises and fears me, and it is right that she should revile me, shun me, I've lost even her pity and she knows me now only as the monster that I am, the final mask has been lifted, she has seen my soul and cringed in horror, and the most sublime moment of my life has been nothing more than a cruel deception

"I have made arrangements for Meg to marry." Erik placed the papers into Mme. Giry's hands. "I have settled a generous stipend on the young suitor, a lesser lord from a respectable family, M. Pardieu. He comes to the opera every single night, reserving one of the boxes. He is respectful and truly enamored of your daughter. I suggest you use whatever influence you have on Meg to accept this suit."

"But, Erik, does she love him? Has she once mentioned a possible marriage to this young man to you? For she hasn't said a word to me."

"Regrettably, no, she hasn't mentioned him. But she will come to love him. I've watched and investigated him. He's kind, intelligent, and hopelessly in love with her." There was a coldness to his manner; his voice was studiously matter of fact. Mme. Giry had been troubled for some time. Something had gone terribly wrong between him and Christine, she knew this for certain. Lately, she had also noted his growing coldness toward herself and her daughter.

"Erik, what has happened?" She assumed the tone she had always used when she dealt with Erik. It was meant to establish that there were ties between them that neither of them could dissolve.

For a moment, she felt him soften. "Madeleine, all hope is dead. Your daughter's in danger of flying too high and burning her wings. I hope to save her from a great fall."

She could tell that there was hidden meaning in these words, but Erik didn't intend to reveal it to her.

"I'll speak with her, Erik. I think I should also meet this young man myself. A mother should have something to say about the future marriage of her daughter, don't you think?"

"Certainly. But I warn you not to throw away this opportunity. I do *not* plan to spend my time as a marriage broker for your daughter. She should better recognize the obligation she owes me in this." Mme. Giry was taken aback by the intensity of this latter remark. She could feel the anger pouring out in these words and in the look of his eyes.

"And if she refuses?" she dared to ask.

"Then she'll be left to her own devices. I'll wash my hands of her and have nothing more to do with her or her career." With this, Erik was gone.

Dearest Christine,

I am to be married. The gentleman whom I must call husband is sweet and kind. It's a match made by my patron, not of my own choosing, but I can't refuse.

He knows, Christine. I don't know how, but he knows.

Your repentant sister,

Meg

Their stay in the country had refreshed and calmed Raoul and Christine, and they were both pleased to be back home in their estate just outside the hustle and bustle of Paris. Raoul was obliged to come into town to settle some business matters so he planned to take the opportunity to visit several of his gaming friends, inviting them to come spend some time with him and his family at the estate. He lunched at the club, and promised that he would pass back later in the afternoon for a few games of cards before setting off for home.

Christine had given him a list of merchandise that she wanted from several shops in the city. Raoul personally discharged one or two of the errands before tiring of them. The rest of the list he entrusted to his manservant. The air was clear and crisp so he decided he would stroll along the river. Memories flooded over him as he drew near the old opera district. The change of environment had worked miracles for him and Christine. They were once more comfortable with each other. They were discussing the possibility of a second child now that little Raoul was precociously growing into a little man. He fidgeted so and no longer allowed Christine to cuddle him like a puppy dog, and she was beginning to miss that tender experience of the babe and toddler. Raoul smiled as he thought of his wife. Upon their return to Paris, she had begun to command the Chagny estate as if she had always been a lady in charge of a staff of valets, cooks, maids, and butlers. She had already hosted several successful dinner parties. At each, she entertained the guests after dinner with her singing. Fortunately in the district there were a number of young families of similar age, so Raoul and Christine were enjoying their new circuit of friends. If it weren't for business matters, Raoul would perhaps be content never to leave the estate, but rather live out his days in the cool shade of his park.

As he found himself nearer the scene of the opera disaster, his mood darkened. Gnawing at the back of his mind was the unfortunate fact that the murderer of so many innocent lives was still roaming the sewers of Paris, free. He tried not to think of the threat the Phantom had expressed in his note. How dare he assume Raoul to be indebted to him. The fact that he interceded that one night tied Raoul's hands as a gentleman. Yet how can one protect a fiend? Did that one act of benevolence absolve the Phantom of all the blood he had spilled? Raoul understood that the only reason the Phantom had protected him was that the monster was still in love with his wife. There was no affection between him and the opera ghost. It was clear that the Phantom spared Raoul only to please Christine.

The sun was about to set, and Raoul decided to hail a cab to return to the club. Christine would be worried if he tarried too much longer. In his path as he turned stood a man. There was an ominous charge to the air. Raoul slowly placed his hand on the hilt of his sword, but he didn't draw it yet. The Phantom had his back to the last rays of the setting sun; the features of his face were cast in shadow. Raoul knew instinctively who he was.

"How goes it with your wife, dear Count?" Raoul noted the sardonic tone.

"Well," was all that he responded. If only he could rid himself and Christine of this Phantom. Every nerve in his body prepared itself for a fight. He hoped all this might finally come to an end.

"I am glad of it." The Phantom showed both of his hands as if to prove to the count that he was unarmed and had no intention of attacking him.

The count edged his way to the side so that he wouldn't be blinded by the last rays of the sunset. As he did so, the features of the Phantom came into sharper focus. He was wearing a mask over most of his face. As before he wore dress clothes and his long black cape. He wore gloves. Raoul noted that in fact his whole body was covered except the area of his lower jaw, mouth, and chin. No other hint of flesh was visible under the wig, mask, and clothing he wore. He knew what hideousness lay buried under this disguise. And this man, who lived in the sewers of Paris, dared profess his love for Christine. It was abominable.

"What do you want with me?" the count challenged.

"With you? Nothing. I want you to give Christine, my former pupil, this note. It is no concern of yours. But if you insist on reading it, so be it. You will have to deal with the consequences." Without an apparent movement a small envelope appeared in the Phantom's outstretched hand. When Raoul didn't reach out to take it, the Phantom nodded to the envelope he still held.

"You must be mad. I'll have nothing to do with you, nor will my wife. Keep your note."

"I regret that you're unwilling to be my messenger. I'd thought to avoid a tiresome journey to the outskirts of town myself. But if that is what you want, I shall oblige you." The envelope disappeared as quickly as it had appeared, and the Phantom turned to go.

Raoul stopped him. "Hold, you monster. Let's have it out now. Draw your sword."

The Phantom's expression was more a grimace than a smile. He put his hand on the hilt of his sword but did not draw it. "Are you sure that you won't carry my little note to your country bumpkin wife?" he taunted.

With this, Raoul drew his sword and ferociously attacked. The Phantom swerved and drew his sword as well. The two men went at each other thrusting and parrying, dodging and slashing. The clang of their swords echoed across the river, the flash of the last glimmer of light flickered on the edge of each metal blade like shooting stars. Raoul was the better trained, but the Phantom drove forward like a demon with a strength born of a complete disregard for his own safety. Raoul kept him at bay and waited for an opportunity to drive the sword up and under the Phantom's guard. At the last moment, however, the Phantom grabbed Raoul's blade with his hand and brought the pummel of his sword down on his opponent's grip. Raoul shocked by the Phantom's daring act, dropped his sword and waited for the decisive thrust. But surprisingly the Phantom drew back and paused. He glanced at the hand that had grabbed the blade; blood dripped from the black glove. He waited for Raoul to pick his sword up from the cobblestones where he had dropped it. Then the Phantom switched his own blade to his wounded hand.

"What is this? Why didn't you strike?"

"I've nothing better to do this evening. I hate for the entertainment to end too quickly, don't you?" There was no mirth in these words.

And again the two men engaged each other, at one moment on the attack, the next on the defensive. Raoul managed to gain an advantage and was pushing the Phantom back toward the wall when the Phantom simply dropped his sword and stood, defenseless, his arms out like a gigantic bat waiting for Raoul to charge forward and thrust his sword to the hilt. Several passersby had stopped to watch the duel. This was Raoul's chance to end it all. The Phantom was unprotected, had dropped all defenses, and seemed to be waiting for the final blow. All Raoul had to do was lunge forward.

He cried out in frustration and lowered the tip of his sword.

The Phantom glared at him. Rage and hatred flashed in his eyes as he stepped forward several paces until their faces were intimately close. There was a murderous glint in his eyes as he looked at his rival. "Why didn't you end it? Here? Now? Why couldn't you just end it for us both?" He spit these words out in a hoarse whisper that only Raoul and he could hear.

"Because that is what you want," responded Raoul coldly, enjoying his slight triumph over the Phantom.

The note floated to the ground in front of Raoul as the Phantom sped off into the shadows of a nearby alleyway. Raoul did not want to, but he couldn't resist stooping for the envelope. It was addressed to Christine and sealed in red wax with a death's skull.

Dear Countess de Chagny,

I would like to address this letter to my dearest Christine, but I've lost that right forever. I've recently become aware of information that reveals to me the error of my deeds. I was deceived, and this deception led me to commit a great injustice. I beg you to forgive me and to forget me.

I hope your husband isn't foolish enough to read this note. It's between you and me. But let me be circumspect, you know of what I speak. My actions grew out of a charade in which you and I were the innocent dupes. When I left the masked ball, I was convinced that you loved me. I only ask you to perhaps consider how ecstatic I was for a brief moment glorying in that deception; it was a wonderful lie if it had not borne such ignominious consequences. I held you to blame for my own disappointment; I thought you purposefully cruel to me. I know now that you are still the most glorious of creatures and that you, too, have been an innocent victim of the deception. The man you last saw deserves your hatred and revulsion.

If you ever think of me, I hope with all my soul, as black as it may be, that it is with some touch of forgiveness. I did what I did laboring under a cruel illusion not of my own fabrication.

Your humble servant,

O. G.

"Have you read this?" Christine folded the note several times and placed it on the table.

"Yes." Raoul waited, but Christine said nothing. "I came upon him in Paris. He insisted I bring you the note. I refused. He challenged me to a fight. At the last moment he dropped his sword. I think he wanted me to run him through." He watched her. Her face was turned away toward the fire so he couldn't see her reaction. "I couldn't kill an unarmed man. He escaped at the last minute before the gendarmes arrived." He paused, hoping that Christine would say something. When she remained silent, he asked, "What is it that he did to you, Christine? What is this note about? Why did he think you loved him?"

"Please don't ask," she whispered.

Suddenly angry, Raoul forced her to turn and face him. "But I *am* asking. I'm your husband. You can't hide these things from me. When you danced, did you tell him you loved him?"

"No! I would never tell him that!"

"Then why does he say that? What did he do that he asks your forgiveness?"

"He attacked me in the woods." She was all of a sudden quite calm.

Raoul stunned drew back slowly.

"Attacked?"

"He tried to force himself on me."

Her former reticence in the marriage bed now made sense to him. "My God, Christine, are you all right? Did he hurt you?"

"No, he was violent with me. He threw me to the ground, but in the end he stopped before he...." She struggled to stay calm.

"But when did this happen? How?"

"The day you went to discuss the repairs to the retaining wall with M. Gautier. He was waiting for me in the grove. He thought that I'd betrayed him again. I can't say more without revealing secrets that aren't mine to reveal. Let it suffice to say that he was deceived by someone and thought that I had pledged my love to him."

"But you had not?"

"No, I did *not* pledge my love to him or invite him to make love to me. But he believed I had. When I didn't come to him, he grew jealous and angry. The day I went to the woods to tell him that he was mistaken, he was beyond rational thought. He lay in wait for me, and when I came down the path he attacked. He meant to rape me. But at the last moment, he stopped. I don't know why he stopped. I couldn't stop him, and he knew it." She seemed relieved to have finally told Raoul what had nearly transpired in the woods. It was as if a great burden had been taken from her chest, and she could finally breathe easily again.

Raoul, however, was stunned. So many emotions warred in his breast. He regretted with all his soul that he had not run the monster through with his sword when he had had the chance. Yet another opportunity to be rid of him had evaporated before his eyes.

"Raoul, I've managed to put this behind me. Can you do so as well?" She touched his arm gently and waited for his reply.

"Why should I? Why shouldn't I challenge him to a duel?"

"No! You mustn't." In panic, Christine grabbed at Raoul's arm as if to stop him from acting upon his threat that very moment. "Please, I want to forget it ever happened!"

"I'm saddened that you didn't confide in me before. I thought our love stronger than that."

She saw disappointment in his eyes and heard it in his voice. A pain clutched at her heart, and she burst into tears. "Please, Raoul, I haven't been myself. I'm so relieved to tell you this now. I wasn't strong enough to face it then. I felt defiled for weeks afterwards. I couldn't get clean. I thought I might never be worthy of you again."

Her tears washed over his heart, and his anger melted away. How could he be angry with her? He embraced her and kissed her what seemed a thousand times. Wanting her more than ever, he picked her up in his arms and carried her to their bedroom.

CHAPTER 9

The Confession

... to thee do we cry, poor banished children of Eve ...

"Inspector, there has been a report of a sword fight along the river where the Phantom has been sighted. Witnesses report," and here the overly diligent officer opened his tablet and read. "A tall man in a black cape and a mask assaulting a gentleman."

"Send Claude with his men to the area. Have them fan out in a search pattern. Be sure to watch the sewer covers. I'll join them at the Rue des guards. We'll narrow this search net soon. It's only a matter of time." Leroux stuck yet another pin in the map behind his desk. Several clustered near the same spot, near the Rue des guards down the river from the abandoned Opera Populaire.

Damn him, damn his lack of resolve, he had every opportunity, why didn't he take it? what more could I have done? blindfold myself? fight with both hands tied? Erik wrapped his kerchief more tightly around the bloody glove and hurried down the alleyway. At the corner of the Rue des artistes were several gendarmes. Obviously they were waiting there for him. He doubled back and turned away from the river planning to circle back, perhaps behind the Theatre Royal, when he heard police whistles and the sound of many boots running in his direction. He had few avenues of choice at this point. He determined to run parallel to the main street and verge off in the contrary direction away from the officers, but as he came to the next intersection he was dismayed to find several officers already stationed there, as well. He suddenly felt trapped. He had been resigned to die at the count's hands. It would have been a relief. But the idea of ending up in the public jail sent waves of panic through him. Brought publicly to trial, placed on exhibit for the Parisian crowds, they would certainly unmask him, drag him through the crowds, strip him of all his dignity. *No, no, no, I must find somewhere to hide, they will lock me in the jail, they will take my mask away, I won't be able to hide from the light, the court room will fill with the curious and morbid spectators, like those who used to come to the fairgrounds and gawk, they'll see my face, the reporters will draw me and publish my disfigurement to the world, Raoul and Christine will appear to testify against me, oh God forbid that I face Christine uncovered, unmasked, to face her testimony against me, she'll call me an animal, she'll forget what sublime music I taught her, she won't tell them how tenderly I nurtured her, how much I gave up when I released her to him, the whole world will know how much I am despised, I must find a way out, it would be better to die at my own hands than to face that.* He edged back into the shadows. Fortunately, it was dark, and the moon had not yet risen. He thought to climb if he couldn't descend into the underground tunnels. Not far was a small church and convent. He easily scaled the low wall thinking that on the other side would be the graveyard. He would hide among the mausoleums. He'd prefer to hide inside the coffin of the recently deceased rather than be taken prisoner.

On the other side of the wall, he dropped soundlessly into a small courtyard enclosed on three sides by a gallery along which was a series of individual rooms. This must be the convent. He crouched and waited for the police to retreat. However, the sound of their boots grew louder, and Erik could tell they were coming in his direction, looking into doorways along the path. They would most likely scale this very wall in search of him. Quietly he stole across the grounds and entered the gallery. He tried one door to find it locked, but the next opened easily, and he slipped inside.

The nun was kneeling in prayer in the chapel of the Virgin, her back to the door. She must have assumed the intruder was one of the other sisters come to join her in prayer. She did not seem the least disturbed by his entrance. Then she must have heard his rapid, heavy breathing for she glanced back over her shoulder. Erik grabbed her from behind, put his hand over her mouth, and with a gesture of his injured hand signaled her to be quiet. Blood dripped from the glove onto the nun's habit. *they'll follow the blood, that's why I haven't lost them, in the garden it will be harder to trace.*

Erik heard the men. They were walking down the hallway outside the cell. He would make his stand here, now. They'd not take him alive; he'd fight to the death. He released the nun, stood, and placed his hand on the pummel of his sword. He wasn't surprised that the nun rose and went to the door, but he was surprised that she didn't scream. Instead, she looked back at him as she left the room and indicated that he should be quiet. He could feel the rush of blood through his body, his heart pounded so loudly that he thought the police surely would hear it, every sound and color was amplified by his tension and anticipation as he prepared to fight to the death. As the door slowly opened, he slid his sword halfway from its scabbard. The nun entered alone, and she was curiously calm.

"You are in need of sanctuary? You have come because God surely meant you to find your way to us."

He wanted to laugh at the old woman, but her smile was so confident that he was baffled.

"Come," she said and offered him her hand. "Don't worry. I know who you are."

"Who? Who do you think I am, old woman?"

"There is no night so dark that a ray of light does not shine somewhere. Now, come. I will wash your hand."

"How do I know that you're not leading me to the gendarmes?"

"Why would I do that? Wouldn't I simply have told them you were hiding inside this chapel and let them come in to take you? You must have faith, my son."

"You're not my mother, and I'm hardly your son!" He meant to sound harsh, but the nun ignored the tone and smiled patiently at him.

"You're injured. You can't leave at this moment. The police would catch you the moment you leave the grounds. Come, let me help." She held out her hand to him in a gesture that reminded him of the open arms of the Virgin Mary carved in stone over the grave of a little boy. All his anger drained out of him and just as he had laid his hand in a moment of black despair in the Virgin Mary's stone palm, he now surrendered his hand to the old nun.

She took him to a brightly lit room with several bare cots, a cabinet with medical supplies, chairs, and a long table. Water basins of various sizes and shapes were stored along the wall; folded linens were stacked on shelves.

"Sit. You're fortunate no one is ill so we have the infirmary to ourselves. Now let's take this old black glove off and see what the damage is." She slowly pulled at the glove until it slid off Erik's hand. He saw the wound was not minor from her scowl.

"It must hurt like the devil."

"Not really. Actually it's rather a relief."

She looked to see if this was merely bravado, but seeing his eyes she understood that it was not.

"What will happen if they find me here? The others in the convent."

She chuckled. "Well, my son, you fortunately went straight to the top this time. I am the Mother Superior of this convent and except for God and the Bishop himself when he visits, no one is higher than I."

"And your God? What would his judgment be?"

"We'll leave that to Him. It is our duty to minister to lost souls, not to sit in judgment."

She prepared the needle to suture the open wound along the palm of his hand. No more than the tightening of the muscles of his jaw suggested he felt the pain. "Well, aren't we brave!" she teased as she finished the last stitch. "I'm used to dealing with many a baby among my sisters in the convent. Taking out a splinter requires two others to hold the third down." She wiped the blood away and wrapped his hand in a fresh white bandage.

"You can take that mask off now." She said this as if she had suggested he remove his coat.

Erik didn't move.

"You don't have to hide yourself here."

"You say you know who I am. If you did, you wouldn't ask me to remove my mask."

"I thought as much. You're the one they say haunts these streets, who lives in the sewers, the ghost from the opera. They say you have led to the deaths of many innocents."

"Don't you fear for your life and the lives of the others living in this convent?"

"Should I?"

Erik didn't know how to answer her. Her lack of fear curiously perplexed and calmed him. Suddenly, all he wanted was to lie down and let oblivion wash over him. She saw his fatigue, and before he even realized she was so near she took his uninjured hand and led him to one of the cots.

"Here is a blanket. Try to sleep if that awful mask will let you. I'll see no one disturbs you until the morning."

"What's your name, sister?" he thought to ask before she left the room.

"You can call me Mother like my girls do." She smiled and closed the door.

"Mother," he barely whispered as he dropped into a deep, dreamless sleep.

"Aren't you ready to take that mask off yet?" Erik woke to see the old nun bent over him peering into his face. "I can see some of the scarring or disfigurement around the edges here." She seemed to be examining him as if he were a specimen under a microscope. "It's bound to be uncomfortable to wear all the time."

"No. I have always worn a mask of some sort or another. It's no more uncomfortable than that wimple you wear."

"Ah, let me tell you something. You think wearing all this is comfortable? You try baking bread or scrubbing floors with all this fabric hanging on you. But I offer it up to Christ as a small cross to bear."

Erik rose from the cot and smoothed his clothes as best he could. The old nun placed a tray on the table and invited him to sit with her and eat. "You must be hungry. You had no supper last night. I love to see a man eat. It is one of God's many gifts, the pleasure of eating. I see that this portion is rather meager for a man of your size. I'll see what I can do about getting you some fresh eggs. Sister Agnes is thrilled to have someone else to cook for. Our order holds to a stark and meager diet so she's hardly able to put her true talents to work for us."

Erik finished the bread and cheese and drank the milk in silence while the old nun continued to talk.

"There are plenty of people walking in broad daylight ugly as sin. There are victims of fire, war, men who have lost limbs in accidents or to disease. You won't shock me; I worked with lepers on an island off the coast of Africa." Given Erik's silence, the old woman reached across the table as if to take the mask off herself.

"No." He backed away out of her reach. Suddenly quite angry, he hissed at her, "If you are so curious to see the freak, I will oblige you with a little peep show myself." He pushed his chair back dramatically from the table and approached the old woman. Looming over her, ominous, he removed the mask and thrust his face within inches of hers.

She flinched as she looked at the lesions and bulbous tissue surrounding his eye, the flattened and corrugated flesh of what was supposed to be one of his nostrils, the irritated and weepy lid of one eye. But she did not look away. "Yes, it isn't pleasant to look at. It's unfortunate because the other side of your face is quite comely. Perhaps it's good that I'm nearsighted. It's all a bit fuzzy to these old eyes of mine." She smiled at him and patted his cheeks with both of her hands.

Erik was stunned by her lack of revulsion. Violent waves of emotion shuddered through his body as he sank to the floor, his face buried in his hands. The old nun patted his shoulder softly, tenderly and waited until his emotions were spent.

"Come, we will sit for a while in the chapel." She beckoned him to follow. Even though he towered over her, she placed her arm around his waist and guided him as if he were a child to the chapel.

"You told the others that I am here?"

"Oh yes, and we are all planning to say the rosary for you this evening. Would you like to join us?

"No. I must leave."

"There are men stationed all about the area. They're convinced you're hiding somewhere nearby. It may even be that they assume you're inside these very walls."

"In that case, why haven't they come for me?"

"The Bishop won't allow it. We're a closed order. The police won't risk problems with the church unless they're certain you're here. In the meantime, do you play chess?"

"No."

"Well, I'll teach you. You seem a bright fellow. You'll catch on quickly. We'll play and have a nice chat. I get so tired of talking with these girls. It's always the same old chatter."

"Remember the knight moves like this, in the shape of an 'L.' You know, you're getting better already, and you've only lost three games. I enjoy playing with novices like you." She gleefully took his rook, placing his king in jeopardy. "Check. Tell me your name."

"I have no name." Erik actually was a very good player, but he enjoyed watching the old woman's glee each time she beat him.

"Don't be ridiculous. You have a name, even if it's only the one you call yourself."

"Phantom, Opera Ghost. Take your pick."

"No. I don't mean those names behind which you hide just as surely as you hide behind that mask."

He kept his gaze riveted to the chessboard looking for some strategy to escape defeat, but this time the old nun had him in a vice. Either he would lose this round or two rounds down the road. Each option led to the same result.

"Is it Jean? Paul? Etienne? Gaston? Robert? Michel?"

"Erik, for God's sake." He ignored her admonishing scowl and tipped his king in surrender.

"Where are you from, Erik? You surely didn't grow like a mushroom in the cellars of the opera house."

"I don't know."

"Who were your parents?"

"I don't know."

"Well, that's interesting. How did you get your name then? Who raised you? Did your mother die in childbirth?"

"No, she didn't."

"Now we're getting somewhere. What do you remember about her, your mother?"

The Mother Superior could tell that he was uncomfortable talking about his past. Yet she had much practice teasing out personal traumas and confessions from her novices over the years. On many an occasion she had sent a young girl packing back to her family to deal with problems that had brought her to the convent. The convent was not a refuge from troubles in the outside world. It was always in the details that she would eventually come to understand her charges and be able to help them find the right path. Although her experience was always with young women, she sensed that Erik was struggling with many buried demons. Perhaps she could help this man exorcise some of them.

"I have some vague memory of a woman." He finally spoke. "I think she was my mother. I remember holding the hem of her skirts. We were at the fair. She told me to wait at the entrance of this tent, and then she walked away. I remember waiting for a long time; she never returned."

"Were you disfigured in an accident or were you born this way?"

"I don't remember a time when I didn't have this face. There was always something covering it."

"They didn't treat you well at the fair?"

Again he did not answer for a long time, obviously struggling with dark memories long buried and the reluctance to relive past pains.

"Well? They kept me in a cage like the other animals at the fair. There was straw on the cage floor, bars. My keeper, Abel, beat me, sometimes with his bare hands, sometimes with a horse whip. I tried to run away several times. I remember he used one of the large cat's collars and leashes to keep me from running when he needed to clean the cage."

The nun kept her eyes on the chessboard and did not speak for some time. "Was there no one who showed you kindness?"

Erik didn't want to remember those days with the gypsies. In his dreams, sometimes images from his childhood would flash by his mind's eye. He tried to recall one that wasn't filled with pain and anger and loneliness. "There was a young girl, an acrobat and trapeze artist, who brought me food sometimes, sweets and scraps. She had bells on her wrists and ankles that made a delicious tinkling sound when she moved. She told me she liked the way they made music when she was on the trapeze. She said she was like a bell hung at the top of the highest steeple. I loved the sound she made. She brought me two tiny cymbals and helped me attach them to a doll that I had. It was a monkey made of burlap, coarsely cut and sewn together."

"Did your mother make it for you?"

"Perhaps. I don't know. It was always with me."

"Then she did love you, it would seem."

Violently he swept his arm across the chessboard sending the pieces clattering to the floor. He stood to his full height and growled at the nun, "She loathed me! She put a sack over my head so as not to look at my ugly face! She took me to the fairgrounds and told me to wait, and she left me. She left me at the fair to be exhibited like a freak. She never meant to come back for me. She might have drowned me in a sack like a litter of unwanted pups, and that would have been a mercy. I would have forgiven her that! My mother …"

"What color was her skirt?" The Mother Superior interrupted using the same tone that she had used before, as if discussing the price of wool or the weather along the coast. She remained unmoved by his anger.

Erik was taken aback by the question and her calm. For a moment, he was simply struck dumb by the absurdity of it all.

"Yes, you heard me. What color was her skirt?"

"What does it matter what color her skirt was? I don't remember such nonsense. I just remember it was the hem of her skirt that I held. I always held it because it was difficult to see through the holes she cut in the burlap bag that I wore over my head so that she wouldn't have to look at me. I didn't want to get lost. I felt safe as long as I held on to …" He stopped and stared out into the room as if looking at something only he could see. "It was gray and blue. Her skirt was gray and blue, striped."

"What else? You remember something else?"

"She must have made the monkey's clothing from the same fabric. No, just the belt. The belt on the doll had stripes of gray and blue, like my mother's dress. This was the only color other than the unwashed natural dye of burlap."

The nun waited.

"The doll might not have been made for me. She might have made it for an older child who tired of it and left it, and I took it up."

"You mean your brother's or your sister's?"

"What are you doing? Why are you doing this?" He was suddenly anxious and confused. What good did these memories serve? It was all conjecture. As if in an attempt to be on firm ground once more, he added angrily, clutching to the only certainty that he had, "She loathed me, and she left me to a fate worse than that of a common animal."

"Did you deserve to be left at the fair?" She persisted in her calm, even voice.

"No. I was a child. I don't know why I was born with this face!"

"You deserved love, to be cared for." He wasn't sure whether this was a question or a statement of fact.

"Yes."

"If you had been bad, you still deserved to be loved. Your mother should still have loved you."

"Yes."

"All children should be loved unconditionally. It's their right. Don't you agree?"

"Yes." The pain was almost unbearable, but somehow he needed her to go on.

"Know that we are all children, all children of God. And as such, He loves us. He loves us unconditionally. He loves us when we are good, and He loves us when we are not good. He loves you, too."

"God's love? That's what you offer me?"

"No, my dear Erik. That is what you always have. All you must do is accept it."

Erik hid in the shadows of the small chapel as the Mother Superior prayed. Through the stone walls of the chapel he could hear the nuns singing a hymn, their voices rising as if one.

Dearest Lord, you must know the purposes of your will, even when they seem strange to us. I pray for this creature who has stumbled upon us in the dark. I do not question why you have given him such a heavy cross to bear; I ask that you make him see that you stand beside him as he carries it, so that he understands that he is not alone. He has done many horrible things, and he is ignorant of your love. If it so pleases you, Lord, shift the weight of this cross from his shoulders and bring him to know your love. Forgive him his sins and comfort him in his despair. Amen.

He must go soon. And yet he felt calm and safe in these rooms with this old woman. She was praying, kneeling, rosary in hand before the shrine of Mary. He stepped out of the shadows and knelt beside her. He didn't pray, but he listened. *Hail Holy Queen, Mother of Mercy, our life our sweetness and our hope, to thee do we cry, poor banished children of Eve, to thee do we send up our sighs, mourning and weeping in this valley of tears, turn then Most Gracious Advocate thine eyes of mercy toward us, and after this our exile, show unto us the fruit of thy womb, Jesus, O clement O loving, O sweet Virgin Mary, pray for us, O Holy Mother of God, that we may be made worthy of the promises of Christ.* She smiled softly to herself and Mary when she felt his hand grasp the corner of her habit. *Amen.*

As she finished and made the sign of the cross, he spoke to her, "I am weary of life, mother."

"I know. But we do not choose the moment of our death. Would it help you to confess and be forgiven?" She could see the doubt in his eyes. "You have to accept that God will forgive you before you can be forgiven."

"The only one I've ever loved despises me. It's her forgiveness that I fear I'll never have."

"Love is not true love if it's given in expectation of something in return. The truest love is that which we give even to those who do not love us, even to those who hate us. Christ's love is the purest example we have of this true love. He sacrificed everything for us. He let himself be crucified for our sins. Take your pain and offer it as a gift to God."

"And what of the deaths I've caused?"

"You'll most certainly have to pay in some way for those sins. If you ask sincerely for forgiveness, it will be yours."

"And I can wipe the slate clean?"

"Before God it will be as if you were newly born. But man keeps another slate, and your crimes can't be erased from that one unless you suffer before man's justice."

"I have to go. It's night. I'll leave by the garden wall."

The old nun watched him place his mask over his tortured face. He knelt before her, bowed his head, and asked for her blessing. She placed her rosary in his hands, and gave him one last embrace as she reminded him that God was everywhere, even in the darkest of nights.

CHAPTER 10

The Descent

> *Be silent in that solitude,*
> *Which is not loneliness—for then*
> *The spirits of the dead, who stood*
> *In life before thee, are again*
> *In death around thee, and their will*
> *Shall overshadow thee; be still.*

"Spirits of the Dead," Edgar Allan Poe

The child was not allowed to play near the stream. His nurse told him to come away from the bank. It had rained for several days, and the ground was muddy. Little Raoul, so light on his feet, had scampered ahead, clutching a huge maple leaf golden and crimson in his hand. The nurse called more and more urgently as she saw the distance between them increase. Her feet sank into the marshy grass and came free of the mud with a sick sucking sound. Little Raoul squatted on the bank of the stream to set his leaf afloat on the water. Then it all happened in an instant. The child was gone. The nurse dropped the bag of toys and her folding stool and ran leaving one shoe embedded in the mire. The water of the stream had begun to rise, and she could see the current. There was no sign of the child. She sank to mid-calf in the mud along the bank and searched down stream. For one moment she thought she saw his hand jut out of the water and then nothing more.

Her cries brought several gardeners to the scene but it was far too late. The body of the little boy would not be found until well into the afternoon and several miles away where the current would deposit him forgetfully near the roots of an old weeping willow tree. Raoul, sobbing, carried his child wrapped in a blanket to Christine's waiting arms. She sank to the floor and rocked the damp bundle until the next morning when Raoul beside himself with grief could stand it no longer. The body would have to be prepared for burial. Her look was wild and her grip so fierce that Raoul needed the help of one of the servants to wrench the child's corpse from her arms. She sat rocking as if she still held him.

The next day Christine had to be dressed by her chambermaid. They fed her bits of dry toast. She barely drank the warm milky tea they gave her sip by sip. Her eyes were what most frightened Raoul; they stared out into vacant space. At one point he brought his face directly in front of hers and grasping her shoulders shook her violently trying to make her see him, for her eyes looked through him as if he were transparent at some spot in the distance seen only by her. He called for the doctor to examine her. But the doctor shook his head and lamented that this was sometimes the toll that anguish took on its victim. He prescribed medicines to calm her, to help her sleep, saying that this was perhaps the only balm he could offer her now. If she did not come out of it in the course of the next several days, the doctor feared she might never recover her wits again but simply remain in this semi-twilight of consciousness.

Raoul attended to the preparations for his son's funeral alone. He asked the nurse to select the clothes in which little Raoul was to be buried, but he dressed him himself, alone, as he thought Christine might have done. Dismissing all those around him, he could hold in his tears no longer and hugged the dead child to his breast and wept inconsolably. The house staff waited patiently outside, despite the sounds of grief emanating from behind the chamber door. After some time, the weeping seemed to diminish, and his manservant knocked softly. No response came at first. Eventually, footsteps were heard, and the young count opened the door for his servant to enter.

The wake began that afternoon, but Christine showed no signs of improvement. She lay listlessly on the daybed in her room until the staff dressed her for the wake and brought her down to the main parlor. Raoul didn't know how long he could delay the funeral to allow Christine to come to her right mind. She must be allowed to say goodbye to her child, he thought. But in this state of mind, it was as if she were unaware of anything happening around her. Gradually visitors from the neighboring estates arrived and offered their heartfelt condolences for the grief of the young couple. Many of the women took turns sitting by Christine, holding her limp hand and absently patting it. The child lay amid freshly cut flowers, garlands of dried aromatic herbs, on a bed of satin cloth. Several candles were his only illumination. The staff busied themselves bringing cold meats and pastries to the buffet for the mourners, pouring brandies for the men and light punches for the women. Raoul sat by the child until one of his closest friends took him gently by the arm to the terrace to get a bit of exercise and fresh air.

Although Raoul tried to pretend that Christine was only grieving, the others could see that she was not responsive. Several of the ladies gathered in a small group and spoke of Christine's shock and wondered what they might do to help her come out of it. When the undertaker came to discuss the arrangements for the funeral, Raoul felt his self-control melting away. Lord Alexander took him aside and told him that he would handle the basic details with the undertaker and that Raoul could sit down and write any specifics that should be followed. Raoul grasped his friend's hand in appreciation, but he refused to retire given Christine's condition. He was the only one who could keep vigil over their dead child.

The Priest had been summoned shortly after the accident. He spoke quietly to Christine, comforted Raoul, and did what he could for the child. He returned in the evening hours to lead the guests in prayer. The funeral would take place the next day at the small chapel in the manor house before the long journey back toward Paris to the graveyard where Raoul's family's crypt lay.

News of the accident had made its way to several of the family's friends in the city, and more people arrived the day of the funeral. Mme. Giry and Meg came that morning and asked to attend personally to Christine. Raoul hoped that seeing them perhaps would bring Christine out of her stupor. Not even Meg could spark the least sign of life in his wife's eyes. It was as if she, too, were lying in the coffin with his son, thought Raoul. Hopelessness sent waves of anguish through his body. At one fell swoop to lose not only a son, but his wife was nearly more than he could comprehend.

Mme. Giry was dismayed at Christine's condition. It was far worse than she had imagined. Christine was young; they would have other children. Little Raoul had been taken from them in a most tragic way, but he had been a happy child. Meg remained constantly by her friend's side, stroking her hair or holding her hand, talking softly and quietly to her.

All of them seemed to have forgotten the nurse who sat wringing her hands, blaming herself for what had happened, until Raoul glanced over in her direction and recognized her despair. At first he felt completely incapable of movement as he listened to the unrelenting stream of sobs, but eventually he felt touched by her share in their tragedy. He went to her and placed his hand reassuringly on her shoulder. His kindness only made her cry more, but she was grateful for his gesture of forgiveness.

"Christine, it's time. Do you want to say goodbye to our little Raoul? They're taking him to the chapel, and then we'll be on our way to the grave-yard." Raoul sat beside his wife and whispered gently into her ear. She must snap out of this, he thought. The doctor had said that the longer this went on, the less hope there was that she would ever recover. Christine continued to look out into the distance, looking at nothing visible to Raoul or the other mourners. What more could he do? Raoul fought the rising panic in his mind. He couldn't lose them both!

The child was now being carried to the carriage that attended outside the chapel. The mourners waited expectantly for Raoul and Christine to take their place in the procession, but Raoul remained at Christine's side urging her qui-etly to respond. There was no use; she remained oblivious to everything around her. Raoul gestured to the servants to help her rise and guide her to the carriage that was to accompany their dead child to the cemetery. The other mourners fell into step and followed the bereaved couple out into the sun-shine.

Mme. Giry and Meg waited for the more illustrious mourners to take their places before they, too, left the chapel. Meg tugged gently on her mother's sleeve and asked, "Does he know?"

Mme. Giry knew immediately of whom she was speaking. "Yes, Meg. He knows, and I've been expecting to see him ever since we arrived. I wouldn't doubt that he'll be somewhere in the graveyard for the burial. I don't think he can resist coming to be with Christine, even if he has to remain at a distance."

"You're worried, Maman. Why?"

"The police have been searching for him. They've gotten closer and closer to capturing him. I fear they might use this tragedy as a chance to lay an ambush for Erik. Leroux is not stupid. He, too, thinks Erik will come to the graveyard."

"Can we warn him?"

"No, ma petite. He needs no warning. He knows that they'll be there wait-ing for him."

"And he would risk this?"

"He would. Of course, he may believe he can escape."

"Maman, what do you think will happen to Christine? She doesn't seem to recognize anything that's happening. She doesn't even look at Raoul."

"Poor man. He's lost them both, I'm afraid."

"She'll recover, won't she, Maman?

"Who can say, ma petite? Sorrow and loss affect us all differently."

there are lilies by the stream and the moss is thick and soft along the bank the sounds of the water rumble in my ears and I think I would like to walk by the river they say it's muddy but I don't care if I get my shoes dirty I will hike my skirts up or wear some of Raoul's breeches I can tie a belt around them to keep them from falling and roll the cuffs at the bottom I used to wear men's clothes from time to time at the opera house Meg and I would play pirates and since I was taller I was always the captain of the pirates and she was my ransomed damsel laughter soft and low rumbled behind the walls where we played he was there listening watching us play our games I want to walk down to the river and show little Raoul the reeds we can sail our leaves with lady bugs as sailors little Raoul likes to splash in the water but we mustn't let him get too close to the water there are so many people now where did they come from? they're mumbling and they put their faces too close to mine and I want them to leave me alone because I'm waiting for Raoul, my little one, to come to me and show me his collection of leaves and it's too loud here for me to hear if he's calling me I don't want to be here I want to go to the opera house where I can listen to the music to the soprano practice her scales I want to take little Raoul there to show him the catwalk and the shadow that walks back and forth on the catwalk the shadow with the voice of an angel that sings to me and little Raoul will listen to his voice and know that there's always music even when the night is dark and cold and I wonder why my babe hasn't come to find me I wait for him so many sad faces and the servants walk by me on tiptoe I want to leave this room that smells like candle wax and dead flowers and my teacher would know how to talk to me he would tell me to sit straight and to practice the scales and that my voice is beautiful to him I sing lullabies to my babe and his eyes smile up at me as if my voice were magic but why do they take me to the carriage? why are there so many people and we can't go now where is little Raoul? we can't leave my babe wants me to take him riding on his pony today we can ride to the far meadow where the ground is not soaked through with so much rain so much rain pounding on the roof on the window making percussion sounds but without a melody we must find a melody to harmonize with the spat-spat-spat-spat of the rain my husband holds my hand how I love him his smooth tender touch little Raoul will grow to be like him with my voice and his father's kind eyes and sweet smile where is my angel? where is the angel who always watched over me? my babe should have an angel an angel to take him to the stream and watch that he not fall in but I don't want to be here, not here, not here, not here, not here, a tomb is open and something is crawling out of the dank hole and it spills out over the marble steps and touches the box why would they put my little babe in a box? he needs a boat, a sail boat, not a box why can't Raoul hear me screaming? I don't want to be here, someone please take me home my little babe and I are going riding today on the pony and my bay to the meadow to pick wild flowers for a grave, no, not for a grave, for the vases in the parlor to replace those dead lilies there are lilies by the stream and the moss is thick and soft along the bank the sounds of the water rumble in my ears and I think I would like to walk by the river they say it's muddy but I don't care if I get my shoes dirty

Raoul takes his wife's arm and leads her to the graveside, the mausoleum where their child will rest. The Priest reads comforting words from the missal. How can any words comfort a parent who has lost his child? The mourners surround the couple, their presence meant to console them. Raoul suddenly feels smothered by the crowd of friends and family around him. Christine stares out vacantly toward the knoll beyond the mausoleum. How can she be so calm? How is it possible that she feels nothing? What can she be thinking, be seeing? Raoul follows her vacant gaze out to the knoll and sees a figure standing looking down upon the mourners, upon the funeral of his child.

The figure does not move. He's tall and dark, the tail of his cape flutters softly in the breeze. Raoul can't make out his features, but he knows who it is. How dare he come to the graveyard as they lay their child to rest in the cold vault! Raoul can't hear the priest's words; he can't take his eyes off the man who stands vigil on the knoll of the hill and watches them put little Raoul to rest among the dead. He stands there like the devil himself waiting to carry off the soul of this young child. Raoul feels overwhelmed by anger that the Phantom dares to stand commanding a view of their tragedy, demanding to play a part in today's grief, their grief. His hand goes to his belt in search of the sword he's not carrying since this is a day for tears and laments, not for fighting and blood. There is no blood to be spilled on the day of his child's funeral; the blood has been stopped cold in the veins of his dead body. Even without a sword, he recklessly slips from Christine's side and rushes toward the still figure on the knoll. The Phantom doesn't move; he waits until Raoul comes within speaking distance.

Raoul stops, his chest heaving from running up the hill. Now the mourners, too, are aware of the presence of a dark stranger on the knoll and mutter among themselves. Some whisper that it's the Phantom, the opera ghost. Others gasp to see the ghost in corporeal disguise before them and wonder why he's come to the child's funeral. Christine's gaze takes on a brilliance it lacked before as it fixes on the dark silhouette that her husband now addresses.

"Why are you here?" Raoul can think of nothing else to say.

The figure doesn't answer, doesn't move. Raoul is close enough to see Erik's eyes behind the ivory mask and discovers that they don't look at him but are trained on the figure of Christine. She and this monster look only at one another. This realization strikes anger intense and hot through Raoul's breast. Suddenly he's aware of the approach of several police officers from various directions narrowing in on the Phantom. Exhilarated, Raoul thinks that finally the Phantom will be brought to justice. The police will bind his hands and drag him to prison where he'll wait for the hangman's noose, a fitting end to this murderous madman. But he sees no fear in the Phantom's eyes which cast a casual glance in the direction of the approaching police. The intruder, in turn, looks for the first time into Raoul's face; there's no mirth to be found in those strange eyes. Raoul feels pierced by their gaze; he's shocked to find there an expression of sadness for him, for the child, for Christine. Then the Phantom whirls around, his cape spreading out like a giant wing, and disappears from sight. The police reach the summit and grab at empty air, and no one can tell where or how the dark figure has gone.

As Raoul looks back toward the funeral cortege, he sees that his wife has fainted.

What can they do for her? Christine stares vacantly into nothingness. The pit of the tomb looms before her, and she's struck with horror. I know that feeling, the feeling of falling endlessly into a black well. No one will be there to catch her. No one understands the deep despondency that drags her down. Her husband stands impotent beside her. He holds her limp hand in his, but his gaze is riveted to the oak coffin. His own sorrow can be heard on the wind as a high keening. No one else hears it, but I can sense it there. He has had a son. He has held the child in his arms. The child has called for him, and opened his arms to him, night after night, day after day. Is it better to have had that love and lose it or never to have had it? Is his pain more intense than mine who will never know such moments? His usually proud stance is bent and broken before the gaping hole in the stone crypt where he is to abandon his child. Yes, I see that his pain is greater. The loss of that child is real; it isn't a product of his imagination like my loss. I will never have a child. His pain is like the pain I feel having known the touch of Christine and yet having lost it forever. In that we are brothers although he would be horrified to think that we shared anything more than our love for Christine and our hate for each other. He would prefer to forget that I've ever held her in my arms and watched her sleep, chaste and protected, in my bed. But it's Christine whom I watch and for whom I fear. Her eyes are wide and unblinking but unseeing as well. She's utterly alone, trapped inside the dark well that is her sorrow. She must see me. She must turn to look at me. Yes, she turns this way. I'm here for you, Christine. I come only because your pain has called to me. I wouldn't be here except that you need me. I understand that you're teetering on the edge of madness. It's a horrible place, Christine. You mustn't go there. I've been there many times, and it's only your voice, your face that keeps me from falling forever into its grip. It is only the memory of you that protects me, shields me from its powerful hold. You must look at me, look into my eyes. They are filled with love for you. There's enough love in my soul to save you from falling. If he can't help you now, do not despair. I'll protect you. I'll bring you to peace if only you let me. But you will have to submit to me; you will have to succumb to the darkness and go there with me. Only if you give yourself to the night, to me, can you hope to strengthen your soul and fight your way back to the light. The darkness will not be so lonely with me by your side. The pit won't terrify you if you know that I'm there to guide you. I am your guide through the darkness. And if you decide to leave me in the end … Well, you can leave me, Christine, but I can never leave you. Your husband has seen me; he clambers up the hill, his hand uselessly searching for his absent sword. Murder even now resides in his heart! He so loves you and so fears me! He has lost everything, and doesn't understand that in this black despair I'm your only hope, Christine. You watch me, you entreat me with your eyes. Yes, my love, I will come for you. Do not fear for his life. He's dear to you, so I won't hate him. I'll fight to control my anger. I'll be your angel in hell. I will suffer, but I will not see you suffer. I will not allow it. You must be safe, my love.

Raoul sits by the fire drinking. At last the mourners have left. He's relieved to be alone. He slumps into the large overstuffed chair holding the flask of scotch in one hand and a half-full glass in the other. He's dismissed his valet and servants and told them not to disturb him. He's made sure that Christine is well attended; upstairs the maids have bathed her and put her to bed as if she were an infant. He's drained of emotion. His body feels numb as if it were made of cotton and wood. He vaguely feels the warmth of the fire as well as the burn of the scotch as it slides down his throat and hits his empty stomach. In part he knows he's numb from the effects of the alcohol. In part he knows he's shut down all his emotions unable to bear it anymore. All were intent on watching him and the dark, foreboding figure on the hill when Christine evidently seemed to whimper and then simply collapsed. Lord Alexander caught Christine as she fainted by the child's graveside.

That dark shape is forever between them. He wonders if the Phantom ever meant to let them be free. Did he let them go that night as if tethered by a short invisible cord, knowing he would only have to tug on it to drag them back within his reach? Perhaps they all were tied on the same tether. Perhaps the Phantom was drawn ineluctably to the graveyard by their misery. Raoul wants to be angry, anything but feel this grief that he manages to put aside only by drowning it in scotch. The Phantom should not have been at his son's funeral.

Raoul had asked Lord and Lady Alexander to escort Christine home. He was unable to leave until the coffin was lowered into the mausoleum and the iron grate closed and sealed. Then, after all the others left, he knelt and cried for his drowned babe, for his wife, and for himself. It was twilight when he finally came back to the estate. Christine had regained consciousness, if that was what you could call it. He was told that she looked around her intently for a few seconds and then settled back into the vacant state that she had maintained since the child's death. She refused to eat but a few crumbs of bread dipped in honey and milk that the maid was able to press between her lips.

What will he do if she doesn't recover her wits? She'll die if they can't get her to eat and drink properly. It's as if she were already dead, already in the coffin. Perhaps he has buried her, too, this day with his small child. Then he thinks of the Phantom, that creature of the underworld. He came to steal them both. Perhaps he already has the child's soul and came to take Christine's at the graveside.

Raoul imagines the Phantom reaching out his hand and beckoning for Christine to come. Her soul rises out of her eyes and mouth like a diaphanous cloud and flies up the hill to the Phantom's waiting hand. He wraps it like a rope round his arm, withdraws it under his cape, and vanishes.

He must find some way to bring Christine back to herself.

Outside the window of the parlor where Raoul sat, the Phantom watched and waited. He saw Raoul take the bottle of scotch with him to sit by the fire. He saw the bereaved father's shoulders slump forward in despair and fatigue. He stood outside the window knowing that the household was settling in for the evening. The servants were finishing their nightly chores, some of them retiring to their quarters, others congregating in the back kitchen to sup, to have a few drinks, and to smoke. The horses had all been brushed and fed and taken to their stalls for the night. The dogs, whom he knew well, were roaming the grounds even now looking for rabbits and squirrels. They recognized him from his many other visits and gifts. His own horse was tethered by the copse of trees in the count's woods. He had walked across the field, along the bank of the stream which now that the rains had ended had returned to its peaceful course. He imagined the child playing by the bank as a swell in the stream rushed past, pushed him off his feet, dragging him down and along its brisk current. He didn't want to think about that. Christine had loved that child; that child had been flesh of her flesh and was now cold and buried in the graveyard. And she lay like death itself incapable even of grief. What could Raoul do for her, lost in his own grief as he was? If this was the life she was meant to live, why could no one revive her? Was she to fade away before their eyes?

If Raoul wouldn't or couldn't stop this, then he must do something.

The Phantom climbed the trellis to the second floor balcony. He easily found his way to Christine's chamber. The balcony doors were slightly ajar to allow a gentle breeze to infiltrate the dark room. He approached the bed and drew back the transparent netting to look down on his beloved. She lay there like that night so long ago now when she sang at the opera and he brought her to his world. There he had shown her his music and told her his dream of their life together. She had swooned when she saw the wedding dress he had taken from the sewing room, a dress that was to be used in the *Marriage of Figaro* perhaps. He laid her in his bed, where he had hoped to find her ever more after that night.

She was not sleeping restfully. Already the toll of these past several days was evident in the dark recesses around her eyes, the sunken cheeks; her slight frame was already showing the effects of not having eaten for some time. Her breath was erratic and shallow. The Phantom knelt beside the bed. He could smell her breath, an aroma of apples and ginger. He dared to bring his lips to her forehead, and there he kissed her gently. She did not stir, but he thought her breathing seemed to calm.

"Christine, it's your angel of music. You forgive me, don't you, my love? I've banished that demon you came upon in the woods. I'm so ashamed that I let you see him! You'll never see him again!" He searched her face for signs of comprehension. Christine stirred briefly and turned her face toward his lips. He leaned in even closer and whispered in her ear. "I live each day in hell without you. I know you're in pain, and I've come to help you. I'll take you to the music. I'll teach you to come to terms with death, my old friend, without fear, without pain. In the dark, you'll again find your child. Do you wish to come with me?" The Phantom placed his lips ever so softly on Christine's. Reluctantly, he rose and stepped back towards the balcony. "When you're ready, I'll know, and I'll come for you, my angel."

Christine stirred for a moment, opened her eyes, but the Phantom had gone.

"What are you planning to do, Erik?" Mme. Giry asked apprehensively.

She had seen him on the hill at the funeral. So had everyone else. She could hear among the mourners the rustle of questions and hearsay concerning the Chagny family and its involvement with the scandal of the opera house. The young count, Raoul, had been patron to the Opera Populaire during that infamous final season when it was plagued by disaster after disaster. Some said that the Phantom had marked Raoul and his family for death. No one understood the enmity, but many professed to have heard some rumor or other that explained it. Of course, several whispered that Christine had indeed been a diva at the opera, and that Raoul had fallen in love with this girl against his family's wishes. Others mentioned that they had heard that the young opera star was the Phantom's lover and that she seduced Raoul for his title and lands. When she tricked Raoul into running away with her, the Phantom declared his revenge against them both. The buzz of whispers deafened her, and for one moment she thought she might shriek. Indeed the world was as cruel as ever it had been when she led that Devil's child to the vaults of the opera house.

At the graveside, Meg had reached for her mother's hand and squeezed it tightly. Mme. Giry could see that she was affected by his appearance, and the knowledge that her daughter had somehow fallen under the Phantom's spell struck her heart like a dagger. She had warned Meg that Erik was obsessed with Christine; he wouldn't give his heart to any but her now. Her daughter's pain broke her heart. But in that moment watching him from the graveside, it was also fear for Erik that stirred both Mme. Giry and her daughter. They knew that Inspector Leroux would be close by, waiting for the Phantom to appear, and here he stood on the hill unprotected in full view of everyone. He might as well have walked into the police station. Mme. Giry couldn't understand why he would put himself in such peril, until she looked at Christine. Yes, of course, it was for her that he stood there so proud, so dark, so powerful. He was to be her strength. Against God and man, he was there saying to Christine, "I endure."

Now Mme. Giry wondered how far Erik would go to save Christine from the madness of her grief. She watched as he inspected the packages she had brought him. Several boxes contained articles of clothing for a lady. "You're mad, Erik, if you think you can do this." She reached out to touch his hand, but he didn't pause in his preparations.

"Is the carriage hired?"

"Yes, the driver will meet you at the bridge as you instructed."

"Did you bring what I asked from the Apothecary?"

"Yes." She knew him well enough. There was no use; she could see it in his eyes, hear it in his tone. Still she dreaded the ends to which he might put the poison. When she requested the powders at the Apothecary's, he had warned her about the poisonous nature of the substance. It worked swiftly. Only then did she intuit what Erik might be capable of.

As he took the phials from her, he saw her concern. "I know that you've always been charitable to me, even when I've been monstrous. This is only a precaution, Madeleine."

She couldn't tell whether he was telling the truth or not. She feared that he wasn't even able to tell himself the truth. "Are you going to kidnap Christine?"

"She's dying. He can do nothing for her. She's mine now."

"You're truly mad, Erik."

"How else can one survive in hell, Madeleine? Christine's only hope is with me in the darkness. You must be patient and trust me."

She watched helplessly as he carried off the supplies and disappeared down the dark tunnel under the streets of Paris.

Raoul requested that Meg remain with them after the funeral with the hope that her childhood friend might comfort Christine and bring her spirits back to her. She tended personally to Christine, woke her in the morning, helped her to dress, brought her tea and toast. She sat by the daybed where Christine reclined, silent and motionless. At times, Christine sighed, but she refused to talk. Even so, Meg noticed that she was different. She still didn't speak, but she was no longer insensible to the world around her. She absentmindedly brought small pieces of toast to her mouth and ate. It was hardly enough to keep a bird alive. However, the vacant stare had been replaced by a willful blindness. She wouldn't look at Raoul or Meg. She insisted on looking out toward the stream that lay in the distance. Raoul ranted and raved at the chambermaid when he saw how his wife fixed her gaze on that fatal point, and demanded that the drapes be closed so that she would not have access to the view of the stream. But when the maid closed the velvet drapes, Christine cried out and flew into a panic and was only calm again when Raoul relented and allowed the drapes to be pulled back.

"I know you've forgiven me, my dearest sister. I can tell in the way your hand lies in mine. You're so far away, but not so far that you aren't aware of us buzzing around you, trying to comfort and bring you back to us. I'll be here as long as you need me." Meg spoke quietly to Christine as they watched the last rays of the sunset in the east. "You sense him, don't you? He's out there somewhere watching us. The police nearly caught him in the cemetery. It was a foolhardy thing for him to do. Such a risk! But he did it for you, Christine. He appeared there for you, so that you would see him and know he was there for you, forever. How I wish things were different! If only he would look at me the way he looks at you!

"He knows it was me that night. I could see it in his eyes, the recognition and the accusation. I don't know how he knew, but something he saw in me told him that it was I who deceived him the night of the masked ball. Since then he's acted so coldly toward me. He insists I marry Etienne Pardieu. I don't want to marry, Christine. I can't imagine lying in anyone's arms but his." Meg stopped to examine Christine's reaction. Her friend continued to look out toward the stream. The only indication that she was listening was the slight tightening of her grip on Meg's hand.

"Christine, if you want me to stop talking about this, you must let me know." Meg waited for Christine to react. Christine seemed to be waiting, too, so Meg continued.

"Etienne is a sweet young man. Blind to everything around him, it would seem. He's no idea that Erik's brought him to me as a substitute, already cuckolded before he's even wed. I'm sorry. I'm speaking like a common whore. But I'd prefer to be his whore than the legitimate wife of any other man. That's how powerful my passion is for him! You must understand this. Your passion for Raoul must be something nearly as fierce as this, isn't it, Christine? Or if not, you must sense the force of Erik's passion for you. I'm afraid I'm as hopelessly obsessed with him as he is with you."

Meg doubted that this was the proper time to talk about these matters, but her guilt weighed heavily on her soul. It was important that Christine understand the truth and that she not fear or loathe Erik. Fighting back her own jealousy, Meg explained, "He thought he was making love to you that night. It broke my heart even at the moment of the most sublime pleasure to hear your name on his lips instead of my own. And yet I couldn't tell him. I wanted that pleasure even if it was meant for someone else. I didn't think how cruel it would be when he learned that those moments of joy were counterfeit. I didn't realize how much he would suffer knowing that he had not made love to you after all. And I didn't realize how it would pain me to see his disappointment and anger. I stole something from all of us that night when I stole his love. It was I who led him to the alcove. I wanted him to make love to me. He would never have attempted it otherwise. Remember the night you spent in his bed, the night of the début? He never touched you; you told me so yourself. He watched over your sleep and held back his desire. Even then he wouldn't dare to be your lover. You must forgive him, Christine. It's my fault that he tried to take you by force. I thank God that something stopped him. Perhaps, at the last moment, he realized that yours was not the body he had possessed that night. I think that is how he finally recognized me. Perhaps his last act of kindness toward me was the night he saved me from one of my suitors at the opera house. That was the moment I thought, 'he knows,' for he glimpsed something on my body, maybe this silly mole at the base of my throat, and looked at me with such surprise and despair. That was also the last time I saw him before he presented my mother with the arrangements for my marriage. She asked me why Erik was displeased with me. She could tell I didn't want to marry the young man and that Erik was forcing my hand for some disagreeable reason known only to the two of us."

Meg felt Christine's hand squeeze hers. A solitary tear fell down her friend's cheek. "Oh Christine, you do forgive us, don't you? I know what it's like to have an unrequited love, to feel a passion so strong that it seems stronger than the will to live. He suffers so for you, and I suffer for him." She could go on no longer. She imagined some softening towards her on Christine's part even though the grieving mother still sat looking toward the stream as if waiting for her child to return from its watery depths.

Each night Meg would come to the parlor after Christine dropped off to sleep to find Raoul, despondent and drinking. He complained of being tired and asked Meg to forgive his lack of civility. One night she sat beside him, even as she had done with Christine throughout the day, until he placed his head in her lap and cried. Tearfully he asked her what he should do. How could he save Christine from languishing before his very eyes? Her only comfort was to suggest that time itself was the medicine that would cure their ills. "You must not leave Christine, Raoul."

"What do you mean? I would never leave her."

"There are many ways to leave someone. You mustn't drown yourself in your own sadness."

Drying his eyes, he looked at the half-emptied bottle of scotch in his hand. "Yes, you're right, Meg. You're a good friend. I've felt hopeless. I have to be strong for her." He placed the bottle on the stand and said goodnight.

On his way up the stairs he thought he heard something, footfalls in the gallery. The hair along the back of his neck stood erect as he sensed someone in the shadows. He bounded up the stairs, two steps at a time, and rounded the corner. There was nothing. He went directly to Christine's chamber and turned the knob only to find it locked from within. A voice, *his* voice, was on the other side. Damn him! How could this be? Raoul ran quickly to the adjoining suite and found this door unlocked. He threw it open to discover the bed sheets thrown on the floor, the bed empty, the balcony doors wide open, and Christine gone. He rushed to the balcony, and there below he saw a carriage speeding down the avenue toward the main gates.

He called for his valet and raised the house in alarm. A groom was sent to bring the count's horse. He was told to waste no time, not even the time required to saddle the animal properly. The count would ride bareback.

Raoul mounted the horse and galloped out to the main road. There was no sign of the carriage. He assumed it had taken the Paris direction and spurred the horse to follow. After several minutes of riding at a dangerous gallop through the darkness, there was still no sign of the carriage. His mount would most certainly have caught up to them by now. Then he noticed down the roadway the carriage stopped, at the edge of the road. Fearing the worst, he dismounted and looked inside. A man lay stunned, his hands tied, his mouth gagged, but there was no one else. The carriage was to take them only so far. The Phantom must have had a fresh mount waiting for him and Christine. There was no way Raoul could find them now. He revived the driver, who could tell him nothing. He had been hired by anonymous note with a handsome retainer, and he had never seen his passenger. In his pocket, he found an additional payment.

Raoul returned to the country manor to find everyone in dismay. Meg handed him a note that the maid found on the balcony after the count had fled in pursuit. Raoul sent for a servant. He would send him to the police to let them know of the kidnapping. As he suspected, the envelope was sealed in red wax with the death skull of the Phantom. He felt bile rising in his throat as he contemplated it. He did not want to touch it much less read it, but he had no choice. It lay in his hand and burned his palm. He broke the seal and read the note.

Count de Chagny,

I've come for Christine. You mustn't think that I do this as revenge against you, although you have met each kind overture on my part with disdain. Let it be understood that if you're reading this note, it means that Christine has come with me willingly.

You've shown yourself incapable of protecting her. She's at death's door; her soul wanders alone in hell. I'm the only one who can find her there. I've always accompanied her in her sorrows and pain. I haven't come to abduct her, but to save her. She doesn't belong to you anymore.

I insist that you not inform the police. They will only prove themselves to be a nuisance. So that you understand the seriousness of my intention, let it be known that I've purchased from the Apothecary a phial of poison so venomous and quick-acting that should you or any police officer disturb us, I'm fully prepared to give Christine a draft and take one myself thereafter. The road to death is not nearly so far or so horrid as you might think. You may doubt that I would poison Christine, but keep in mind, dear Count, that I'm a desperate man. Some would even say that I'm mad. So be it. If I am mad, it is the world that made me so. It is the loss of Christine that has driven me to insanity.

You stole my Christine from me, but she's not happy. It's time that she return to me. Once she's healthy again, I will allow her to choose and will abide by her decision. If she should want to return to your side, I won't prevent her from doing so. If she decides to stay with me, you shall not interfere or if you do, I will fight you to the death.

O. G.

Raoul let the letter fall on the floor where Meg picked it up and read it quickly to herself. She wanted to comfort Raoul, but she had nothing to say that would change the terrible reality that the Phantom had taken Christine under the city to his abode.

What would he do to Christine? wondered Meg. What if she awoke in terror and begged to be released? Would Erik, once he had her with him, have the strength to renounce his hold over her yet again? Would he expect Christine to accept him as her lover? If she rejected him, how would he react? What if she never came out of this malaise? Would Erik bury himself along with Christine in the bowels of the earth?

"You must take me to them, Meg," Raoul insisted.

"What?"

"You or your mother knows the way to his lair. You must lead me there."

"But I can't," Meg stammered.

Raoul shook her roughly by the shoulders and snarled, "You must." Meg was shocked by his violent manner.

"But you read the letter. He has a poison. He'll hear you long before you draw near. He'll poison Christine and then kill himself."

Raoul examined her intently, wondering if she believed what she was saying. "You think he would do that? You think he's capable of killing the only thing he's ever treasured?"

"What choice would you give him? Raoul, you don't know the hell he went through after Christine left with you that other time. I do. I think he would rather die than go through that again." She pleaded with him. "Raoul, please, you mustn't ask me to betray him."

"I can't just let this happen, Meg. He's insane. Christine's sick; she needs to be here. Perhaps I didn't do enough for her, but she's my wife. It was *our* son that we buried two weeks ago. He has no right." Overwhelmed by despair and frustration, Raoul picked up one of the straight-backed chairs and flung it against the wall. Crystal and porcelain broke as it flew past the China cabinet spilling its contents to the floor. He stormed out of the room, through the foyer, and out into the first rays of dawn.

He called for the messenger to return. For the moment, he wouldn't inform the police. Instead, he would ride to the opera house and search himself or lie in wait until Erik came up to ground level for supplies. He wouldn't sit back idly while Christine suffered who knew what horrors in the Phantom's kingdom in the sewers of Paris.

He called his valet and told him to pack his valise. He gave instructions that his solicitor was to secure an apartment overlooking the devastated ruins of the opera house. Each day he would expect his mail to be brought from the country estate in case the monster contacted him again. There, in the apartment, he would take up vigil, and sooner or later he would find a way to rescue Christine.

The Phantom wrapped her in furs, placed her upon the saddle, and mounted behind her. She didn't resist, but lay back against his chest, enclosed in his arms as he spurred the horse on to Paris. The carriage driver wouldn't tell Raoul anything, but then again there was little that Raoul didn't already know. The letter would make his intentions clear, but Raoul would have already realized that it was he who had taken Christine in the dead of night from her bed. He wouldn't believe, of course, that Christine had come willingly.

Yet, Erik had spoken to her in the night, telling her he would take care of her, that she would come to love the darkness and find peace with death. She had been asleep at first, but slowly she opened her eyes and saw him in the half light of the moon as it shone into the bedroom. He waited for her to struggle, to protest, but she simply lay there looking up at his masked face. Was she in her right mind? He wanted to think so. He caressed her cheek with his gloved hand wanting to feel her warmth through the fabric. She didn't draw away from him in fear. He smiled and told her that they would take a short journey, that he would take her to his world. For a moment, he saw doubt flash across her brow, but he put his finger softly to her lips and begged her not to worry. He had always loved her. Then he asked her if she would come with him to be his bride in hell. She let him lift her in his arms from the bed and carry her from the room to the waiting carriage.

There inside Erik rested her upon the seat and ordered the driver to give full rein to the horses. Behind them, the lights of the house receded into the darkness.

Erik didn't approach the entrance to his underground tunnels directly, but chose a labyrinthine route through many different neighborhoods until finally arriving at the site of the old opera house. Circling to the burned-out stables, now long abandoned, he came to the barricade. Lightly he dismounted, leaving Christine seated upon the horse, and removed the cross-beams that blocked the entrance. They were only loosely nailed. He had made sure that they gave the impression of being firmly in place if anyone passed by. Once the doorway was cleared enough to allow the horse and Christine to pass through, Erik told Christine that he would join her inside after only a brief wait. Erik lit a lamp hung inside the stable and returned the exterior planks to their original positions. Then he let himself into the opera house again through one of the many grills on the basement windows. Quickly he maneuvered through the narrow crawl spaces until he emerged inside where Christine waited in the saddle. She seemed relieved to see him approach. From there, the Phantom led his bride down the many passageways to the underground grotto where he had taken her after her début at the Opera Populaire. He passed the organ which lay mildewed and broken, the reams of music, the model sets he had fabricated for Christine's performances, to a series of shattered mirrors.

Here he dismounted Christine, leaving the horse to find his way back to the street where the groom Erik hired would find him. She stood weakly in his embrace. Her weight against his side, the feel of his hands encircling her waist, her head cradled against his chest filled him with joy. He picked her up in his arms and carried her through the shattered mirror, down through his labyrinth to his new home, the one he had prepared especially for him and his bride.

CHAPTER 11

The Bride in Hell

When the stars threw down their spears,
And water'd heaven with their tears,
Did He smile His work to see?
Did He who made the lamb make thee?

William Blake, "The Tiger"

Was this moment always before us? we played our elaborate games only to find ourselves here again in this damp, dark womb all that happened between was a dream, a wonderful dream, but a dream nonetheless he has always been there that day when my babe was washed away by the stream he was there to lay him on the grassy bank to close his watery eyes who better than my demon in hell to lead me to my child? who better than he to bring me his bones? we will sit upon the dank earth and lovingly caress those bones and I will tell him stories of my dead child only he loves me knowing the death's skull lies masked behind this flesh only he would lie with me as I rot and kiss my bones here in this dungeon we will embrace our sorrow we will glory in our madness. As it was meant to be I will be his I will be the bride of horror

He lays her on the bed he has made for her. Bouquets of crimson roses, their thorns stripped from their stems by hand, crown the pillows, exhaling their soft aroma. Flickering candle flames cast mock water currents in shadow and light upon the roughly hewn stone of the ceiling. She wonders when he will lie down by her side. She hears his steps retreat and ever so softly the notes of a melody he used to play for her when she was but a child, bereft of father, in the opera dormitories. That melody stopped her tears and rocked her to sleep each night. That was the end of her loneliness. She grew wrapped in the love of those songs from her angel of music. She thought it was her father's spirit, but it was this abandoned creature who took pity on her. Raoul had been wrong; he is more than just a man. Now she understands that he *is* the angel that her father sent. Here in the darkness, she feels calm. Her child lies in such darkness.

She waits and listens for him. He comes to the bedside and brushes the hair from her face. So rarely she has seen him smile. Yet now she sees a smile upon his face as he brings her something to drink. His eyes are soft when he smiles.

She accepts the offerings he brings her. She's grateful that he doesn't speak. He plays his music for her, haunting sounds that vibrate across the stone of this chamber, sad, sad songs, and others that rise sharp and clear as if beating against this underground prison, as if seeking to fly to the heavens. He places the music in her hands, as if asking her to accept his gift to her, but she drops it to the floor where the sheets scatter. The smile leaves his face, replaced by sadness. He dissolves into the shadows, but she knows he's still there. His eyes burn into her from the darkness. When will he take her to her child?

He takes the damp cloth and wipes the sweat of slumber from her limbs; he tends to her as if she were a child. He pulls her from the bed and forces her to walk, to place one reluctant foot in front of the other. They stroll down the cavernous arteries of this dead world until she feels her limbs tremble, and he picks her up effortlessly into his arms and carries her to bed. She sleeps and sleeps.

When she wakes, he is beside her. Their eyes meet briefly, and she wonders what she sees in those dark orbs of his. He turns his face away, as if he were caught. She senses he has been by her side for a long time. She feels the warmth from his breath on her cheeks. Again he pulls her to her feet and forces her to walk with him. He's strong. She feels the animal strength restrained under the linen shirt. His arms, like the crossbeams of a fortress, keep her from falling. She hears his heart beat deep and even in his chest. And she wonders when he will fulfill his promise to her.

it is as if she were a painting of her true self, she lies there and only the faint rhythm of her breathing gives sign that she's alive and I recall the mannequin that I used to dress as if she were Christine and I reach out to touch the lace that trims her gown, but I know that I mustn't for this is not a doll but my beloved Christine and I content myself with hours of contemplating her face a face so lovely that I want to cry as I look at it but she stirs not she lies as if dead and I must bring her back that was my sole purpose in bringing her to this world to the comfort of the dark where only my eyes can see her pain she needs to regain her strength to want to live again to turn her thoughts away from death and the dying to find the music again to feel again I force her to walk up and down my passageways I bring her food and make sure she eats I play my music for her and I think I could be content to live the rest of my days in this way here with her by my side but it's a pale reflection of life the one I offer her down in this hole I remember her début at the opera house she was glorious such life such joy in her voice the life has gone out of her and perhaps she's nothing more than that counterfeit that I used to invite into my fantasies I must revive her somehow I must

She waits and listens for him. He sees that she looks for him, but she refuses to speak. She's stronger every day that passes, but he can't bear her silence. He brings her to the organ and sets her in the chair before the stand where he has placed his music. It is the aria he has been playing for her, the new opera, the *Phoenix*. He plays the first chords, and waits for her to intone the notes. She stares unseeingly at the music. He plays the chords again and signals her cue with a slight nod of his head. She sits as if deaf and mute, as if all the music of the world had been silenced. If he cannot touch her with his music, she will be lost to him! Again he plays; his fingers fly across the keys. Again and again he starts the aria, and Christine lets the notes fade, unsung. Again he plays, crashing his fingers onto the keyboard. Again, rising and bringing his fists down over the keys. Her silence frightens and angers him.

"Sing, damn you! Sing!" He shouts at her, his fists clenched tightly shut. She stares through the music, but her breathing is shallow and rapid. "You do hear me! You pretend to be oblivious to everything, but you hear me." Erik pushes the music stand to the ground sending the sheets in a flurry across the stones and walks away from her.

"Why do you wear the gloves? You take them off only when you play." The sound of her voice stuns him. He stops, anxious for her to continue speaking.

"Why do you wear this silence, this mask of madness, Christine?"

Her expression darkens, and she points at his large, powerful hands as he comes toward her. "You have strangled people with those hands. You hide them to hide your crimes."

Shocked by her cruel directness, Erik steps back from Christine. There is a demonic fire that blazes behind those eyes, those celestial eyes, that burn into his soul.

"Wrap those hands around my throat and strangle the life out of me. Take me to my child," she insists darkly, fixing her gaze on his hands.

"No!" he roars at her. Stopping his ears with his hands, he flees from the chamber.

How long had it been since he stormed out of the chamber leaving her sitting next to the organ? Staring at the sheet music that was scattered on the floor, she found herself humming the melody. It was beautiful, one of his best pieces. She bent and picked up a sheet of the score and studied it carefully. Perhaps he wasn't returning. She pushed herself up from the chair and slowly walked to the bedroom. There was no sign of him there, either. So she lay on the bed to wait. Suddenly, he loomed over her, black and ominous like a crow, the only light emerging from the glint in his eye and the flash of a grimace across his mouth.

Startled, she gasped. He drew even closer to her face and taunted her angrily, "You came with me, Christine, because you think that this monster will end your suffering. You have no forgiveness for me. I can never be anything more than that hideous monster! You expected me to reunite you with your dead child?" Mockingly, he imitated her, "Erik, the monster, will snuff out my lights. I can ask my monster to do this for me."

She dared not interrupt him. As quickly as it had appeared, the anger in his body melted away. "Was that the reason, Christine, you came with me?" He knelt beside the bed, took off his gloves revealing large, strong, handsome hands. He briefly brushed his fingers over her long, tapered hands. He spoke not so much to her as to himself. "A monster? Is that what you need me to be, Christine? Am I to go on playing this same role forever and ever? Will the curtain never fall?"

In her hand, he placed the ring that Raoul had once upon a time given to her. In a moment of compassion, she had given it to him, this lonely creature. At the time, she did not quite understand its meaning, but it had bound them together somehow just as surely as her wedding ring bound her to Raoul.

how do I help her? what does she want from me? I fear the answer more than anything she wants her own death she looks to me for release she is trapped like me in some dark, deep cavern and she calls to me her monster to lead her to death I could do this for her I have the poison we could both end this now we would lie in each other's arms and not alone in the dark no one knows about these rooms only Madeleine and Meg could hope to find their way to this sanctuary if some day someone were to come upon us they would find our skeletons entwined and think that we were lovers lovers in death if not in life and if the old woman is right? well if Christine flies to heaven to be reunited with her child then I will most assuredly be dragged off to hell what am I to do? am I never to have her love? not in life nor in death?

What's he waiting for? she thinks as she lies upon his bed. When he plays the music, she's calm, and she nods off to dreamless sleep. She wakes to see him sitting next to her. He no longer smiles nor speaks. He feeds her from his own hand, and she silently eats. When will he fulfill his promise and take her to her child? She wants nothing else.

No one comes, not even Raoul. Poor man, he will grieve. She mustn't think of Raoul, it will weaken her resolve.

Poor Erik! Reluctant monster! There's but one more favor he must do for her.

She avoided his eyes as he placed the sheet music again in her hands. He demanded that she sing. He started the aria from the beginning, waiting for Christine to enter on cue. She felt his anger in the notes. Again he started the aria from the top, and still she sat silent in the chair. Pushing back the stool so abruptly that it toppled over, he grabbed her and lifted her from the chair.

"It's your child you want, you say?" He spat the words into her face. "I must be your demon, your gravedigger?" He dragged her down the tunnels away from the chamber on and on, never relenting in his pace even as she stumbled. He held her firmly so that she never fell. He dragged her like a madman until they came finally to a wrought iron gate. They must have walked the length of the city to arrive at this point.

At the gate, the monster pressed her to the wall and leaned his body into hers. She felt his breath hot on her face as he stared into her eyes. The rough surface of the wall dug into her shoulders. She thought for a moment that he would strangle her then and there and leave her body to rot in the tunnel. But even as she waited for his grip to tighten on her neck, she felt him pull away from her. Instead, he opened the rusty latch and opened the iron gate. "You want your child? You want to look on him, hold him in your arms?" She understood then where they were.

He beckoned her to enter the crypt. Past granite slabs, past effigies of long dead relatives of Raoul, he guided her to the child's coffin. He brushed from the cold stone the dust and cobwebs that had already formed across its surface.

"Is this what you want, Christine? This? Is this your child, the one I saw from the woods clinging to your skirts, the one who gathered sticks and leaves and set sail to them in the fountains? This is the child that nursed at your breast?"

She rubbed her fingers over the granite inlay where his profile had been etched by a skilled artisan. The coffin was small, too small. There should be no need for coffins this small!

"Come. Do you want to play with dead things? Isn't that why you came down to my world to be with me? To play at death? Shall I open the coffin, Christine, so you can see what the worms have done to your little Raoul? Shall I place him in your arms so you can sing him to sleep once more?"

She drew back from the crypt, fearing his wild look, listening to his wild speech. Erik grabbed her by the arm and forced her back to the cold rose marble of the crypt in which the coffin lay. "No, Christine, you must not turn away; you must see what waits for us all."

She struggled to be freed from his hold. She clawed at his hands and beat him with her fists, but his hand gripped her arm as if in a vice.

"No," she screamed as he pushed at the slab covering the child's coffin. "No, no, no, please, don't!" Panic seized her as Erik pulled and jerked her back again to the opening. With one hand he worked at the coffin lid, prying at the lip. A slit of darkness revealed itself as the lid began to give way to Erik's efforts. "I beg you leave my child in peace." Unable to bear it, she felt her legs give way under her. Erik let the weeping mother crumple to the floor of the mausoleum.

He waited while she abandoned herself to grief, crying the tears that had been locked away until then. As her grief abated, he held out his hand to her. Eventually, reluctantly, she accepted it and stood. He closed the slender gap that he had opened in the coffin, replaced the heavy marble slab, and led her from the crypt.

"Now. We are done with this morbid fascination with death, are we not, Christine?" He used his teacher's voice as he had when she was his pupil. "Let us return to the piece I have written for you."

She nodded her head slightly and followed Erik back the long walk to his chambers.

she calls me death, she calls me monster and comes to hell to find her lost child not thinking to return to the daylight not caring that she leaves those behind her that would rather choose death than see her die and she doesn't know the weight of darkness and she doesn't understand what it is to be damned she thinks she will find relief in this world of darkness with me and I had thought she was in love with darkness with the sensuality of this world that I could offer her with the music and with the passion that I have for her but it is the dead thing that brought her here the death's mask not the face of the man hideous as it may be or beautiful that it may wish to be that brought her it isn't the man it is the Phantom that she sought and that she wishes will choke the life from her so that she too may lie in the cold cold ground and it's with the warmth of a man's soul that I love her she pushes me away she refuses my gifts she accuses me she glares at me she demands that I crush that throat which brought forth such glorious sounds such angelic notes and I've no choice but play the part of the demon and drag her to the grave if only I can make her see the cold hopelessness of lying with the worms then she may come to her senses and choose life if she looks death in the face she's so young and she can be happy but not with me I've seen her lie in my bed and I've thought of the days that stretch out before us and she will wither here with me in the darkness I can't bear to watch this happen to her I've found the child's grave, the poor dear little child who had such a brief moment of life but so much love I'm astounded at the gift of a mother's love the love I see in Christine for her child I wish I might remember such a love I take her drag her down the passageway to the crypt I will fulfill my role as devil's child I will be her monster and I will be cruel and force her to see her dead child and know that she's taunting death itself she must recant and she will and when she does I'll lose her forever she'll wish to return to the light to Raoul to her life in the sunshine she'll return to his bed and have more children and I'll be left here in this dark hole to die I can't keep her here once she recovers from this death wish I push her against the stone wall and hold her here delaying the moment that will take her from me forever I take this moment and it will be mine and then I open the iron gate and drag her to his coffin she cries such tears it is done she will not wish for death now she will mourn but she will live and our time is done

"Please sit down, Count. I have promising news." Inspector Leroux drew architectural papers from his desk and spread them out before Raoul. "We received word from the night watchman at the cemetery of St. Isidore. Several nights ago as he made his rounds he saw lights in one of the crypts."

"In the Daaé mausoleum?" Raoul asked expectantly.

"No. The Chagny crypt where you recently buried your son. Forgive me for my directness, but we have no time for the demands of etiquette."

"Yes, yes. Go on."

"The watchman, of course, is superstitious like most of his class and did not inspect the crypt. He fled as fast as he could. It was only because my officers have been combing the area making inquiries that this information came to my attention. He says that as he fled, he thought he heard a woman's voice."

"Christine? What was she saying? Could he make out the words? Is she all right?"

"Unfortunately, he said that she was crying rather hysterically. He thought she was greatly agitated. He also mentioned hearing a man's voice, but he couldn't make out what he was saying."

"My God, what can he be doing to her?"

"Of course, Monsieur, and that is why I have brought you here." The inspector spread what appeared to be a draftsman's papers across his desk. "In the municipal archives we have finally located the original specifications for the underground system of channels that lie under the Church of St. Isidore. Interestingly, the system lies under the oldest of the crypts, including your family's. It was perhaps a system of defense constructed many years ago linking the Church with the estate of Lemontre. It connects many of our most ancient edifices. This may be the map to the Phantom's very lair. We will employ blood hounds, starting at the crypt since obviously this is one spot along the routes that may lead us to him. We don't have anything with the Phantom's scent to offer the hounds, but I think I can count on you to bring some article of clothing recently in contact with your wife. We'll track her and find them both."

"No, you must not!"

Bewildered by his reaction, the inspector demanded that he explain himself.

"He'll hear the dogs well before we find him. He's sworn that he'll poison my wife and thereafter himself if we come anywhere near his lair. I won't let you risk my wife's life."

"What do you expect us to do, Count? Wait until he decides to turn himself in? He's a murderer, and it's my duty to find him and bring him to justice."

"Inspector Leroux, we wait. We wait for him to come up to the streets, and we apprehend him there. Then we take the dogs into the sewer to track my wife. Either he will tell us where she is or the dogs will lead us to her. Either way, we must have him in our custody before we attempt to search the underground tunnels."

"Very well, Count. We will continue our vigilance at the old opera house as well as at the new opera house where Mlle. Giry sings nightly. I have found out that one of her sponsors is a strange, unknown man. I assume it's the Opera Ghost himself. I can't prove anything, but I know that Mme. Giry and her daughter must be accomplices to this murderer. Someone acts on his behalf in the outside world."

She walked behind him, curiously relieved, through the narrow galleries. He listened to her footsteps behind him and when she tired, he gathered her into his arms and carried her. She trusted these arms; she understood him now. He glanced at her from the corner of his mask, his eyes so beautiful. She smiled at him, finally at peace with herself and the world. When he laid her on the cushions of the bed, she bid him sit beside her.

"I know my child is not in that crypt. He's safe now from torment. You've helped me recover from my desperation. It's because of you that I'm myself again." Christine could see his body tense; he must have known what she was about to say. Yet he was silent.

"I want to go home, Erik. You must take me back," she said softly.

"We will not talk of this now," he answered hurriedly, avoiding her eyes.

His panic crackled like a magnetic charge across the air between them. But she must return. Raoul would be frantic, imagining horrible, unspeakable acts. He knew only the violent, evil face of the Phantom. She longed to return to her husband, to comfort him in his grief now that she was able to deal with her own.

She watched Erik's inner struggle, lamenting that she had to cause him yet again this pain.

Suddenly, his agitation subsided replaced by a strange mad exhilaration. He told her that he had a plan. She would learn his new opera, and they would travel to Italy where she would perform it in the best opera houses. She would sing in an elaborate mask so no one would know her, a mask of white and gold plumes. He would give her a new life, a life on the stage.

She watched him pace wildly round the room spinning plans that seemed drawn from a gothic romance. He would become an eccentric lord, no one would know why he wore a mask, he would rent a chateau in the country, and Christine would live with him. He would be her teacher. But he would expect no more than this from her, that she accompany him and sing his operas in the great palaces of Italy and Spain. She would be the crown jewel of society. But she would always return to him. She would sing to him, and he would be content to sit with her in the evenings and listen to the music, his music written only for her. They must begin training now. As he spoke, he became more and more agitated, until the fever of madness seemed to burn itself out, and he simply stopped in midsentence. When she looked into his eyes, she could see that he knew his hopes were fantasy.

Unable to bear his desperate attempt to hold her to him, she rose from the bed and went to him. She pleaded with him to listen. He didn't have to hear the words to know their meaning. Wanting to stop her from speaking, pierced by sorrow, he bent his face towards hers and kissed her lightly on the lips, knowing that she wouldn't go to Italy with him nor would she accept a new life on the stage as his Phoenix. She didn't push him away. She felt his silent tears mingle with hers and course down their cheeks pressed one to the other.

He struggled to find the words, but there were none. He pulled away from her embrace and ran down the dark tunnel away from the light.

never to love never to have what others take for granted to lie in the arms of a lover to be alone and walled away in a crypt as if dead but trapped in a body that feels the most exquisite sensations the touch of a breeze the movement of the fabric across the skin the sounds of music rising like vibrations in my blood and never to feel the pleasure of another's touch again I think I will go mad and I cannot keep her by my side if she asks to go I won't be able to deny her and I'll have no hope of living anything but the life of the undead here in this grave never to love or be loved I cannot bear it I cannot I want to know that joy again the joy the pleasure the sensations that stirred and demanded satisfaction the intensity of touch that I felt for the first time in the arms of my counterfeit Christine if only I could return to the dream and relive that illusion

He had to get away from her. He couldn't bear her look of pity. He ran down the tunnel deeper and deeper into the bowels of the city. He ran until the darkness was less and less broken by the infrequent air shafts leading to the streets above. He ran to blot out thinking until exhausted he slowed to a walk. But he pushed on with no regard to his destination only to find that he had doubled back toward the barricade at the Rue des artistes. Near the barricaded shell of the destroyed edifice, his kingdom of music, stood several of the inspector's men. He easily slipped past them and emerged into the darkness of the street. Over his shoulder loomed the corpse of the Opera Populaire: all those dreams of grandeur turned to ash. Ahead rose the Opera National above the squat cafés and shops along the avenue.

The performance would be finishing. Meg would be taking her final bows. She always waited for him in her dressing room. No matter how late he was, she greeted him with a smile and listened to his remarks on her performance. Would she welcome him now? Would she welcome him if she knew what torment brought him to her door? In her arms, he might find relief from the desires that plagued him. Would she accept him if he came to her tonight? If he asked for her body, would she lie with him again as she had at the masquerade? Would she give herself to quell the passion he felt for another woman? To ease the pain of lust that was driving him mad?

He slipped into the crawl space between the walls and found his way to the backstage dressing rooms. He waited while the stage manager checked the props and chatted with several of the chorus girls. Word came that the lights had been extinguished, and only a few of the singers lingered behind, some entertaining guests discreetly in their rooms. The laughter and quick banter of the after performance elation faded as the corridors cleared. The lights dimmed except for the few emergency lamps left always lit for the custodial crew that would soon begin cleaning the hallways, stage, and auditorium. Cautiously, Erik tapped open the door and entered the now deserted corridor. He made his way along the passage to the rooms. There he found the hidden door that adjoined Meg's dressing room. Sliding it gently to the side, he stepped into her room. Meg sat at the dressing table in her robe, removing her make-up. She saw his reflection in the mirror before she heard him.

"Erik. The police are watching the opera house day and night. They'll find you."

"No one saw."

"What have you done with Christine? Is she all right?"

"Do you think I'd ever harm her?"

"No, of course not. I know you'd rather cut off your right hand than harm her."

"That would be a poor price to pay."

Meg waited for Erik to continue. Instead he seemed to listen to something that only he could hear. Suddenly, he drew back behind the screen and into the darkness of the corner of the room. The knock startled Meg. Before she could answer, Inspector Leroux and two officers came brusquely through the door. The inspector cast a disappointed glance around the room.

"I'm not used to receiving uninvited guests in my dressing room. What do you want, Inspector?"

Leroux addressed the young woman with a scowl. "Mlle. Giry. It is a serious offense to protect a known criminal. I can't stress how severely the judge would treat you if he found you had helped this madman escape our attempts to apprehend him."

"Monsieur, I understand your dedication to your duty, but you can't think that I would help a murderer."

"Why not, Mademoiselle? After all, he is your secret patron, is he not? I see you're surprised that I've found this out. I don't know what power this demon holds over you all, but he holds no such power over the law. We will bring him to justice with or without your assistance. And that day, I'll insist the full weight of the law fall on his head and on those who have protected him." Having edged closer and closer to the screen, the inspector pushed the edge with his foot toppling the screen forward into the center of the room. It crashed down upon the couch revealing nothing more than a wire stand on which Meg had draped her costume and the bare wall of the room itself.

Meg had barely managed to stifle a cry of warning when she was relieved to see Erik had somehow vanished from the room.

"How dare you, Inspector Leroux! Would you like to check the drawers of my vanity, too? Perhaps the Phantom can shrink to the size of a mouse and is hiding among my undergarments."

"I hope your mother can understand the serious nature of this game and talk some sense into you. Good evening, Mademoiselle."

With that the inspector left the room followed by his two officers. Meg sank to the seat overcome by the sudden pounding of her heart. Slowly and silently, the wall panel shifted and from the shadows emerged Erik. He came to her, holding a finger to his lips for her to be quiet. He knelt beside her and awkwardly stroked the blond tresses that fell about her shoulders. She wanted nothing more than to throw herself into his arms, but feared that this would drive him back into the shadows. As if he could sense her desire, he stood and pulled her to her feet.

"Meg," he whispered. "Meg," he repeated in a gravelly whisper deep in his throat, but could not continue. Instead he wrapped her in his arms and pressed his lips against hers hungrily.

As suddenly as he had embraced her, he released her and stepped away. But before he could disappear completely, Meg dropped her robe from her shoulders. In the candlelight her body shimmered in milky waves as she stood silent and naked except for the blush of passion that spread gradually across her face and throat.

Wordlessly, he reached for her.

"This time without masks, without disguises." She melted into his arms and sought his mouth. This was the body that he had held and known. He felt drawn to her, even against his will, against his reason. Gently he caressed her, his gloved hands tracing the curves of her breasts, her waist, her hips.

"Take off your mask," she urged, her voice soft and moist on his neck.

"No," he moaned as he lay her on the couch and leaned in against her.

She kissed his neck, his cheeks, his mouth holding his masked face in her hands. She felt his whole body tense and move again as if to pull away from her. Knowing his ambivalence, she held him tightly and willed him to stay. "Let me give you what Christine can't. I love you. I can be content with this if this is all you can give me, your need and your passion, even if it's for her." She pulled at his clothes, loosening his shirt until she managed to slip her hands under the fabric and against his naked skin. "You're warm, solid, real. There's no phantom here."

He could restrain himself no longer. She helped him disrobe; he cast his gloves to the side and ran his bare palms, his fingers along her body wishing that his hands could delve into her very soul. Kissing her passionately, he lifted her body to his until there was nothing between them to hinder their desire.

Lying asleep in each other's arms, their limbs intertwined, their breath merging in the syncopation of shared dreams, they were unaware of the horror that accosted Mme. Giry as she beheld her daughter in the arms of the Phantom.

Erik emerged from the darkness of the tunnel to find Christine asleep in his bed. This would be the last time that he would keep watch over her. When she woke, it would be over. He would take her tonight to the streets above where Raoul would most certainly be watching for her. He had resolved to renounce his claim on her and withdraw forever from her life.

She stirred and gradually opened her eyes to see him studying her face. Immediately, she sensed a change in him. The madness that tortured him the night before had disappeared. A strange calm had descended upon him. Yet in his eyes remained a passion tempered by restraint.

"Tonight I take you to Raoul."

She wanted to ask where he had gone, but he walked away into the adjoining room. There he sat at the organ and began to play a movement from his opera, the one he had written for Christine. She came up behind him and picked up the libretto he had shown her day after day. Sweetly she sang the Phoenix's song of rebirth while he played the chords. After the final note faded, Erik rested his hands on the mute keys. Christine gazed at them. They were beautiful, large and broad, and she had seen them move with hypnotic grace. Now they lay still on the white keys as if they rested on a lover's body. Something had changed. What had happened? Her mind could almost grasp it, but not quite. About him lingered the traces of a perfume that she knew but could not place. As she tried to remember where she had smelled that scent before, he spoke.

"Christine, you must forget me and all this."

"Erik, I won't ever forget you."

Taking her hand and placing it over his heart, he promised her, "You will always be here, Christine, and here in my music."

"What will you do?"

"Do you think I've the right to hope for happiness someday, perhaps with someone else?"

"Someone else? Is there someone else, Erik?" Sadly, she thought how unlikely it was that he would ever be happy. His destiny was to remain hidden in this underworld or risk being brought before the courts for his crimes. What hope could he have of happiness? Who would willingly share this hell with him?

"There is one who would gladly come with me. We would go to Italy or Spain. Perhaps we might have a chance at happiness where no one knows me. She might help me find some way to exist outside this world."

"Surely Mme. Giry won't agree to leave Paris."

"No, not Mme. Giry. The only world she ever offered me was this illusion of life." He indicated with a sweeping movement of his hand the vaults and sewers of Paris. There was bitterness in his voice. The rescue Mme. Giry had offered had turned into another prison.

"Then who?"

Instead of answering her, he simply looked into her eyes. Surely she knew of whom he spoke. And then it came to her that he meant Meg. The blood rose in her face as she realized what he planned. He wanted to drag Meg into his nightmare world, subject her to his dark, unnatural passions. She was horrified to think that her friend would end up in this underground realm, fleeing from the authorities, as paramour to the Phantom.

Erik saw the incredulity and disgust in Christine's expression. He sensed her opposition, her building outrage. He had no right to seek happiness. He was bewildered and furious that she thought him undeserving of pity, that she condemned him to loneliness and abandon. Like the whole world, except for Meg, she considered him unworthy of the smallest compassion, the least hope of comfort.

In a rage, he rose from her side and with huge strides paced back and forth across the room like a caged leopard. "And why am I not allowed to want? To desire? Why am I forbidden the pleasures of the flesh that any other man enjoys as his due?" He roared at her; anger distorted that small segment of his face not covered by the mask. Alternately approaching and retreating from Christine as she cowered on the bench, struck with fear by his frenzy, he growled, "If Meg will love me, even with this face, why am I not permitted to lie in her arms?" His anger began to dissolve into anguish. "I am not a monster, Christine! I am not a monster! I am a man. I need and want and love like any man. If Raoul were here caught in this hell, if he were condemned to this dark loneliness, this unending solitude, wouldn't you cry out in outrage to heaven against that injustice? Would you not try to bring him solace, some consolation for the loss of his humanity? How can you look at me and deny me this one mercy? I've given up so much for you, Christine." He bemoaned her apparent lack of understanding, and his anger gave way to sorrow and self pity.

She felt the horror and disapproval drain from her heart as she listened to his pleas. She regretted her coldness toward him, her lack of compassion. "Forgive me, Erik. I hope with all my soul that you find happiness. Yes, you should go with Meg, if she's willing to be your companion, and you should make a life together somehow, somewhere."

It took several moments for him to gain some control over his violent emotions. Christine waited cautiously. Gradually as Erik calmed down, she came to his side. He reached out for her hand and brought it to his lips as she wiped the tears from his face.

"Mme. Giry. The Inspector will see you now."

CHAPTER 12

The Prisoner

Erik had asked her to sing to his accompaniment one last time before he was to lead her to the streets above. He was aware that the count waited and watched from rented rooms overlooking the river and theater district. After their song, Erik would take her to Raoul. Christine sang like the angel she was, and for this reason, neither Erik nor Christine heard the gendarmes as they approached. Out of the corner of his eye, Erik saw the shadows swim across the cavernous wall. He stopped playing in mid note. Encircling the room, their weapons trained on him, were as many as twenty armed men. Christine froze in shock until she heard Raoul call to her. She ran to her husband. Before she could explain that Erik was about to deliver her to him, Raoul pulled her safely away from the trap. She tugged at his sleeve, entreating him to do something. But Raoul did not understand her meaning.

The count stood by to watch events unfold. Christine was safely in his arms. At last, he would be rid of the Phantom. As long as the Phantom lived, he'd have no peace of mind.

Erik saw only one choice. The police were cautiously closing in on him. He dashed to the cabinet where he had stored the phials of poison he had commissioned Mme. Giry to acquire for a desperate situation. Such a situation now loomed before him; there was no escape. He would gladly take the poison. He was prepared to die rather than be chained and dragged off to prison. The entire periphery of the cavernous chamber was lined with gendarmes. There was no time for leave-taking. He would never again touch Meg or feel her touch on his body. He would write no more music. He would no longer hear

Christine's voice. They would back him into a corner, subdue him, and carry him off to prison.

He opened the phial and lifted it to his lips.

"Stop him!" Leroux picked up a stone and threw it across the room at the Phantom's hand, striking the phial. It shattered against the floor. Merely a drop had reached Erik's tongue, not enough to kill him, perhaps only enough to make him ill. His hand bled from the broken glass, and he licked the blood hoping to rescue yet a few more drops of the metallic-tasting venom.

The police officers closed the circle and grabbed him from behind. The Phantom bent forward and then quickly arched his back throwing several of his attackers against the cavern's wall. Others latched on to his arms, and he swung violently against them, sending his body like a battering ram into theirs. One fell to the ground with a sick crunching sound as if his ribs had broken. Leroux urged the others on as Erik vaguely heard Christine screaming in the distance. His feet suddenly were whisked off the floor, and he felt himself caught in a head lock by a large, burly officer. Several others managed to hold his arms. He was hardly aware of the snap of the bone as the gendarme bent his arm back at an unnatural angle. Then the dizziness washed over him as his stomach cramped and convulsed in waves of nausea. The poison perhaps would be sufficient after all, he hoped against hope. He prayed for death. The air was pushed from his lungs as he crashed against the cave floor. Fists pummeled his face and body. Someone kicked him several times until blackness mercifully took him away to some empty corner of nowhere.

Raoul had to restrain Christine physically as Leroux's officers beat the Phantom pitilessly. Only when he lay limp and bloody on the floor did Leroux order them to desist. Christine buried her face in Raoul's shoulder when she saw Erik covered in blood lying as if dead at Leroux's feet. The inspector bent to check the prisoner's pulse and finding it still beating, even if erratically, ordered his men to bind him and take him to headquarters.

Raoul was concerned only with Christine's safety. She had come back to him. She was responsive and seemed uninjured. Nothing else mattered to him.

Christine watched as the officers pulled Erik's broken arm behind his back and tied it tightly together with the other. Blood oozed from his mouth, and the visible portion of his face was red and swollen. As they yanked him to his feet, he stirred and cried out from a sudden sharp pain. She squeezed Raoul's arm and whispered in a pleading tone, "Please, do something. Don't let them do that to him." Even though Raoul was appalled by the policemen's brutality, he was just as reluctant to intervene. He couldn't understand why she insisted on defending the Phantom; she knew what he was capable of, indeed what he had already done. Instead of interceding on the Phantom's behalf, he told Christine the police were only doing their duty. He was a dangerous man, and force was necessary to subdue him.

"You can't be serious," she responded, incredulous at his lack of pity. "They've beaten him nearly to death."

The police officers proceeded to drag him down the tunnel to the streets above. Raoul could see the prisoner's head sway, then lift as if he were regaining consciousness. Then he could see Erik's body convulse and hear the sounds of vomiting as his body reacted to the ingested poison.

"Get him to a doctor," Leroux hastened to say. "He won't escape that easily. The monster must stand trial."

To calm Christine, Raoul agreed to do what he could for Erik, but first he was determined to get her out of this hellhole and to safety. As he led her through the tunnels toward the street level, she suddenly pulled away from him and ran back toward the music room. There, Raoul found her gathering the Phantom's sheets of music to bring with her. "It may be all that's left of my angel of music," she said as if in apology as she returned to Raoul's side. "You will see to it that they treat him humanely?"

Raoul struggled with his annoyance. He tried to remember that Christine had been in a very different state when the Phantom carried her off. Now his wife had returned to him, and he was uncomfortably aware that he might owe a debt of gratitude to the Phantom for her recovery. "I can't do anything at this moment, Christine. But if it will make you happy, I'll try. Now, come. I must get you home."

"I've missed you so, Raoul."

"I feared I'd lost you forever, Christine."

"No. That's what you must understand! Erik never intended to take me from you forever. He meant to bring me back to you." She wondered if Raoul believed her; she hoped he did.

Erik was dimly aware that he was being dragged down the passageway. He was faint from the agony spiking along his arm through his shoulder and down the side of his chest. Each breath brought a shudder. His lungs rattled audibly. Each movement of his chest reminded him that they had broken his ribs. He couldn't raise his head, blood dripped into his eyes, and he could only barely make out the damp uneven stones of the floor as he was pulled forward. He slid in and out of consciousness.

He heard the officers as if they were on one side of him only. The sounds coming from the opposite side were muffled, and he thought perhaps his ear was damaged for he felt as if it were wrapped in cotton. He tried to stand, to put his feet beneath him so he could bear his own weight, but an officer drove the butt of his rifle down into the small of his back leaving him incapable of thought much less movement.

"Let's see his pretty face," laughed one of the gendarmes as they approached the wagon and threw him into the back. Hands grappled at his face. Then Erik felt cold air where his mask had always been. Blinking away the film of blood from his eyes, he saw the officers' sickened grimaces as they looked at him.

"Oh my God he's ugly!"

"Ugly enough to cause a pregnant woman to miscarry!"

"My mask. Give it to me," he feebly managed to say, but his hands were bound. He licked his swollen, bloody lips. "Put it back."

They only laughed at him.

He lay in his own vomit, the arcing cramps finally subsiding. The doctor's emetic had been forced down his throat, and he had expelled everything in his system. His throat was dry, hot, and raw from the gastric juices that had surged up with each nauseous convulsion. He had dirtied himself, his bowels dissolving into liquid as they, too, pushed the poison and the medicine from his lower intestinal tract. If only he had been able to take the full dose, this would all be over now. He would be beyond their grasp. Yes, they would have had the pleasure of filing past his corpse, of putting his deformity on display, but he would have been blissfully beyond their derision and their disgust, the pain and humiliation.

He opened his eyes to find himself lying on the cell floor. No window, only bars on one side, like the bars of his cage at the fair. There was even straw scattered thinly beneath him to soak up the puke and urine and blood and shit that he lay in. The opposite walls of the room were stone. The floor itself felt cold and damp against his feverish brow. His lips throbbed, his ear ached, and he knew he must be deaf now on one side. This distressed him more than the pain in his arm. They had thrown him in the cell. He lay on his broken arm, and the pain kept him from moving. As long as he could lie still, he would be all right. He could stand the pain if he remained perfectly still.

The squeal of an iron door opening on rusty hinges pierced the silence of the cell. Hands pulled him roughly to a standing position. He could not stop the scream that scalded his throat. Without heed to his pain or to the filth of his soiled clothes, the guards escorted him down the hall to a room where the inspector and state prosecutor waited.

They sat him at a simple table in the Spartan room. The inspector stood while the prosecutor sat in a corner, far from the table, inserting pinches of snuff into each nostril, obviously disgusted by the smells emanating from the prisoner's body. Erik sat as straight in the chair as his pain would permit. Aware that he was trembling uncontrollably from head to foot, he raised his head and summoned as much control as he could to face his tormentors. The prosecutor at first repelled by the prisoner's face, as well as his present condition, stared at him with morbid curiosity. "I say, Leroux, what could have done that to his face? Indeed it's the whole side of his head as well. Might it have been a bad burn?" The gentleman took a monocle he held on a gold chain round his neck and brought it to his eye. He approached Erik to get a better look at the disfigurement, but the inspector stopped him before he came within an arm's length of the prisoner.

"Stand back, Monsieur Barnet. He's quite dangerous."

"But he's manacled, Leroux, and beaten within an inch of his life. I'd say by the looks of him that all the fight had gone out of him. Surely he's no threat now."

"You wouldn't think to look at him, but he put five of my officers in the infirmary. One of them is in a coma even as we speak. So don't underestimate him. He's one of the strongest men I've ever seen. His threshold for pain alone is amazing." Leroux to demonstrate punched the prisoner's broken arm. He fell from the chair and winced, but he swallowed the scream that swelled up from his gut. "You see? Any other man would have passed out from the pain. His arm's broken in at least two places."

"Will you need the doctor to reset it now?" The prosecutor squirmed with delight in his chair anticipating being present as the doctor worked on the fracture.

"Reset? The arm hasn't been set for the first time yet. We called in the doctor to deal with the poison, nothing more. He tried to kill himself, you know. He'll get medical attention for the rest once I'm done with him."

"Oh, I see. That way the doctor can deal with the whole mess at one time, n'est-ce pas?" The prosecutor returned to his seat in anticipation of a long night ahead.

Leroux called in two officers to lift the prisoner from the floor. Erik held his breath until the two men managed to set him properly on the slats of the chair.

"Now … are ready … down … business … the scribe … confession … start … and … the events of … deaths … you are also charged … say?" Erik saw the inspector's lips moving; two fleshy worms undulating across a cruel face. The words, however, were unintelligible. Like the peaks of mountains a word would rise above a constant hum only to sink down into muffled buzzing. He squinted in an effort to see the inspector better. Perhaps he would be able to make out the missing links in the long statement the inspector seemed to be making for Erik's benefit as well as for the prosecutor. A scribe sat in the corner. He must have come in as the other officers left for Erik had been unaware of him until he followed the inspector's line of vision toward the back corner of the room. He understood what was happening in spite of the fact that he was having trouble hearing what the inspector was obviously dictating.

The inspector was still speaking, but Erik interrupted him. "I need to rest now," he said and laid his head on the wooden surface of the table. No sooner did his head touch than he fell into a black void. Just as suddenly, a blinding pain seared across his forehead like a white light bouncing off the metallic surface of a knife blade. His eyes burned as he blinked them. Leroux held him by the collar of his bloody shirt and with his fist struck him once again. Then someone threw cold water onto his face. He choked and sputtered the bloody water mixed with saliva and mucus.

Suddenly the pain was excruciating, but he forced his eyes to focus on the inspector, and summoning every ounce of hatred and anger in his body he fixed his eyes on him and glared. Consciously, he forced himself to breathe deeply and evenly in spite of the broken ribs that threatened to pierce his very lung.

"Now, that's better."

The inspector sat close to Erik, and the sounds of his voice faded in and out slightly but were audible. "Let us resume the statement. Do you have a name other than Opera Ghost? Oh, yes, that's right. Mme. Giry said your name is Erik. No last name, just Erik."

Madeleine? Dismayed, Erik searched the inspector's face for some explanation. Bewilderment and doubt began to overwhelm his senses blocking everything else from his mind.

"How do you think we found you, Erik Opera Ghost? Or do you prefer Erik Phantom? I like that. Yes, that will do. It almost sounds like a real name for a real monster, don't you think?"

Slowly the thoughts formed themselves in his mind like the fingers of those who used to come to the fair to touch the Devil's child through the bars of his cage. Madeleine? Madeleine had spoken with the inspector? Betrayed by Madeleine? She had given him his name? She had led the police to his chambers? How could that be? She had always protected him. She had hidden him from the carnival people, from the authorities; she had saved him from certain death when he was a child. Not Madeleine! She would not do that. She was ...

The inspector saw the prisoner tremble convulsively as he took in the information.

"She was not very happy with you when she came to my office quite early this morning. She told us everything, where you were, how she acted as your liaison with the world outside, the general nature of the underground system of tunnels. Of course, I could put her in prison for aiding and abetting a criminal, but the state will show its appreciation of her cooperation and her testimony at the trial and not press charges against her."

In response to Erik's shocked expression, the inspector clarified, "Oh, yes, M. Phantom. She is willing and eager to testify against you at the trial. You must have done something to destroy her loyalty to you."

She had been his only family. Yet she had betrayed him, knowing that they would hunt him mercilessly like a dog and exhibit him before the mob and hang him on a public gibbet for all to see.

"Do you confess to the murder of Joseph Buquet?"

"Yes," the prisoner answered. What did it matter now? His throat burned when he spoke. "May I have some water?"

"Do you confess to the incident of the chandelier, maliciously loosening it to fall in a filled amphitheater knowing that it would certainly kill many of the opera spectators?"

"Water, please." His tongue lay dry and swollen in his mouth.

"Answer the question. Do you confess to the murder of eleven strangers in the opera house the night of August 12, 1870?"

"Yes."

"Did you attack the Count de Chagny on several occasions including this past March 25 outside the gaming rooms at his club?"

Erik listened confused and realized the inspector was talking about the night the count had been attacked. Erik had been following him, waiting for an opportunity to slip his note in the count's pocket. Raoul killed one of the assailants himself but was too tipsy to deal with the other two. He surely would have been seriously wounded, if not killed, had Erik not intervened, in spite of himself, and saved his rival's life.

"Did you attack the Count de Chagny on several occasions including March …"

"No. I …"

The inspector struck him with his fist in the ribs.

"Shall I repeat my question?"

Instead of answering the inspector's question, Erik asked, "Did the Count de Chagny himself say …?" Again the inspector hit him. Erik doubled over in pain unable to finish.

"Answer the accusation."

In a barely audible whisper, Erik managed to reply to the slander the count and inspector had trumped up against him. "No."

"You did not attack him and kill three other men that had come to his assistance? Think carefully, Monsieur Phantom, before perjuring yourself," the inspector whispered, his mouth close to Erik's ear.

"You attacked him again, witnessed by several passersby on the river road. Is that not true?" Speaking loudly enough for the scribe who dutifully committed the accusations to paper, the inspector circled behind the prisoner.

This time he did not wait for Erik to answer.

"You also attacked and raped several young professional women of the night in the Rue des Misericordes last autumn. They are eager to identify you. In addition, I can't prove it, but we're certain that you drowned the Count de Chagny's son, pushing the child into the swollen river. We may get the nurse to testify to this; she was after all in the area."

"No, no, no, no, no!" Erik objected.

The inspector motioned to someone behind the prisoner who brought to the table a small metal vice with a large screw on one side. The officer unshackled the prisoner's hands from behind his back and brought them forward to the table where the manacles were again locked in place. The movement of the broken limb sent flashing lights of pain across Erik's vision yet again. On the inspector's signal, the officer placed Erik's little finger in the depression of the vice and began to turn the screw. Erik felt the increasing pressure as each side of the metal contraption bore down and crushed the bone of his finger.

It was a long night. The inspector had begun to tire. He wiped the sweat from his brow with his damp handkerchief as he told the officer to proceed to the fourth finger. Each time the prisoner passed out, they would bring him to with cold water or smelling salts. The stench in the room was becoming unbearable. As Erik bit down hard to stifle the animal sound that threatened to escape, the prosecutor could bear no more. "Monsieur Inspector, I'm already late for supper. It's well past 8:00. I simply must go."

"Do you confess?" The inspector banged his fist on the table where Erik's head had fallen and willed him to answer.

"Water." The prisoner did not so much say it as mouth the word.

The session was over. The prosecutor had tired of the repetition, and Erik had again passed out. The inspector couldn't afford to have the prisoner die on him now.

"We'll start again in the morning." The officers came into the room and lifted the prisoner from the chair. "Clean him up. He stinks to high heaven. Have someone come in and clean the interrogation room as well." As a last minute thought, he ordered, "No water and no food."

Madeleine Madeleine Madeleine come get me please come get me let me out please come oh please come Madeleine it it it they have broken my arm, my fingers, please help me please you can't leave me here like this they will break me inch by inch it hurts it it hurts all over it hurts but Madeleine you can come and oh you brought them to me you told them where I lived where I hid safe safe safe from them from them all Mother Superior please those things they say I did I didn't do them they want me to confess I killed Christine's babe they want me to confess that I raped those women I admitted that I murdered Joseph Buquet he deserved it Mother he watched the chorus girls dress through a hole in the wall he himself made and he forced Marie Jeanne to do despicable things with him and she was only a child I saw him leering at Christine, I knew he planned to wait for an opportunity and that he would corner her somewhere dark and quiet and force himself on her he thought he could outwit me he watched me and followed me he came close to finding the way to my secret apartment under the cellars I don't regret choking the life out of that vermin he deserved it I did it to protect Christine and myself I regret Mother Superior I truly repent the other deaths the innocent deaths those who died that night when the chandelier came crashing down those deaths I have on my head I don't even know who they were they were innocent and if I am to suffer it should be for those deaths not for the invented crimes the inspector wants to heap on my head mea culpa, mea culpa, mea maxima culpa what was that prayer you taught me Mother? Oh, but my Madeleine led them to me even though she knew they would torture me I thought she loved me just a little she protected me she brought me to the wardrobe rooms to find clothes and to pick out my first mask, a beautiful gold and silver mask, the mask of Apollo, so beautiful when I put it on I was handsome I could look at myself in the mirror and Madeleine smiled at me and called me her Greek God oh Madeleine it hurts and you have left me here with the pain in the filth I can't stand my own body my head wants to explode with the pounding inside my throat is raw and dry I call for water but no sound comes out this body this charnel house this prison that I flee unendingly and never escape will the pain wash my guilt away Mother? how much pain must I endure to wash those eleven souls from my conscience? I can't believe you led them to me Madeleine my Madeleine I showed you my first compositions and I drew my first designs for the opera and showed them to you always to you to make you smile to make you proud of me to make you see that I was capable of beauty creating symmetry in form harmony in sound that I was not an animal that deserved to be beaten and locked away in a cage I learned to speak like a gentleman to please you and how to carry myself this accursed body like those who came to the opera each night and to appreciate beauty I wanted only to create beauty to surround myself with beauty to wrap myself in the arms of beauty to worship at beauty's altar and now you send me back to the cage to the whip to the chains to the ugliness to the pain to the fear and I don't understand I need you to come for me Madeleine to lead me out of this pain to make me understand why you betrayed me I need you to come to stop the pain the fear I never told you how frightened I was in the cellars of the opera house where you hid me I didn't want you to be angry with me to send me away to bring them to find me I cried night after night until I decided to make the cellars my stage and you watched me steal pieces of scenery and smiled and laughed when I described my rooms and your laugh echoed in my ear at night when I sang so that I wouldn't hear the scratching of the rats along the wall and now you've brought them and let them take me to the cage and I try not to cry, I'm sorry, Madeleine, I'm sorry, please let me come home ...

The guard heard him call for water, but orders were orders. Perhaps in the morning they could bring him some along with a bit of dried bread. The guard was used to watching over drunks and thieves who settled down for the night and slept. Sometimes a prisoner would cry quietly in his cell, such sadness was to be expected. After all these men had committed crimes and must suffer for their acts. But this was beyond anything he had experienced before. The prisoner was half dead. He lay in the dirty straw unable to move for the pain. The inspector had insisted, "no food, no water." So his hands were tied. He couldn't go against orders. But it was cruel, it was. Even a pack animal is given water as he grinds out his work day. A criminal must pay for his crimes, but there should be dignity and humanity in a society's justice.

He didn't care what the inspector said. Once the shift changed and night settled in he would take a jug of water to the prisoner and give him some to drink. As ugly as he was, he was still a human being.

An hour later, the young guard found his opportunity. He cautiously unlocked the cell and knelt beside the prisoner to offer him water. It was soon clear to the guard that the prisoner had been tortured and was unable to lift himself to drink, so he dipped the hem of the prisoner's shirt in the water and brought it to his lips for him to suck. As his lips were moistened by the cool water, he began to stir. He took the wet cloth in his mouth and pressed his tongue against it. Slowly he lifted his head enough to take the cup, with the guard's help to steady his trembling hand, and brought it to his lips to drink.

They had told him the prisoner was the Opera Ghost and that he was horribly disfigured. The descriptions could not quite do him justice. The guard found it hard to look at his face, especially since the beating had left cuts and contusions even on the so-called normal side of it. So this was the demon that had viciously killed so many, he thought to himself. The gazettes were filled with stories of his evil. They made him sound supernatural. Yet the prisoner that lay on the straw floor, cradling his swollen hands to his chest, had nothing supernatural about him. The guard prided himself on his knack for knowing people. This man was no devil. There was more evil among his fellow officers than in this creature. He had seen several of Inspector Leroux's key officers on more than one occasion delight in mistreating the inmates. They enjoyed their power. But he had never seen the inspector condone abuse of this sort with any of the other prisoners.

"Thank you," whispered Erik hoarsely and laid his head back on the cold stone.

"Don't tell anyone I brought you water. The inspector expressly forbids it. He'll have my neck for it if he finds out, and I'll be without a job besides."

The prisoner moved his head just enough to acknowledge the guard's warning.

The guard imagined that the prisoner's position might be uncomfortable and thought to move him so that he wasn't lying on his broken arm. But the prisoner yelled out in such pain that the guard stopped immediately. Besides the strange angle of his arm, four of the prisoner's fingers on his right hand were swollen and bruised. Perhaps he would expire before morning. It would be a blessing for him, the guard thought.

No one told Meg about the commotion in the streets. The audience was seated, the curtain was about to rise, and Meg had assumed her mark on the stage for the first act. Only Mme. Giry knew what was happening a bare three streets down the way near the old opera house. She knew because she had betrayed the Phantom and had told the inspector how to find him. She watched the policemen enter the tunnels and waited until they emerged again dragging Erik's limp and bloodied body. She was shocked to see how they had beaten him. She had imagined him emerging from the tunnels, tall and proud, escorted on either side by two men wary of his powers. He would walk with dignity, even with defiance. Of course she imagined him wearing his cape and mask, not stripped to his linen shirt and breeches, the shirt torn open and bloody. His head dangled limply. Suddenly the enormity of her betrayal hit her. She regretted her anger. She had turned him over to the authorities.

But she had found them wrapped in each other's arms, naked in the early morning. He had taken advantage of her daughter to satisfy his lust. He didn't love Meg, but used her because he couldn't have Christine. She had to protect Meg against him. He would not drag her down into his nightmare, not her daughter. It was him or Meg, and she had to choose Meg.

Raoul had warned her. He was mad. He had killed. He had destroyed the opera house because he could not have the woman he wanted, a woman who did not love him. She had protected him long enough. It had to stop sometime, and she had drawn the line in the sand. Here and no farther. Yet he had taken her daughter to his bed. Now she understood why he had arranged the marriage for Meg. He planned to marry her off so that he could enjoy her safely as a mistress. It was he who had betrayed her trust. Even so, she cringed to see him taken away to the prison, beaten and defeated, humiliated. No one must know what had happened between Meg and the Opera Ghost. He would be taken to court and most certainly be found guilty. The sentence would be death by hanging. As angry as she was, she would not watch him hang. That she couldn't bear. He had been just a child, like a young brother to her, like her monstrous child. As the wagon disappeared down the street, Mme. Giry could no longer repress the pangs of remorse. Oh my God, she thought, what have I done to you, Erik?

"Maman, what's happening? Someone said the police have captured the Opera Ghost. Is it true? Has anything happened to Erik?" Meg had heard the steady rise in volume among the audience during the intermission. Word had filtered in that the Opera Ghost, the Phantom, had been tracked to his underground lair and had been carried off in chains to prison. He was, even now, supposedly behind bars.

"The police found Erik in the tunnels and have taken him to jail." She whispered this to her daughter and tried to steer her to the dressing room. They must avoid a public scene at all costs. No one must know that the Phantom was in any way connected to Meg.

"Oh my God! What are we going to do?" Meg became hysterical. Her mother told the assistant dresser to leave so that she and her daughter could be alone. She closed and locked the doors behind her.

Firmly, she grabbed her daughter by the shoulders and shook her until she stopped ranting. "Control yourself and finish dressing for the final act. You have an opera to perform. We can't do anything for him. He's lost. You must make up your mind to forget him, ma petite."

Horrified and struck dumb, Meg stared at her mother as if she were a stranger. What was she saying? How could they simply abandon Erik? Her mother placed the costume over her daughter's head and tugged it down into place. Stepping behind her, she began to lace the bodice tightly. Incredulous, Meg thought back to that very morning when she woke to find Erik still sleeping by her side. She woke him with gentle kisses. Naked in each other's arms they caressed and kissed again and again. Was that to be the last time that they would ever make love?

Her intuition told her that her mother had something to do with Erik's capture. It was her coolness, her apparent lack of concern for Erik. This was not like her. Her mother had always defended him, even in the face of overwhelming evidence of his wrongdoing.

"Maman, what have you done?" She felt the tears pour from her eyes as she recognized the guilt on her mother's face.

"I don't know what you're talking about, Meg." Mme. Giry insisted on ignoring her daughter's accusations. She had not thought this out. She had only thought of the need to get the Phantom away from her daughter, to save Meg from his lust. Now she realized she would have to face her daughter's anger, too. "Quickly, finish your make-up. Dry those eyes. The Finale is not tragic. You mustn't cry; your eyes will be puffy and red."

"You couldn't have, could you? You couldn't have turned Erik in to the police! I can't believe you would betray us like that."

"Betray 'us'? I betrayed no one."

Her daughter was not fooled by her denials.

"Very well. Sooner or later you'll have to know. I have to appear in court and testify against him. I did it for you, my love." Seeing that Meg did not accept her excuses, Mme. Giry snapped at her, "I found you both this morning, there, on that very divan. I will not let him ruin your life!"

Meg struck her mother across the face sharply with her open hand. Mme. Giry was so shocked that she didn't know what to say. Meg struck her a second time full across the face with her outspread hand.

"Get out! I never want to see you again."

"Well, at least they brought a doctor to the cell finally this morning to set his fractured arm. That's what I heard at the club. Of course, it had to be broken again since it had already been a week and the bones had begun to knit incorrectly. I don't think you want to go into details with your wife. It was pretty nasty. They must have tortured him over the course of several days. Most of his fingers on one hand are broken, as well as a couple on the other hand. The doctor fixed those as best he could and bound his chest. He has broken ribs as well. The damnedest thing is he must be strong as an ox because the doctor said a lesser man would have died. He expects the prisoner to recover eventually unless of course the torture continues or he's hanged before he can heal."

"Why torture him? The evidence from the Opera house is overwhelming. And since when do we condone torture in this country? What did François say?"

"Said the inspector wants a confession, complete and detailed. According to François, he's accusing your Phantom of every unsolved crime of the last four years. The prisoner confessed to some, but remains adamantly against accepting the guilt of the others, the trumped-up charges."

"What are these so-called false charges?"

"Woooo, it's quite a list, Raoul. One in particular that I think you might find upsetting. The inspector claims he drowned your child."

"What? That's ridiculous. We know exactly what happened. The nurse was there. It was an unfortunate accident."

"I know. Personally, I think Leroux is carrying this whole thing too far. There may be political motives. François thinks he wants to make this a stepping stone to political appointment. He also accused the Phantom of attacking you."

"Well, that's true. He did. He attacked me in the graveyard four years ago and again … Well, actually on the river byway I would have to admit that I challenged him."

"Fact is Leroux's accused him of having attacked you the night of the card party."

"That's preposterous! Even though I hate to admit it, in point of fact, he saved my life that night."

"So you've told me. According to the official confession Leroux is trying to torture him into signing, the Phantom attacked you with intent to murder. Three men came out to your defense, and he killed them and left *you* for dead."

"My God!"

"The judge won't hear the case until later this year, probably in autumn. By that time, you should be prepared for the worst. The prisoner may well be dead by then. They tend to waste away in jail, and given the animus against him, I wouldn't expect him to survive the spring."

"We must do something, Lord Alexander." Christine entered the salon. She had been listening in the hall.

"Christine, please. I told you I'd handle this."

"But you haven't! Torture, Raoul? They've broken his fingers, left him without medical treatment for days. It's barbaric; he can't be treated like that. I don't care how monstrous his deeds. I have to see him, Raoul. You must arrange a visit."

"Don't be silly. That's impossible."

"Actually, that's not true," interrupted Lord Alexander hesitantly. "The jail is planning special exhibition hours for the public. Anyone who can pay the entry fee can get a look at the Phantom of the Opera starting next week, every Wednesday up to the trial date." Lord Alexander knew the effect this might have on Raoul and Christine, especially Christine, but there was no use hiding the fact. It was common knowledge, and the police had even begun to post notices around town to advertise. Even he felt sickened by the state's complicity in this ignominious treatment. Christine was right. In a civilized society, such things were not done.

"Oh, Raoul. They've put him back in that cage from which he fled so many years ago. How will he bear their stares?" Raoul went to Christine's side to comfort her, but she irritably pulled away from him to stand by the fire.

"My darling, he knew that sooner or later the police would apprehend him." He had meant to suggest that the Phantom was prepared to face this ordeal. "After all, he is guilty. He knew the risks, the consequences of his crimes."

"And what of the crimes society has committed against him? He has lived his whole life condemned. First in the cage, then in the vaults of the opera house. For the first time, he was reaching out for some semblance of a real life with …" Christine's tears wouldn't allow her to continue.

She left the room visibly upset. Raoul made his apologies to Lord Alexander, but the Lord had some inkling of the troubles the young couple had experienced.

"Have you had time to reconsider your plea, M. Phantom?" The inspector had resigned himself to the fact that the prisoner was capable of suffering whatever torture he could devise without acquiescing to his demands. He had assumed that he could break this lunatic in the first hours after capture if he struck suddenly and hard enough. The judge would overlook a few broken bones, swollen eyes, any number of bruises and cuts invisible to the public and hidden under the prisoner's clothing, but he would have no patience for missing digits and limbs or premature death.

He had also withheld food and water, but to no avail since the sisters of charity attended the prisoners every day and personally made sure that each man had his cup of water and his crust of bread. As long as Erik had these, he could outlast the deprivations imposed by the inspector.

Incredibly, Erik had recovered some of his physical strength. When the doctor finally was allowed to set his broken bones, he seemed to have survived the worst and was now apparently rallying. The dizziness was less and less a problem as his damaged eardrum seemed to be mending. He had regained some hearing in the injured ear, although sounds were still muffled and fuzzy.

"I asked you a question."

"I confess to the murder of Joseph Buquet, and I accept the responsibility of those who died in the opera house the night the chandelier fell. That is all."

"Pierre, bring in the young ladies."

The officer opened the door and allowed three young women to enter the interrogation chamber. They lined up against the wall facing the prisoner. Erik could tell from their worn dresses, gaudy make-up, that they were the prostitutes that he was accused of raping. Nervous, one chewed compulsively on her fingernails; her eyes darted back and forth between Erik and the inspector. The older one set her arms jauntily akimbo on either hip and defiantly stared at Erik in fascination. The third kept her eyes firmly focused on her shoes and slid slightly behind the nervous one as if wishing to disappear. It was obvious to Erik that these young women had been coerced or paid to testify against him. He ignored their stares and kept his eyes trained on the bare wall directly before him. There was after all nothing that he could do to put an end to this circus show. The freaks were all present; let the festivities begin, he thought to himself.

The inspector addressed each woman individually and asked her to look closely at the prisoner. This brought on a round of nervous giggles from the younger ones. Then the inspector asked each one to say if the prisoner was the man who had attacked and raped them in the Rue des Misericordes.

The nail biter recited her rehearsed testimony. "Yes, M. Leroux, this is the monster that beat and raped me."

Next Leroux expected the older prostitute to make her declaration. The scribe, as always, diligently wrote down the testimony.

"Well, it would be easier to say, M. Inspector, if I could see his goods, so to speak. I know I could recognize *them*!" The older woman laughed at her own bawdy joke.

At the slightest nod of the inspector's head, two officers pulled Erik to his feet. As they seized him, the prisoner reared his head back into one officer's face breaking the man's nose and busting his lip. Then, in spite of the fact that the other officer gripped the arm that the doctor had recently set in plaster, Erik rammed his entire weight into the officer's chest, sending him reeling backwards into the wall. The three prostitutes screamed in terror as Erik broke free from the immediate restraint of these two men. The inspector, however, had blown his whistle and drawn his billy club. He crashed it over Erik's head. At the same time several other officers in response to the alarm entered the room and wrestled the prisoner to the floor.

The older prostitute was so unsettled by the violence of the scene that she yelled above the tumult that it was just a joke, she didn't need to see his goods after all. The prisoner was certainly her rapist. She wanted nothing more than to finish her job and leave before all hell broke out.

Erik lay panting under the weight of four policemen. The one whose nose he had broken kicked him repeatedly in the ribs before he was pulled by his comrades from the room.

"Resisting an officer of the law in his duty and assault on an officer of the law are severe crimes, M. Phantom. You are all witnesses. The punishment is within my purview, and I sentence you to be flogged. Get him out of here. Take him to the courtyard. Thirty lashes on the back." Erik coughed up bloody spittle as the officers dragged him by his legs through the corridor to the courtyard.

The special group that had paid their entrance fee to see the Phantom of the Opera in the flesh pressed as near to the bars as the cordoned off area would allow. The Lords had promised something that would deliciously frighten their ladies and mistresses, the Phantom unmasked, in chains! The trip to the cells itself was nearly worth the admission. A young urchin accepted pennies from the gents to tell them the story of the mad genius of the Opera House before they were allowed to descend into the dungeon. The gentlewomen were aghast at the filth and squalor of the Parisian cells. When they walked down the final corridor and reached the last cell in the block, the cell where the Phantom was kept in isolation from the run-of-the-mill criminals, they expected a dramatic spectacle. They were bound to be disappointed to find the man leaning into the corner of the cell, his face turned away from the bars and thus invisible to the privileged party of spectators.

"Why won't he turn around?" asked a particularly disappointed mistress as she brought her perfumed handkerchief to her nose to ward off the evil smells of the enclosed space.

"Yes, we didn't pay to see his back! Let's see the face!"

"Make him turn around. Guard! You, guard! Come here and make this prisoner turn and face us."

Although most of the spectators were bored rich gentlemen and ladies, a few special friends had been invited to spice up the party. The virtuoso pianist from Prague, for one, had been invited to the showing and later to dinner and after dinner games. And at the last minute, the diva from the Opera National had expressed interest in coming along, too, for the freak show. M. Pardieu was somewhat uncomfortable joining the group since he didn't believe it was right to enjoy the misery of others and since Meg's erratic behavior toward him had him at his wit's end. She had repeatedly postponed the announcement of their wedding as well as the wedding itself, and suddenly she was hanging on his arm insisting that he ingratiate himself with Lord Saussiere so as to obtain this invitation. And now here they were in this God awful pigsty tormenting this wretch for their morbid entertainment. He wouldn't have believed Meg capable of such pitiless fascination.

"Mademoiselle Giry, perhaps if you sang the monster might look this way. According to the lad's story, the Phantom was an opera buff and that's why he haunted the Opera Populaire."

When Erik heard her name, he turned and sought her face among the crowd. Delighted with the change in events, the men applauded in appreciation, and several women pretended that they might faint. Meg pushed the others aside, unconcerned with their puzzled reactions, and pressed against the loose cord until her hands touched the bars of Erik's prison. Erik looked only at her but remained fixed to the spot at the back of the cell.

"Erik! Let me touch you!" M. Pardieu's mouth dropped open in disbelief as his fiancée pressed even more urgently her body against the bars as if she would melt through the iron and into the monster's arms.

"Go away!" Still frozen to the spot, he tried to ignore her as if he addressed the general mass of people.

"Erik! Please! We may not have another chance!" She begged, tears openingly falling down her cheeks.

Incapable of resisting, he came to the bars of his cell and reaching his good arm through them wrapped Meg in his embrace. Several of the ladies in the crowd fainted in earnest this time as the Lords indignantly called for the attendants. Erik pressed his face to the cold metal as did Meg, and their lips met briefly before the attendant grabbed Meg and pulled her away from the cell door. Desperately, Erik called out to her. He strained his body against the bars and reached to pull her back, but she had slipped out of range. She called to him hysterically as they forced her down the hallway, away from him. Oblivious to the gaping stares of the spectators, Erik slid down the length of the bars onto the floor still calling for Meg and reaching and finding nothing but empty air.

"Christine, they had him on display like an animal, and …" Meg burst into tears and couldn't go on. She tried to explain something to Christine, but she was distraught and incomprehensible.

Christine had forgotten old grudges in the face of Erik's capture. She was ready to forgive both Meg and Erik each and every trespass. Raoul didn't understand how matters could so drastically change for her. Even though he was willing to intercede on the Phantom's behalf, it was only to put his wife's mind at rest. As far as he was concerned, the man was a criminal and should be put away for life. In fact, Raoul considered that Erik should perhaps have always been locked up. He was clearly mad and had committed a serious crime even as a child. Yet Christine insisted on ignoring his crimes.

Raoul was compelled to relent somewhat in his condemnation of the Phantom when Christine attested that only he had been capable of guiding her through her grief for their son. It was true that she was her old self again, but Raoul was haunted by those missing days she spent in the Phantom's lair. Nevertheless, he knew better than to ask her or to reveal his suspicions and fears to his wife.

Meg had come to stay with them. She came in tears from the first day. Meg confided in Christine that Mme. Giry had betrayed Erik's whereabouts. Raoul, of course, was already aware of this and had told Christine. Meg also explained to Christine why her mother had done so.

"I've paid one of the night watchmen who's in charge of the rounds to keep me informed of Erik's wellbeing. He's already shown some kindness to Erik."

"How did you know he was sympathetically inclined toward Erik?"

"He approached me. Erik sent him after I …" She broke down into convulsive sobs again, and Christine had to wait for her passion to subside to hear the rest of the story. "I made Etienne take me to one of the showings at the jail, Christine. I told him I wanted to see the Phantom. He was appalled and tried to convince me that it was lurid and cruel. You can't imagine the humiliation. When we came upon his cell, he was hiding in the corner. He kept his back to us the whole time. He just stood there. I could tell he was standing as still as he could, trying to maintain some dignity, trying to ignore the gross comments the Lords and Ladies with their finery and perfumes shouted out at him. If they had had rotten vegetables, I think they might have thrown them at him to see his reaction. He was dressed only in his shirt and breeches. They had even taken his shoes away from him. He was dirty, unshaven. Oh, Christine, they'd taken his mask away. He was so vulnerable. Someone in the crowd mocked him and asked me to sing for him because he had been an opera buff. When he heard them say my name, he turned toward us. His face was swollen, bruised, cut. I couldn't stop myself. We tried to embrace each other but the guard pulled me away and threw me out of the jail. All the way down the hall I could hear him call for me. I can't bear to think of him being there. You have to help us. You have to make Raoul do something. Surely he has powerful connections. Erik asked the night watchman to send me word that he was all right. Here." She rummaged through her pockets and pulled out a dirty scrap of paper folded several times and with trembling fingers unfolded it and handed it to Christine to read. "It's not in his hand; his fingers are too injured for him to hold the pen. The night watchman had to write it for him."

My dearest Meg,

I dictate this hastily to a guard who has taken pity on my condition. He will see that you get it. There is no hope for me. Leroux is determined that I will hang. I have confessed to my crimes, but he insists on foisting others' crimes on my head, too. I suppose he would like to paint me as black as possible or perhaps he simply wants to clear the books on crimes he is not able to solve otherwise. Please know that I had nothing to do with little Raoul's accident, nor did I rape the prostitutes that they have brought to testify against me. I attacked Raoul in the graveyard many years ago when I first lost Christine, but I have on several occasions since then avoided attacking him or even interceded to protect him. I expect no gratitude from him, but I am loath to be forced to expiate a crime I did not commit. I need you to know this. At the trial, they are bound to portray me as a monster.

I must be honest with you; this is no time for deceit. I have always loved Christine. I am resigned to the fact that she does not love me. If not for you, I would never have known the full expression of love that we are capable of. You are the only one who has given me my humanity. You are the only one who has brought me to peace with my body, such as it is. I am incredibly grateful to you for having loved me. Please forget me. Please be happy. I will not die well if I believe you will never be happy again. Your most humble and loving, Erik

Raoul was successful in closing down the freak show. Lord Alexander and he penned several articles for the gazettes protesting the mistreatment of prisoners. They also spoke to many an influential barrister at the House of Justice decrying the barbarous nature of the spectacle.

Finally Raoul secured written permission from a sympathetic barrister, the Honorable Pierre Henri, to visit the prisoner, including a guarantee to complete access and rights to procure appropriate treatment of said prisoner. With the legal writ in hand, Raoul set out, somewhat reluctantly, to fulfill his promise to his wife.

The count heard the commotion well before he and Inspector Leroux arrived at the Phantom's cell. In spite of bandaged hands and a plaster cast immobilizing one of his arms, the prisoner had barricaded himself in the corner behind the wood framed cot and thin mattress. Several guards had just entered the cell to subdue him. They pulled the bedding away from the corner revealing a wild man. Raoul was amazed at the transformation the Phantom had suffered. His ominous dignity, the still menace of his stature and gaze, all this had disappeared and been replaced by a brutal, desperate, animal violence. This, too, was power, but a power out of control, born of panic and hopelessness.

One of the guards pushed the prisoner back hard against the stone wall. He groaned in pain and immediately collapsed to the floor. The guard had been rough, but the assault in and of itself did not seem that severe.

"What's going on here, sergeant?" asked Leroux.

"I don't know sir. He went berserk when he saw you and the gentleman coming down the hall."

From his position on the floor, the prisoner turned toward the wall away from them all. The soiled rag that had once been a shirt slipped off his shoulder revealing a portion of his back, and there Raoul glimpsed the fresh welts from a lashing crisscrossing older wounds just beginning to scab and heal. On the shirt itself were evident fresh and old stains of blood. A growl emerged from the corner startling Raoul in its ferocious intensity. "Go away, Count. You have no business with me."

Raoul forced himself to recover from his initial shock. In this one glance at his rival, he knew more than he needed to know about his recent treatment. He looked in recrimination at Leroux who, in turn, serenely watched the prisoner. Appalled, Raoul recognized the pleasure the inspector obviously felt as he witnessed the Phantom's suffering.

"Have your man open the door."

Leroux at first refused. It was absurd to put the count in danger. The prisoner was deceptively strong. It took four to five officers to subdue him in spite of his injuries. "I won't hear of it, Count."

"It is not a request, M. Leroux. I demand you open the door and let me enter the cell to interview the prisoner."

Begrudgingly, Leroux indicated to the guard to do as the count had requested.

Erik groaned again as he heard the iron door open. Here was Raoul to gloat over his defeat, to strut about glorying in his triumph. The count finally had his nemesis where he wanted him. Not only would he delight in his death, his punishment, but he longed to witness his humiliation, to see him crushed, slowly, painfully. He would leave him no dignity, nowhere to hide, no respite.

Suddenly looming over him was Raoul. The bars were behind him, and the count was in the cell just inches from him. Summoning all his strength and wits about him, Erik pushed himself off the ground. He steadied himself by bracing his uninjured arm against the wall, and although somewhat awkwardly he managed to stand, stiff and erect, and face his adversary, his tormentor, his judge and executioner. For that was what Raoul had become. He had gone to the very portal of hell to drag the Phantom to his death.

Raoul had forgotten the hideous disfigurement the Phantom always disguised behind his masks. Now he winced as the prisoner recovered his customary air of defiance and stood, unmasked and unprotected, before him. Pure
hatred filled the prisoner's eyes as he cast his sights past Raoul, beyond the
bars, at Inspector Leroux. Raoul sensed that Erik's brave show of dignity was
costing him dear reserves of physical strength through pure will and was about
to crumble. He hates me, thought Raoul. And why not? I have played a key role
in his demise.

"I've come to check on your condition. There've been rumors that you've
been tortured."

Erik only glared at him; a slight smirk played at the corner of his mouth.
Raoul noticed that Erik was trembling uncontrollably. At any moment, his
knees would surely buckle.

"Leroux, bring us two chairs, please."

"It is expressly against policy to allow ..."

"Bring two chairs now. I don't intend to remain standing while I interview
the prisoner."

The guards brought two simple wooden chairs and set them next to the two
men. Raoul sat first and waited for Erik to do likewise.

They sat facing each other. Raoul now found himself at a loss for words.
Suddenly, he regretted coming. He should never have promised Christine that
he would intervene in this matter. How did she imagine that the prisoner
would react having his rival as an advocate? What hypocrisy he must feel this
to be!

Erik began to whisper. At first Raoul thought it the wild utterances of a
madman, but soon he realized the tremendous effort the Phantom exerted to
address him in such a way that only the two of them would hear.

"You think you've won. You think you took her from me." Erik imbued each
word with a challenge. With his bandaged hand, the four broken fingers tied
together, he tapped his scarred forehead. "Christine is here. Last night, she
sang to me. You will have to bash open my skull and dig her out with your bare
hands to take her away from me." Raoul restrained himself from rising to the
challenge. Why the devil had he come?

Several minutes passed as the two men sat gauging each other. Almost
against his own will, it would seem, Erik spoke to Raoul again, "Water."

"What did you say? Water?" Raoul noticed Erik's dry cracked lips. He sur-
veyed the small space of the cell. The straw was old and dirty, the simple wood
framed cot and soiled mattress had been returned to their place, a bucket with

a lid rested in the opposite corner as far from them as it could be. He knew from the smell that it wasn't drinking water but the accumulated urine and feces of the last day or so. No water, no cup, no blanket to protect against the chill dampness of the cell.

"Leroux bring us both some fresh water, please."

Within minutes the guards brought two tin cups and handed them to the count and prisoner. "Leave us alone now." Leroux was about to protest when he realized it would be of no use. The guards locked the two men in and retreated down the hall after the inspector.

Erik held the cup unsteadily in his crippled hands. His trembling spilled half the liquid down his shirt as he brought it to his lips. Raoul took the empty cup from him and put his full cup in its place. Erik held it for a few seconds. Raoul turned away, embarrassed to see that the Phantom, this man who had ruled over the Opera House as his private domain, was moved by his simple gesture of kindness to silent tears. He listened to the sounds Erik made as he drained this cup of water, too. Several spasms of coughing followed and gradually subsided.

"You have done your duty, Count. You can in all good conscience say that you performed your charity to this monster. You've come and inspected the conditions under which the state treats its more dangerous charges. Nothing untoward has been found. God knows we convicts must be treated firmly. Christine doesn't need to know the details." These words from the prisoner's lips—so close in tone and content to Leroux's—felt like a slap in the face to Raoul.

"You truly mistake my intentions. Yes, I'm here mostly due to Christine's insistence. But I confess I'm not so cruel that I enjoy your suffering."

"Did you not testify that I attacked you the night you were wounded outside your club? And that I also viciously murdered the three men who came to your assistance? Does your need for vengeance against me push you even to perjure yourself? Do you so desire my destruction?"

"No! I didn't accuse you of that. I won't testify to that lie."

Erik was visibly surprised. "Then Leroux himself or someone else plots my vilification. As if my true crimes were not enough to damn me to the hangman's noose."

For some time, the two men sat in silence. Raoul, anxious to discharge his duty, finally spoke up. "Christine wants you to know that Meg has come to live with us."

At the mention of Meg's name, Erik's defenses completely crumbled. Giving in to despair, he pitched forward in his seat and buried his face in his hands. Awkwardly, Raoul tried to find a place on Erik's body that had not been bruised or cut to put his hand to comfort him. Instead, he drew his chair even nearer in an attempt to calm him. Erik fought to compose himself.

"She's well. We'll look after her. I'll look after them both. I know that … I know you and Meg … have been … have become close."

Erik interrupted Raoul urgently. "I've so little time now. I've so much in here." He drove his fist against his chest as if he meant to pierce his heart with an imaginary dagger. Unable to sit quietly, tormented by so many strong emotions, Erik rose unsteadily at first from the chair and paced the width of his cell. In spite of his injuries, his body moved gracefully like that of a panther. "I'm so confused. Christine and Meg are both locked inside me. I ache and, oh my God, here I am revealing my soul to the last man on this earth that would pity me. So you see, my dear Count, you have indeed won. I have no more defenses. I stand before you a pathetic mockery of my former self, and you see me for what I am, unmasked and unable to control myself. I would to God there were someone else I could pour my soul out to, not you. Not you!"

In spite of his antipathy, Raoul was moved by Erik's torment and his honesty. How difficult it must be for him to stand so naked before his enemy.

The prisoner returned to his seat next to the count and continued, "You cruelly robbed me of an easy death so many times. You force this long humiliating journey on me when I can no longer fight back … Well, so be it …" Erik slumped in the seat and seemed no longer to be talking to Raoul, but to himself. "Meg and I dreamed … a foolish dream that we might flee to Italy, buy a small villa in the country. I would be an eccentric recluse, and she would perform on the stage. We might yet have made a life …"

Raoul didn't know what to say. He waited for the moment to pass. Finally, the words seemed to rise of their own accord, surprising him as much as Erik. "We've both suffered and fought too long, you and I. We share a love for the same woman. Instead of rivals, in these last days surely we can put the rancor aside and be as brothers." Not until Raoul heard himself say these words out loud did he truly believe them.

A heaviness that Erik hadn't even realized weighed down his heart suddenly lifted, and he looked at Raoul in amazement and gratitude. "Yes, we'll make a pact. I won't die alone. I will leave a brother and his wife, behind me … I have a request, selfish perhaps, that only a brother or dear friend could carry out for me. I fear that I have ruined Meg. You must insist M. Pardieu keep his word and marry her. They won't be able to harm her if she's Pardieu's wife. You must protect her against Leroux, against the society that will certainly shun her if they find out …"

"She's already told us that she intends to marry no one if not you."

"Oh, God, please. I beg you to talk some sense into her."

"Don't you wish to marry her?"

"Please, don't ask me that. What do you want me to say? I'm already a dead man."

"If a secret marriage between the two of you could be arranged, would you marry Meg?"

"For what remains of my miserable life? To wed little Meg? To make her a widow? The Phantom's widow? What advantage would that be to Meg?"

"Before God, she would be your wife. Your … time together would be sanctified."

Erik hung his head in thought for what seemed an eternity before speaking to Raoul again.

"This could be done?"

"Yes, I believe I could manage this."

"As my wife, she would inherit my money?"

"Why, yes."

"There are bank accounts outside Paris that the state can't touch. Meg's mother knows where they are and has access to them. These would be hers. If Meg is foolish enough to have me. But she must swear that after I am hanged, she will not grieve. She will remarry."

Raoul started to rise, but Erik called him back. "Before you go, there are many things left unsaid between us that need to be said. I loved Christine from the day she came to the opera house, an orphan. I heard her cry every night. I was but barely grown myself. I had already spent several years in the opera house. I understood what it was to be an orphan; I understood her loneliness and grief. At first she was such a young thing my feelings were more like those of an older brother or guardian. She missed her father; she needed his protection. I let her think of me as she wished. I didn't mean to deceive her. But as she grew to be a young woman, I felt the stirrings of a passion for her that I myself couldn't comprehend. I thought it was the music, beauty itself, but I know now that it was also my need as a man that drew me to her. Please, bear with me. I know this is uncomfortable for you. If you had not come along, I might never have recognized the true nature of my passion for her. I might have been content with her as my pupil, my adored diva. The music might have been sufficient. But when I saw you and Christine that night on the roof of the opera house, having fled my monstrosity ... You kissed and pledged your love for one another. It overwhelmed me with jealousy and desire, and I knew all that my situation was denying me."

Raoul squirmed in his chair as he listened to Erik. This confession threatened to revive his own jealousy once more. Erik saw the warring emotions in Raoul's eyes. "Please, listen, just a little longer. There was a time I could have ... there was a time my lust threatened to overwhelm all other emotions, drives, reason itself. But there was always that first love for Christine—a pure love unsullied by lust or selfishness—underneath it all. That love I still have for her, the love of a guardian, a guardian angel, her angel of music. Meg has helped me see what I will never have with Christine. She has given me a glimpse into a man's life, not a monster's. I now know how complex love and desire are. Meg has helped me to bear Christine's loss. As her husband, you must believe me when I tell you that Christine has always remained true to you and your love even when she has loved me, not as a lover but as that creature who accompanied her through her sorrow, her loss of a father and home, her loneliness."

All the doubts and suspicions that had tormented Raoul since Christine had returned to their home were dispelled. Ironically, he would never have been so reassured if anyone but this man, whom he had hated so violently, had proclaimed Christine's faithfulness. There was no way he could express the depths of his gratitude to this, his former, enemy.

"Before you leave, a final request. Can you take a message to the Mother Superior at the convent of St. Isidore? Can you tell her I'm grateful. If she might come to the sentencing, just the sentencing ... I think it would help me if she were there when the judge ..."

Raoul admired Erik's resignation before the ineluctable specter of his own impending death. "Of course."

They both sat silent yet a spell longer. Then Erik asked, "Have you seen Mme. Giry?" His tone was neutral, but Raoul understood how betrayed he must feel.

"No. We haven't. I'm sorry, Erik. Her betrayal must have been a tremendous shock to you."

"Yes. But I've had much time to think while here. I believe I know why she did it. If you have the chance to speak with her. Tell her ... Tell her I know she will testify against me ... and that I ... I am sorry. It is hard to think she would do this ... But tell her I am grateful for the life she tried to give me. Ask her to forgive me for ... whatever horrible crime I did to lose her ... protection. Now go. I am very tired."

Raoul had left him a bundle of fresh clothes. Erik tore the brown paper from the bundle and spread the articles out one by one on the soiled mattress. Two fresh shirts, a pair of breeches, a dark vest, a starched collar, a black waist coat, undergarments, stockings. Wrapped between the vest and waist coat, Erik found two white masks, one shaped like a half moon that would cover only his disfigurement, another half mask that would cover the entire upper part of his face; a comb and brush were also among the articles. Erik ran his finger tips, the most sensitive part of his injured hands, over the masks.

Since Raoul's visit, the guards' treatment of him had improved. Fresh water was always available, his bucket was removed and emptied twice a day, he had been given a blanket for the cot, and he was fed now twice a day a stew which included a modest portion of fatty meat and vegetables. He already felt the effects of the improved diet on his strength and state of mind. The guards had allowed him to bathe the day before for the first time in the two months he had been locked up. The itching had become almost unbearable. For the first time in many nights he had slept comfortably.

The night watchman had given Erik the sign that it was time to get ready. He carefully put on the clean, freshly ironed clothes laid out before him. As he buttoned the vest and arranged the stiff collar, he realized to his amusement that Raoul had forgotten that he had no shoes. He brushed his hair without benefit of mirror. It had grown down past his shoulder, and he thought it might have looked dashing to tie it back in a tail as a seventeenth-century pirate might have done. He knew that there was only so much he could do to improve his looks without benefit of the magic arts of the theater that he had always used. He considered the masks, wondering which he should choose.

Unexpectedly early he heard footsteps coming down the hallway toward his cell. He stepped back in the corner wondering if Leroux had found out the plan and had come to drag him to some other cell in the prison. He quickly made his choice and put on the smaller of the two masks. It immediately gave him a feeling of strength and wholeness. Then he caught sight of the night watchman accompanied by two other men and close behind them appeared a vision. There stood Meg luminescent as if the light surrounding her emanated from her own body. Her blond tresses were piled in elaborate braids on her head, a diamond tiara, her crown. The wedding dress was peach and white lace, her arms were covered past the elbow with elegant white gloves, a blue sash caressed her incredibly narrow waist. On Raoul's arm glowed Christine, their matron of honor, in peach and blue.

Erik felt the blood rise to his face unbidden as he glanced at Christine, but he forced himself to lock his gaze on his bride. Through the bars, he took Meg's hands in his. The Priest had agreed to perform the briefest version of the service given the circumstances and the danger. When it came time to exchange banns, Raoul stepped forward as best man and placed the ring in Erik's hand. He recognized it as the ring Raoul had originally given to Christine and that Erik had once stolen from them. He placed the ring on Meg's finger, and the Priest pronounced them husband and wife. The night watchman escorted the Priest from the prison, and Raoul and Christine discreetly turned away as Meg and Erik pressed their bodies against each other through the bars and kissed.

Raoul reminded them that they didn't have much time and that each moment they stayed put them in danger of discovery. They all had agreed to this plan; it had to be done quickly. There would be no wedding night. Such a risk was out of the question. Yet Erik didn't realize how difficult it would be to see Meg so briefly and have to watch her go. Not only would he not lie with her as a husband, but as he held her he could barely feel her for the bandages on his hands. Angrily, he stripped them from his fingers. He could hardly move them, but at least he could feel the skin of her face as he held it in his bared hands; the sensations were heightened—his fingers sensitive and aware of every texture—by the fact that they had been wrapped for several weeks.

"You must be reasonable, Meg. Do as Raoul says."

Raoul gently took Meg by the arm to lead her away when she shook loose of him and clung to the bars of Erik's jail. He returned her kisses, and then collecting all his strength and resolve he pulled away from her arms and retreated to the back of the cell.

Meg called to him in tears, but did not resist as Raoul pulled her from the cell and back down the hallway.

CHAPTER 13

The Trial

For Mercy has a human heart,
Pity a human face,
And Love, the human form divine,
And Peace, the human dress.

William Blake, "The Divine Image"

In his dream, she came to him. Stars studded her hair, and light blazed out from her eyes. She melted through the bars of his prison and took his hands and kissed each tortured finger. Bones mended and glided painlessly in their joints. Her healing touch, her palms, ran down his chest and pressed his sore ribs into place, and he drew in her breath, sweet with cinnamon and cloves, without pain.

He reached for her hand and brought it to his twisted, lacerated face, and she smoothed the skin around his eye and erased the red and weeping welts, the bulbous growths. He touched his face and found it whole, smooth, unblemished.

Embracing him, her arms wrapped round his back; she sealed his open wounds and whispered in his ear that it was their wedding night.

In his dream, she came to him.

In his dream, Christine came to him and made him whole.

In his dream, Christine came and was his wife.

It would be over soon, he kept telling himself. Time pounded away at his soul, chipping away at it bit by bit, threatening to leave him completely hollow inside. It would be a relief, he told himself. A moment of pain, then blackness, then … perhaps forgiveness. In his mind he remembered, he rehearsed, the notes of the song of the Phoenix. It began with fire and pain, a staccato of tortured notes cutting across a low ominous field. The sounds would oscillate between fortissimo and pianissimo as if they mimicked the very fires in which the Phoenix burned. Suddenly a sustained rest would, in its absence of sound, take on a corporeal weight as if it were sound and stillness simultaneously—death. Then, the movement of healing, of the gradual rise from nothingness, would begin with one simple longing strain, a note so pure it had always been inside the listener's mind and only now perceptible. Other notes would join until woven together they would fly up like the Phoenix itself, glorious and beautiful, powerful and wise, old and yet new again. Erik's fingers picked out the notes, gliding over the empty air on his phantom keyboard. His eyes closed, he imagined the sensual contact with the keys. As the notes grew shorter, more rapid, his fingers failed to obey, and the pain brought the music to a standstill beyond which he could no longer push.

Simpler pieces he could play, but not the complex compositions that he had composed and performed in the underground grotto. His fingers would never heal enough to allow him the virtuosity of movement across the keys that was the soul of his work. Incapable of bearing the silence any longer, he began to sing, to fill the emptiness of the cell, to fill the emptiness of his deathwatch. In the day, he would listen with his inner voice. Only at night was it safe to make those notes audible.

The night watchman heard him sing the first time several days after the clandestine wedding service. At first only snatches of song reached his post along the corridors of the prison. Eventually he sat back and listened for hours to an ongoing performance of arias from many different operas. He didn't know the names, but some of the melodies he recognized from versions popularized in the dance halls and bars. He thought perhaps the other inmates might complain in spite of the incredible beauty of the prisoner's voice and its soothing effect. Most of the other prisoners were in cells far removed from the Phantom's since the inspector had insisted on the prisoner's isolation. If any of them did hear the Phantom's song, they never complained even when he sang late at night or in the wee hours just before dawn. He supposed that the prisoner's voice affected them in much the same way it affected him.

The night watchman was surprised when the count arrived unannounced with a companion. He had never meant to allow this to get out of hand. After the night of the wedding ceremony, he had vowed that he wouldn't risk his position any further. But the count had insisted. He was willing to pay, not that the night watchman had expected to make money from the prisoner's misfortune. Yet to be honest, the money was welcomed. His salary was not generous, and he had mouths to feed, more than he could comfortably support on these wages alone. But he needed to be cautious. He couldn't afford to lose his position. Work was hard to come by. And what if the inspector decided he had broken the law and put *him* in jail? No, that would be more than Christian charity required of him, he was sure!

"He's not expecting you. I thought it was tomorrow you were coming!"

Raoul understood the guard's anxiety, and he couldn't afford to alienate him with rash carelessness now. He would still need his help in the near future. He placed the bag of coins in his hand, and pressed his arm in a gesture of reassuring friendship. "It has to be tonight. My friend will need about an hour or a little more. Can you manage?"

The guard looked at the count's companion, a young man, slight in build, completely covered with a long riding cape and hood. He had never seen this person in the count's company before.

Raoul could tell he was worried and hastened to add, "It's all right. We'll be very quiet. My friend will visit for as brief a time as you specify. I'll remain here to help you keep guard."

"What? You're not going in yourself? Just this young man?" This was even more curious than he had at first thought. Yet the count had this way about him. He certainly was an important man, a powerful man after all, but it was more than that. He told you everything would be all right, and damned if you didn't believe him! It was something about his face, such an open and matter-of-fact face; it gave you confidence.

The night watchman was surprised to see the count lead the young gentleman by the hand down the passageway.

They heard the Phantom singing before they reached the cell. Raoul had heard Erik sing only once, on the stage, in the performance of *Don Juan Triumphant*. He couldn't deny that he had a beautiful voice, an extraordinarily seductive voice. He shivered slightly at the memory of the effect the Phantom's voice had worked on Christine. The performance of the opera was supposed to be a trap, but it appeared that Christine had been the one to fall into the trap instead of the Phantom. Even from his place in the opera box overlooking the stage, Raoul had sensed the magnetism of his rival. It was dubious that Christine had simply acted the part of the young virgin seduced by the infamous Don Juan. Raoul's heart had been in his throat as he watched her give in to the Phantom's power.

The song the prisoner was singing abruptly stopped as they drew near the cell door. The guard's keys tinkled metallically as they swayed in his hand. Wordlessly, the night watchman unlocked the door, and the young gentleman entered. The guard could see that Erik was as puzzled as he had been and wondered again if this was such a good idea. But the count simply nodded his head meaningfully at Erik and urged the guard to follow him back along the way they had come.

Erik didn't move. Nor did the young man until the footsteps faded away in the distance. Only then did Meg remove the hood that had covered her features so completely. In that moment, Erik realized why Meg had come in disguise. The guard would never have left a woman alone in the cell with the prisoner. When Erik still remained aloof and failed to greet her with anything more than stony silence, a dark warm blush rose to her face.

Finally, he spoke, but the tone was curiously detached. "You shouldn't have come, Meg."

"I couldn't stay away."

"Call them back. Now." Dropping the indifference in his tone, he spoke gently, softly, but it was as if words and tone had no relation to one another.

She couldn't tell if he was angry or sad or anxious. He seemed somehow dejected. As unexpected as her arrival was, she believed he would be comforted, if not pleased, to see her. Disguising as much as she could her disappointment, she unfastened the cape and laid it on the cot. She wore a simple linen shirt and breeches.

She wouldn't kiss him, not until he asked to be kissed! Instead, she simply came to his side, letting the back of her hand barely touch the back of his as it rested quietly by his side. Unable to remain silent—the precious moments they were stealing were slipping unused from their hands—Meg addressed him in sweet defiance, embarrassed to make explicit the reason for this visit. "You're my husband, and we haven't had our wedding night."

Instead of the effect she hoped this would have on him, he drew away from her.

Biting her lip, fighting to keep the tears from her eyes, she turned to gather her disguise about her once again. "Very well. I'll call for the guard to say our time is up."

But as she started to go, the Phantom blocked her way. He seemed massive and dark; a strange kinetic force emerged from his stillness. She suddenly felt quite afraid of him, without knowing why.

"You come to make love with a monster? A monster who doesn't love you?"

He edged closer to her forcing her to step back into the depths of the cell. She couldn't take her eyes from his which had grown dark and sinister in the gloominess of the prison. The angry rictus of his mouth added to the hideousness of his deformed face. All of a sudden, she saw herself locked in a cage with a murderer, a man who professed he didn't love her. Was this Erik unmasked? Was her beloved a mere show of light and shadow, a phantom, an illusion that she had forced this crippled, twisted monster to embody? This was a stranger!

"I married you to give you something. To make amends for my past. To save you from being ruined. I owe Madeleine that much! You go too far; you ask too much of me. All of you! I've tried to be a man!" These last words rang out with desperation, and she glimpsed behind the menace yet again the man she loved.

"I don't care. All that may be true, but I know you love me. You can deny it, but I won't believe you."

"Love? Is that what you call this insistent, selfish drive to possess you, even now, here in this dank and merciless cell? This yearning of the body to have its pleasures? This need to join one flesh with another? At any cost? With no hope of future?"

"Erik ..."

"Don't call me that. A gargoyle, a demon, doesn't need a name! You're a stupid, foolish child who has been burned for playing with fire."

Their voices had reached the guard post, and the night watchman knew that he had been tricked into allowing yet again a woman into the prison. Raoul demanded that the guard remain at his post and let him go to the cell. He'd be sure to quiet them down.

"Erik, don't talk about yourself that way! And I'm not a child. I'm a woman who wants this moment, even if we have no future!"

"What will it take, Meg, for you to see, to really see?"

Neither spoke, but there was an ominous edge to the respite. Raoul stopped just outside the cell to listen to the curious silence. Ever so gently, Erik brushed Meg's cheek with the back of his hand. But the look in his eyes was cold as he softly spoke again, "I dreamt the other night of my wedding night. I dreamt."

"I've dreamt of our wedding night, too, Erik. Raoul and Christine have risked much to arrange this brief moment for us ..."

"Christine!" The one word fell from his lips as if it had been torn from his body.

"Oh, my God." She understood it in his look, in his tone, the way he said her name. She always knew it, of course. She wrapped her arms around herself refusing to give in to her grief, never once taking her eyes from his.

He had prayed that this moment wouldn't come. He wanted so much not to hurt her. And here she stood in torment because of him. Yet he knew he couldn't save her from this truth. Raoul, too, stood ambivalent, indecisive outside the cell door, out of their sight and waited, unable to back away.

"I love you in much the same way you love her. I can expect no more from you than you can expect from Christine." All the emotions seemed to drain from Meg. She draped the cape on the cot and sat, no longer looking at her bridegroom nor dreaming of wedding night kisses.

Erik was moved by her constancy in the face of his cruelty. Was it wrong? Was it cruel to love her if his love was less than complete, a love that existed in the shadow of his overwhelming obsession with Christine? If she truly loved him the way he loved Christine, then she must suffer terribly. He would be dead soon. Would it be so wrong to give in to his desire, to seek solace in her embrace, and to make love to her? If she wanted him, knowing that he loved another, was it wrong to go to her? Was it cruel to steal some comfort in these last days of his life? To lie in her arms, to take what she so wanted to give to him?

Silently, he came to her side. He wouldn't think. He would look at this beautiful, sad creature and not think. He would comfort her. He would let his arms fold her to his chest; their faces would draw near, and their breathing would find a harmony as if their two bodies were one. "Forgive me, Meg," he repeated over and over as his mouth pressed against hers. "Forgive me. Stay, if only for a little while." He whispered into her hair as they held each other, as they sought comfort in each other's arms, "My darling, my wife."

Raoul discreetly backed away to leave no witness to their sad consolation.

"It was lovely," Meg said shyly. "At first he was surprised and angry that I had come."

"Angry? But why?" Christine arranged some of the freshly cut spring flowers in the vase and continued trimming the stems of the others on the garden work table. The two women had agreed to meet in the morning in the greenhouse. Meg had returned in the middle of the night just a few hours before dawn and had gone directly to her room. All morning, Christine had waited anxiously to talk with Meg about the rendezvous she and Raoul had arranged. Raoul had come to bed, exhausted, and as Christine cross-examined him about the way the arrangements had gone, he had responded in short, clipped answers and pleaded with his wife to let him sleep. Raoul still slumbered when Meg came down to have breakfast in the sunroom. Christine had watched her friend for signs of how the tryst had gone. She had barely restrained herself while the servant served tea and toast. As Meg drained her cup, Christine pulled her from her chair and dragged her off to the greenhouse where they could be alone and talk.

"I don't understand. Why would Erik be angry?" she repeated when Meg did not answer.

"Oh, it's complicated. I think he was afraid to be happy." Meg looked away from Christine and fiddled with the leaves of an acacia plant. "But eventually he came round."

When she saw Christine's smile, she couldn't help but burst into giggles.

"Tell me," Christine whispered conspiratorially as she would do when they were children in the opera dormitories lying side by side in their beds.

"I can't."

"Why not? We're both old married ladies now," she teased.

"Then you tell me first! Tell me the last time you and Raoul … You know." Meg challenged.

"Oh, but that's not the same. We're just old married folks. You just spent your wedding night."

Without warning, Meg's face crumpled into tears. Christine was shamed by the absurdity of their adolescent banter. "Oh, Meg. I'm sorry. I'm so sorry. I just wanted you to forget the rest."

"My wedding night! Celebrated in a damp, cold dungeon, on a dirty mattress, with a man who will surely be condemned to hang!" An angry note crept into Meg's voice as she continued, "Of course, you would expect a story from me about the transformative power of love, wouldn't you? Let's see. This is the story you want: I arrived dressed like a boy, and Erik asked Raoul, 'Who is this young man? Why have you brought him to my cell?' And then I removed my cape, and he swept me up in his arms, and we made love again and again until Raoul came and from around the corner, for he didn't want to intrude on our privacy, he reminded us that I had to leave. But the time we spent together will fill our hearts for eternity, and not even death …" Meg broke off and sat down among the lilies to wait for the emotions to pass.

Christine was angry with herself. She had hoped this chance to be together would be comforting and joyful, but how could it be anything but bitter-sweet? Erik would eventually be taken to court to stand trial for the murder of many people, a crime whose guilt he could not escape. There was no verdict but a sentence of death awaiting him. He was locked away in prison, and Meg was desperately in love with him and had to wait out these final days knowing that it would only end in separation and death. Perhaps this indulgence made it even more painful.

Collecting herself little by little, Meg insisted on continuing, "No, Christine. My wedding night wasn't exactly what I had planned." There was a subtle change in mood as she remembered those last moments with Erik. "But we did make love. He was wonderful, so gentle and so caring. He took such pity on me."

"Pity?"

"You're surprised?" Confused, Christine heard an edge of anger again creep into Meg's voice. "Even now, Christine, you stand between us."

Christine was unprepared for Meg's attack and appalled that her secret fears were realized.

"His wedding night!" The sarcasm twisted Meg's features into a face Christine barely recognized. "He, too, had dreamed of it. He had dreamed of spending it with you, Christine! And he told me so. He told me to go away and said he didn't want me there."

Still Christine couldn't find any words. She wanted Meg to be quiet, but she was incapable of stopping her or walking out of the greenhouse to avoid hearing her.

"Oh, Christine. Why do you hold on to him so? Why can't you let him go?"

"I am … I don't hold on to him. I don't understand." But a voice inside Christine understood perfectly what Meg was saying.

"Can't you be honest at least with yourself? I know you love Raoul. And even though I know Erik does in some way love me, too, he will never let go of his obsession with you as long as you …"

"What? Say it! Explain what you mean!" Why she was insisting on hearing more, she couldn't say. Her heart was lodged in her throat, yet she was compelled to hear it spoken.

"As long as you feel something for him. He senses it, and he can't let go of a desperate, woeful hope that someday …"

"Don't be absurd! I've never given him any cause to … to think that I … I would return his love." Christine clutched the newly cut gardenias. The skin of her hands was slick with their moisture. White petals fell like snow about her feet.

"When he looks at you, he sees it in your eyes."

Christine turned pale. She feared for a moment that her heart had stopped beating. She felt stripped naked in the garden, and she wanted to flee from the room, but Meg stopped her and threw the words at her friend as if they were an accusation.

"We made love. He made love to me in spite of his love for you. He's mine. I love him, and you can't have him, Christine. You can't have them *both*."

Erik was dressing when Leroux came to the cell. As he buttoned the vest and straightened the starched collar, the inspector had the guard open the cell door. The barrister that Raoul had hired had explained calmly and kindly the process that was about to begin after these many long months in prison. As part of his counsel, the barrister had encouraged Erik to make a good entrance, as if he planned anything less.

"That won't be necessary." The inspector nodded to the two gendarmes that accompanied him. Evidently they had already been given their instructions. Erik did not resist as one unceremoniously ripped the buttons and pulled the vest from his shoulders. Next the officer unfastened the high white collar and wadded this, too, with the vest and threw them on the cot. The other officer lifted his hand to Erik's face to remove the mask, as well. Reflexively, Erik's hand darted up to stop the officer's hand. In spite of the fact that his fingers had been repeatedly broken in the first days of incarceration, he locked the officer's wrist in his grasp making the poor man cry out in pain to be released. Leroux struck the prisoner across the jaw with his billy club, and Erik staggered letting loose of the guard's hand. Before he could recover, Leroux himself grabbed the edge of the mask and pulled it free.

"You're a prisoner, a common criminal. How dare you act the grand lord with me! You don't even have a last name! An illegitimate spawn of some whore, you strut about with these counterfeit props pretending to be a gentleman." Erik knew better than to respond. He simply wiped the blood from the corner of his mouth with the back of his hand and stared straight ahead at the cell door. Beyond this door were the men who would escort him to the courthouse.

"You sicken me. You were born in the gutter. You lived in the sewers, and yet you put on these airs. It's time you faced the world as you truly are and let them see you, the so-called Phantom, as what you are. No ghost, no phantom, no supernatural creature, no genius, just a bloody, heartless murderer. I'll see you stand before the citizens of Paris and see you tremble in fear. I'll watch you dirty yourself at the end of the noose when we hang you in the public square."

Leroux said nothing Erik had not already imagined night after night in his dreams. He only hoped Leroux was wrong when he described him cowering before the mob. He intended to face the last days of his life with dignity. Each nightmare, each dreaded image of the trial and execution he allowed to play itself out unimpeded, uncensored, in an effort to steel himself against the inescapable events to come.

Leroux allowed him to wear the fresh shirt and breeches the barrister had left for his court date as well as a pair of simple slippers, nothing else. Unmasked, his lip already bruised and swollen, Erik faced the squad of men that surrounded him. His only desire was that the trial end swiftly.

In spite of the barrister's attempts to build a defense, Erik was uncooperative. He wanted no defense. He resolved to plead guilty. Let the prosecutor heap testimony and evidence on his head. Then it would be over. Then and only then would the mercy of execution bring this horror to its end. The sooner he was released from this body, the sooner he would be released from this life's sorrows. No more longings, no more false hope, just silence and darkness. He couldn't imagine more torment than the life he had already led. Surely not even a vengeful God could torment him more than all his fellow men had already done.

Not all the dreams or nightmares of a lifetime could have prepared him for the reception he met when the guards opened the side door to the courtroom exposing him to the galleries. After weeks of reading lurid, sensationalist reports and editorials in the popular press, the Parisian citizens had swarmed to the courthouse for the spectacle. They lined the surrounding balcony, filled the seats, and stood several rows deep behind the benches. Even now some recently arrived spectators elbowed and pushed their way into the mob to find some place from which to look down on the notorious Phantom of the Opera.

The crowd immediately shrieked and shouted when the unmasked Erik stepped through the doorway into the courtroom. Panic seized him before he could compose himself as he saw women faint, children hide their faces in their mothers' skirts, men screw up their faces in hate and revulsion. One voice, a shrill woman's, called out above the general din that the Phantom had stolen her baby away. Others emboldened by the anonymous accusation screamed out various crimes the Phantom had committed against them. "He raped my daughter. He beat me in the alley and stole my purse. He slit my father's throat under the bridge. He set fire to my home burning my wife and children alive in their beds." Erik involuntarily cringed at the wall of hate crashing in on him. Without thinking, he dug his heels into the floor in a vain attempt to resist being pushed forward into the amphitheater where he would be at the epicenter of such loathing. His gaze darted wildly, like the eyes of a trapped horse in a stable fire. Only when it lit on Meg did he manage to quell the rising panic and his impulse to struggle against his captors. Next to her Raoul looked disapprovingly at the crowds.

Making a gargantuan effort, Erik faced the vituperation of the mob, rose to his full height—a good head above most of his guards—and slowly walked forward to the box where the accused was to stand during the proceedings. He shook off the guards' hands and stepped inside the box opposite the bench, which the judge subsequently occupied.

His Honor took up the gavel and instructed the public to be silent and keep order. Something hard hit Erik on the side of his head, near his temple, a small stone thrown from the gallery above. Another projectile was flung but glanced harmlessly off the wooden railing that enclosed the prisoner. Outraged by the lack of decorum among the spectators, the judge threatened to clear the balcony if the crowd did not control itself. "This is not a circus," he angrily declared, to which an anonymous voice from the crowd replied, "Well, then what's that freak doing here?" The entire courtroom burst into malicious laughter until the judge struck the gavel so hard that it threatened to splinter.

Erik could see Raoul and Meg out of the corner of his eye. Meg brought her handkerchief to her face to hide that she was upset. Even Raoul seemed affected by the abuse the crowd heaped upon the Phantom and was puzzled that he had not worn the garments so carefully selected for his appearance before the judge. The count understood the popular association the common man made between ugliness and evil. The judge, who was supposed to be immune to such facile prejudices, did nothing to hide his revulsion as he examined the disfigured prisoner brought before him.

A trickle of blood ran down the side of Erik's face from the cut where the stone had struck. He stood as if oblivious to it. He turned to glance briefly at Raoul and Meg, and tried to be glad that Christine wasn't with them. It was better that she stay away. He trained his look on the judge. From that moment on, it was as if he had recovered his mask and again stood on the catwalks of the opera house. He raised his head as if in challenge and waited stoically for the farce to continue.

"M. Reyer, you were the lead conductor at the Opera Populaire during the time in question. Is that not so?"

"Yes. I was the principal conductor for two decades at the Opera House." M. Reyer was obviously proud of his artistic career, but nervous to be on the stand in the courthouse at the Phantom's trial. His nervous tick of bringing his handkerchief repeatedly to his mouth annoyed the prosecutor, who studiously avoided looking at him.

"M. Reyer, in your own words, tell us what you know of the Opera Ghost."

"M. Prosecutor, I know very little. I'm sure you could find others at the Opera House who knew much more than I." He laughed nervously from behind his handkerchief.

The judge admonished the witness. "Answer the prosecutor, M. Reyer, or you will be held in contempt of court."

"Your Honor, of course. Well, theater people tend to be superstitious. Each and any theater in Paris has its ghost or phantom, sometimes several. The Opera Populaire was no exception. But in the past ten years or so there were actual signs that ours might be more than the product of a fevered imagination."

"This ghost went on a killing spree, did he not, M. Reyer?"

"Actually, my first inklings that there was such a … thing … as the Opera Ghost was when he required M. Lefevre to pay him a salary. He also required that Box five remain at his disposal, but no one ever saw anyone occupy the box. On one occasion when the previous manager admitted a couple to the box, they were told by an unseen voice to get out. I've never seen a lord and lady move that quickly!"

There was laughter in the auditorium, but the judge swiftly raised his gavel silencing the throng.

"So he was obviously violent, dangerous. He held power even over the manager himself."

"Yes, rather. M. Lefevre realized that it was easier to pay the salary and respect his wishes. As long as he did so, nothing untoward happened. In point of fact, for years we worked together quite smoothly …"

The prosecutor interrupted the conductor and asked in spite of himself, "Worked together?"

"Quite right. He was a musical genius, there was no doubt of that. It started with minor compositions that simply appeared on my music stand, songs that were exquisite in their harmonies, their clever surprises, melodies that stayed in your mind well past their performance. Soon he was leaving entire operas for me. We staged several under an anonymous name." M. Reyer reddened as he realized that he had admitted to being the Phantom's artistic partner and promoter under oath in a court of law.

The prosecutor was beside himself with annoyance at the babbling of the old fairy whose evidence he had previously thought so ironclad and prejudicial to the Phantom's case. This nostalgic bit of drivel threatened to put the Opera Ghost in a very different light from the one he preferred to cast upon him. "M. Reyer, we are not concerned with the accused's musical talent. Can you please speak to the matter at hand? When did you realize that the Opera Ghost was not only real, but dangerous?"

"Dangerous? Well, he had certainly turned troublesome in the last three or four seasons. It seems our diva fell from his good graces; he felt she had persisted beyond her prime to dominate the stage and was impeding the advancement of other talents. Accidents began to happen. Scenery collapsing during rehearsal narrowly missing the diva. Costumes ripped to shreds moments before opening night. Hardly dangerous, but annoying to say the least."

Exasperated by the conductor's refusal to get to the point needed, the prosecutor demanded that he speak of the murder of Buquet and the disaster of the chandelier.

Erik had avoided looking directly at the witness through much of his declaration. Only when M. Reyer spoke of the musical compositions did he find himself drawn to look at the conductor. M. Reyer's opinion was one that he had esteemed. He recalled how delighted he had been when M. Reyer presented his first opera to the manager and suggested they perform it. Music had become his salvation. M. Reyer's recognition of his talent had inspired him to dedicate his life to the opera house and to music. Erik could tell that the conductor was uncomfortable and reluctant to testify against him. It touched him, but he held back his feelings. On this pillory, he couldn't afford to give in to his emotions.

"Did the Opera Ghost or did he not strangle Joseph Buquet and then mercilessly drop his body, hanging by the neck, from the overhanging catwalk to the stage below where he expired before a full house of appalled spectators?" Dramatically, the prosecutor declaimed the accusation, raising his arms high above his head as if the Phantom were among the public in the balconies and then bringing them crashing down toward the floor in an arc to suggest the imaginary fall of Buquet.

"Well, I imagine Buquet was already dead when he fell, but yes, I get your point."

Irritated that the conductor's remark might dampen the drama of his gestures, the prosecutor glared at the old man. M. Reyer ignored him, waiting for the next question.

"And the night of the disaster?"

"Well, we were playing his last opera, *Don Juan Triumphant*, which is actually a very unusual piece, quite daring in its discordant use of contrapuntal notes, not melodic at first but in a strange way always flirting with the edge between the musical and the non …"

"M. Reyer! We are *not* here to try whether or not there is any musical merit in the criminal's compositions! The court couldn't care less whether or not the Phantom can compose a good opera!"

M. Reyer was offended by the gross manner in which the prosecutor had addressed him.

"Will you continue? But I charge you to stick to the point."

"Very well! What was I saying? Oh, the night of the chandelier, we had all set a trap to catch him. We assumed he would be somewhere in the house observing his opera. As you know, we artists are somewhat self-absorbed by nature. Then again, we knew he would not miss a performance by his pupil." Again having feared he had said the wrong thing, the conductor stopped, drew his handkerchief to his mouth, and moaned.

"This pupil was at the time Mlle. Daaé. Is that correct?"

Reluctantly, the conductor nodded his head.

"Please answer audibly for all to hear, M. Reyer."

"Yes."

"The Phantom had an obsession with this young singer. Is that not the case? Go on, M. Reyer. Answer the question."

"Yes. Well, why not? She was a glorious talent. He had been grooming her for that spot for several years. Without his guidance and help, she would probably have remained nothing more than a chorus girl." Once again, he feared he had said something indiscreet. He looked apologetically toward the count whom he thought he might have offended.

"What did the Opera Ghost do that night?"

"Oh, everyone knows this already. Why should *I* have to say it!"

"Please, M. Reyer."

The judge warned the conductor that if he continued to avoid answering the prosecutor's questions in a direct and clear manner that he might be playing his future music in a jail cell.

"Yes, your Honor. I do apologize. I'm trying my best to answer completely and honestly the prosector's questions. Well, to get back to the opera. The Phantom surprised us all. He took the part of Don Juan and appeared on the stage. He had never done anything remotely as public as this before. He actually sang the part! I knew he was a genius, but such magnetism, such presence!

The whole auditorium was mesmerized by his masked appearance and his voice. He *was* Don Juan! It was uncanny. I still tremble—look at my hands—when I recall that voice."

The prosecutor began to object, but realized that it was no use to interrupt the imbecile. It was best to let him conclude one way or another.

"Anyway, he was singing with Christine, I mean with Mlle. Daaé." The conductor looked conspiratorially at the count who he expected would be pleased he had used Christine's maiden name to protect her current identity. "They were all searching everywhere in the building for the Phantom, except where he actually was. He was there, before all our eyes, on the stage! That's when she ripped his mask off so that the police and everyone would realize it was he! He may have seen this coming, as well. At any rate, he had a diversion, the chandelier, to cover his disappearance with the young lady."

"A diversion? You make it sound so harmless. What were the consequences of this *diversion* as you call it?"

"Well, most of us got out of the way as best we could. A few were trapped and unable to get out of the path of the chandelier."

"Eleven people were killed, were they not?"

"Yes, unfortunately. I don't know if he meant to ..."

"That is all, M. Reyer."

Several other witnesses, less favorably disposed toward Erik, testified against him. It was established beyond any reasonable doubt that Erik was the Opera Ghost, the so-called Phantom of the Opera, that he had murdered Joseph Buquet, and that he had detached the safety chains harnessed to the chandelier, cut the only cord sustaining it, and caused the deaths of eleven people in the audience that night. Erik was not paying attention to the series of faces he saw before him on the stand. In his head, he reviewed the notes of a possible composition, one that would sadly never be committed to paper, never be performed on any instrument but that of his mind.

He was tired. It was required that the accused remain standing in full view of all, but custom allowed the judge to temper this with mercy. Often the accused was permitted, after a brief time standing, to occupy the wooden chair in the cubicle. But the judge, in this case, had refused to give him the customary permission to sit.

Lunch interrupted the unending repetition of testimony. Only then was Erik escorted from the courtroom and permitted to sit while he ate a modest stew in an adjoining room. His barrister was the only person, other than his guards, that was present.

"Erik, I would like you to take the stand in your own defense. It's our only hope to move the judge so that the sentencing might be more lenient."

Erik brought the soup to his mouth, bit off a portion of the bread, and ignored the lawyer. He seemed not to have heard a word his barrister had been saying. "We could plead insanity. It might save you from the gallows. After all a life in a cage and then buried under the …"

With a smirk on his lips, Erik finally interrupted, "Save me from the gallows? Instead, I suppose, my sentence would be incarceration in the madhouse! I would rather they draw and quarter me in the public square. I would rather be burnt at the stake. I would even rather be subjected to another torture session with Leroux and then burnt at the stake than live one day in a madhouse. Under no circumstances will you plead for *that* 'mercy'!"

Once again in the courtroom, Erik felt his knees buckle and the blood rush from his head when he heard them call Mme. Giry to the stand. He hadn't seen her since well before her betrayal. He looked away, hoping he wouldn't have to see her as she drove the final nail into his coffin. Mme. Giry took her place beside the judge and was sworn in. The moment he heard her voice, he turned to look at her in a reflex he couldn't control.

She was small, oh so very small. She sat stiff, completely motionless; her face was held down as if she were looking for something in her lap she might have dropped. She desperately avoided meeting anyone's eyes, especially his. She seemed to have aged ten years, her face was gray, and her hair had lost its luster. She was so vulnerable that he felt in spite of himself the urge to run to her, to protect her.

The prosecutor circled around the desk as he directed his preliminary questions to the witness. She answered so softly at first that the judge had to instruct her to speak up and repeat her answer again so that the court could hear. Erik could see her hands tremble.

She doesn't want to be here, thought Erik. She's scared or she's filled with regret. Look at me, he urged mentally. Suddenly that was all he wanted. He needed to see her eyes and for her to see his. Then he would know. Then he would reach into her very soul and know. And he prayed that he would see there some hint of love, some desire for forgiveness from him, some recognition of the pain that she had caused him.

"Answer the question, Mme. Giry."

"Yes, I had served as the Opera Ghost's liaison to the outside world. I delivered notes; I collected his salary and deposited it for him. Later I would do his errands, the purchase of provisions once a month usually."

"Why did you bind yourself to this freak, this monster?"

Shocked by the phrase the prosecutor used, she looked up from her lap at him. In the next instant, her eyes met Erik's.

"He needed me," was all she could manage to say. Erik looked away for only a moment, trying hard to control his emotions. When he raised his eyes again to the witness stand, Madeleine was still looking at him, a terrible sadness in her eyes.

"When did you realize that he was insane? Out of control?"

Erik looked away. What could she say?

"M. Lefevre had always upheld the terms set by the Opera Ghost. It was when the new owners took charge and decided to disregard every aspect of the contract that we...."

"Dear, Mme. Giry, you speak of this 'contract' as if it had the binding force of law when in fact it was nothing more than the demands of a fiend! He threatened death and destruction to anyone who thwarted him, who refused to do as he said. Is that not the case? Have I stated it well?"

"No, Monsieur. The contract was modest, a reasonable negotiation, and M. Lefevre had profited greatly by it."

"Come now, Mme. Giry, you don't expect us to believe that ..."

"He would do things that caused annoyance, but nothing that hurt anyone until ..." Suddenly she realized that the pit she had tried hopelessly to skirt loomed ineluctably before her. There was no way that her testimony would save him now. Pained, she sought Erik's eyes.

"Until?"

" ... "

"Mme. Giry, must we remind you that you are under oath and must answer the questions I pose here today? You were about to tell us about M. Buquet, were you not?"

"Joseph Buquet spied on the chorus girls in their dressing room through a peephole he had carved in the walls. He had molested several young girls, mere children. No one could prove anything. The Opera Ghost was trying to protect them and himself."

"We are not here to try M. Buquet, who is unfortunately unable to defend himself against accusations since his neck was crushed in the fall from the flies of the Opera House. Now answer the state's question. Was this man before you," and here the prosecutor dramatically swiveled round and with out-stretched arm theatrically indicated Erik, "the one whom we know as the Opera Ghost and the Phantom of the Opera, and was it he who murdered Joseph Buquet and caused the deaths of eleven innocent souls during the final performance of the Opera Populaire?"

From his cubicle in the center of the floor, Erik could bear her distress no longer and shouted at the prosecutor, "Stop harassing her! Her testimony is unnecessary. I have already confessed that I am guilty of those deaths!"

In outrage and amazement, the crowd broke into a loud clamor. The judge banged his gavel repeatedly on the bench and indicated that the prisoner was to be restrained. "Order. Order. Or I will clear the courthouse! Restrain him. The prisoner will not speak!" The guards who had been by Erik's side had already laid hands on him to keep him from bolting from the box. One now took a cloth, wadded it, and drove it forcefully into Erik's mouth, and then tied another cloth around his head to keep the gag in place.

Mme. Giry broke into tears as she saw the guards silence Erik.

Once order was again established, the prosecutor repeated the question to Mme. Giry, who wracked by sobs, barely managed to reply. "Yes, he is the Opera Ghost, and his acts unfortunately led to the deaths of those people."

One after another, they had taken their turn accusing Erik of rape. In their modest new dresses bought by the prosecutor, it was hard to imagine that these women were prostitutes until they opened their mouths to give testimony. Then by their manner and speech it was clear that these were not the respectable young ladies that they were purporting to be. But in spite of their gross comportment and vulgar descriptions, the audience was willing to recast them as unfortunate virgins of the working class. They enjoyed the lurid stories of the Phantom's sexual incontinence. He had stalked these women, one after another, and forcefully dragged them under bridges, into sewers, and even to the ruins of the opera house itself where he raped them again and again before they managed to escape.

The rapt attention and obvious enjoyment of the mob reminded Raoul of the reaction of the audience the previous season to a theatrical rendition of the gothic novel, *The Monk*. So patently obvious was it to any sane individual that these women were lying that the Count de Chagny could not believe the judge would allow such a travesty to continue. Yet he did. In the interval in which the witnesses stepped down from the stand, the mob of spectators in the balcony gave vent to their bile and shouted down their insults to the prisoner.

The prosecutor, pleased with his case, announced that the state had concluded. It then fell to the prisoner's barrister to plead the case for the defense. The barrister rose in his place before the judge, adjusted his pince-nez on the bridge of his nose, and cleared his throat. The crowd gradually quieted down, curious to hear what he would say on behalf of a criminal so obviously guilty. Before addressing the court, the barrister looked back once more at Erik as if waiting for a sign. Receiving none, for Erik sustained his look with cold ferocity, he sighed and began. "Your Honor. I have a difficult task before me. Difficult because my hands are as tied and my mouth as gagged as that man's behind me who stands before you and accepts the most heinous displays of our society's disdain. Does he deserve this ... lack of Christian charity?" There rose a general murmur of outrage from the galleries at the obvious sarcasm of his remark. Erik leaned forward, wrists bound, and gripped the rail with white knuckled fury as he waited for the barrister to conclude.

Addressing the public, the barrister rebuked, "Do not fear, you will have your spectacle." Then throwing his hands up in the air as if to say he surrendered, he again addressed the judge. "My client refuses to allow me to present a defense, which is not to say, and I want this to be clearly understood by all here today in this courtroom, that there is no defense to be given. Quite the opposite, I assure you. He has pleaded guilty. In spite of that initial plea, he has been subjected to a steady stream of vitriolic haranguing from the prosecutor who has wasted a large sum of public moneys on mounting a public case which did not need to be made. The prisoner, I repeat, pleads guilty. Guilty to what? Well, one might just as well be sentenced to die for five counts as well as for two. Has he committed crimes, including murder? Yes, he has. He has never denied this fact. And he is prepared to suffer the state's judgment. But here today we have seen such a brazen miscarriage of justice that I am appalled to practice in this hallowed place the profession that I have always held in the highest esteem."

There was a general uproar in the courtroom. The judge banged his gavel as much at the barrister's remarks as at the angry display of the spectators. The prosecutor's objections were drowned out by the general melee of voices. "Does the defense rest?" demanded the judge after bringing the courtroom to order once more. He was growing weary of the whole circus.

"Unfortunately, we do, your Honor." And with that, the barrister lowered his head, removed his pince-nez, and let out an audible sigh.

"The prisoner is to be withdrawn. I will deliberate the verdict tonight, and we will reconvene tomorrow morning." All stood as the judge retired from the room.

The guards surrounded Erik and ushered him from the courtroom.

CHAPTER 14

The Sentence

When the grim Darkness overspread the Earth, then, with every horror of thought, I shook—shook as the quivering plumes upon the hearse. When Nature could endure wakefulness no longer, it was with a struggle that I consented to sleep—for I shuddered to reflect that, upon awaking, I might find myself the tenant of a grave. And when, finally, I sank into slumber, it was only to rush at once into a world of phantasms, above which, with vast, sable, overshadowing wing, hovered, predominant, the one sepulchral Idea.

"Premature Burial," Edgar Allan Poe

How much longer will he be able to hold up? wondered Raoul as he watched them escort the prisoner once more to the box. For that matter, how much more would Meg be able to stand? She sat beside him in the gallery on the main floor wringing her hands compulsively. She chewed on her lip making it bleed yet again. Even from this distance, Raoul could see the physical toll the trial had begun to take on the Phantom. Amazingly in spite of the loss of weight and his haggard expression, the prisoner was an imposing figure. Perhaps all those years creating and wearing his disguise, embodying the legend of the Phantom, had instilled in him this strength, this presence. It was as if he had created a role and that role had, in turn, created the man who stood before them all.

Raoul saw how affected Meg was when they brought Erik into the courtroom. He had tried to prepare her. She immediately noted the slight stiffness in his walk, the unnatural way he held himself, and the bruising along the left jaw that extended down his neck in a purple crescent.

"How could they, Raoul? How could they beat him even now? He can't defend himself."

"One of the officers said he went berserk when they left the courtroom after yesterday's final testimony. He attacked the guards in the squad, crashing into them like a wild man with all he had in him. Shackled as he was, he injured several of them before they managed to restrain him."

Meg didn't ask Raoul why Erik had done what he did. They had both seen him struggle to control his anger in court during the state's case, especially the false evidence brought against him.

The judge hadn't arrived yet. Raoul searched the crowd. Would she come? It was the one request Erik had made for this day, the day he was to be sentenced. How Erik knew the Mother Superior of the Convent of St. Isidore, Raoul couldn't guess. Yet when he asked for an interview with the nun and explained that it concerned Erik, she admitted him without hesitation to her office. She warned him that she'd have to beg special permission from the archdiocese to attend the trial. The order was, after all, cloistered. Only in extreme cases were any of them, including the Prioress herself, allowed exceptions.

All rose as the judge entered and took his place at the bench. All but the prisoner were allowed to take their seats to wait in great expectation for the verdict and sentencing. Raoul wondered at the suspense that filled the amphitheater, as if there were any doubt as to the outcome. Erik in subtle glances toward the crowds scanned their faces. At one such moment, he caught sight of Meg and Raoul and lingered for a moment on them. Not satisfied he continued searching. Raoul knew he was searching for the nun. Raoul was also anxious to find her among the crowd. He wouldn't forgive himself if he were unable to fulfill this one request Erik had made. Meg grabbed Raoul's hand as she sensed Erik's rising panic. And then suddenly Erik's gaze fixed on some object, and his breathing visibly calmed. They followed his gaze to the upper balcony where among the rabble stood a woman dressed entirely in white, the Mother Superior herself from the order of the Convent of St. Isidore. She seemed to glow among the drab colors surrounding her, and Raoul wondered that she had not been easier to spot. She held in her hands a black rosary with large beads, and her lips moved in constant prayer as she held Erik's gaze and smiled tenderly down upon him.

The judge struck his gavel several times even though the entire courthouse was silent in expectation. "The court has found the defendant guilty of twelve

counts of murder and three counts of malicious and violent sexual assault."
Meg broke down and cried into her handkerchief. Erik cringed as he witnessed
her distress. As the judge prepared to read the sentence, he again sought out
the comforting presence of his guardian angel, the prioress of the convent.
"The prisoner will be taken to a place of public execution and hanged by the
neck until dead. Sentence is to be carried out tomorrow at dawn. And may
God have mercy on his soul."

The crier dismissed the barristers and told the crowd to clear the court as
the officers seized Erik and dragged him from the box. Before Raoul could stop
her, Meg cried out across the courtroom for mercy. Erik, hearing her plea,
momentarily stumbled. Raoul silenced her by burying her face in his chest and
holding her tightly against him.

"Meg, don't. He can't be strong unless you're strong."

When they looked again toward the side door, Erik was gone.

The judge and deputies of the court filed out of the room taking no heed of
Meg's desperate tears. The barrister for the defense was the only court official
who lingered behind as he gathered his papers together. Meg tried to push
Raoul away. She hated him at that moment. She hated the fact that he could sit
there while Erik was taken from her. She hated that he was calm when her
whole world had come crashing in on her. She hated that he would be here the
day after tomorrow and the day after that while Erik would be lying cold in his
grave.

He let her push and strike at him until she wearied and simply cried. "Meg,
there's another way. You must believe me."

Tomorrow he would die.

He sat with the pen and ink and paper the guards had given him upon
request. He lifted the pen several times and held it poised over the paper to no
avail. He was vacant of words, bereft of language. To whom should he write? To
Meg? To Christine? To Mother Superior? It struck him that he preferred to
write to Madeleine. There was no comfort he could give to Meg or Christine.
Mother Superior didn't need his words; she understood what he was facing, his
fears.

He pushed the writing materials to the floor and lay on the cot. All he
wanted to do was sleep. Let it be over soon.

"Phantom. Did you ask for a priest?"

The guard who woke him from a shallow sleep was not the kind night watchman that had accompanied him for so much of this final journey. Erik was in the holding cell, the one in which those condemned to die the next day were kept for their last night. He sneered at the guard instead of answering him.

"Well, there's a priest and altar boy here to give you your last communion, I suppose. Didn't know monsters could be Catholics!" Laughing at his own joke, he gestured for the other guard to let the priest and altar boy come forward.

It occurred to Erik that Mother Superior might have asked a priest to visit him this last night before his execution. In this case, he would let the priest perform his rites. Although he felt he was beyond redemption, he wouldn't want her to be disappointed. If she thought he had some chance of salvation, he would respect her beliefs.

The guard opened the door and let the priest and young boy enter the cell. "When should I come back, Father?"

"I'll call out when we're done, my son."

Erik recognized Raoul's voice immediately! Only after the guard had left, locking the main door to the corridor behind him, did Raoul remove his hood and cloak. "I've brought your wife, Erik." Raoul took Meg's cloak and hood from her. There she stood dressed this time like a young altar boy.

"Why?" Erik was distressed and angry that Raoul had smuggled Meg into his cell.

"Erik. We have a plan to help you escape." Meg rushed to speak.

"It's useless." He did not address Meg, but spoke directly to Raoul. "You should not have come, and you should not have brought her. Call the guard. Tell him I refuse confession. It won't be difficult for him to believe. They all think I'm in league with the devil anyway."

"Wait. Meg is telling you the truth. We have a plan. You will escape tomorrow when everyone sees you die on the gallows."

The dawn's early rays filtered through the bars of the deathwatch cell where he was to pass his last night in this world. He could hear the approaching march of the execution squad.

He had slept but poorly. The harness chafed his skin. Raoul had himself fitted Erik with the protective brace, a heavily reinforced girdle that fit snugly under his arms, hidden under the coarse material of his shirt. It was meant to support his weight just enough to keep him from strangulation or worse during the hanging. The theater people had taught Raoul how it was to be worn and how it worked. The mechanism involved the harness and an attachment invisible to the spectator that linked the harness to the hangman's rope. Even as the noose encircled the neck, the invisible wire, attached to a spot on the rope itself inches above the noose, held the condemned's weight under his arms. Between the two—the noose and the safety wire—he would appear to hang but his weight would be shifted from his neck to the upper portion of his chest.

How many had been bribed to achieve this piece of thespian magic, this theatrical stunt? Certainly the technical assistants at the theater might have extorted some money for their cooperation and silence if they had realized why the count wanted use of the contraption. Then there was the hangman himself and the doctor who would pronounce Erik dead and make sure that his body was taken away before anyone else could examine it. Raoul was to claim his body as an act of charity. From there, it was only a matter of Raoul's own most trusted servants and transportation out of Paris, indeed, out of the country.

What if it all went wrong? What if the contraption failed? He would fall to his death. If he was fortunate, his neck would snap. He was a large man, surely his weight would suffice to wrench the various vertebrae asunder, and sever the spinal cord. He had heard stories of the days of the guillotine when severed heads rolled to the feet of the crowd and gazed up in shocked awareness, mouths gaping open and closed like beached fish drowning in air. Could death be that slow to know itself? And if his neck didn't break, his weight would pull the rope taut around his throat crushing his larynx and closing his windpipe. His face would turn red, then purple; he had seen this on Buquet's vile face. Fortunately, he would be saved the humiliation of crying out. No human sounds would escape that unforgiving embrace of the rope around his neck. The pain would be excruciating, the panic to breathe, the awareness of no escape. But it would not last forever. In the face of all this, would he be able to stand before all of Paris and let them put the noose around his throat?

What if Raoul had lied? Nonsense. To what end? Christine would never forgive him. But there were too many involved in the plan. Raoul had been foolish to attempt a rescue. He should have told Meg to insist that Raoul let events unfold as they ought. If anything happened, if Raoul were imprisoned for attempting to help him escape, Christine would be left without protection. That must not occur. What had he been thinking? To put this plan into effect was to jeopardize Christine's happiness.

The cell door opened, and Leroux entered to supervise the transfer to the gallows in the public square. Erik's hands were manacled behind his back, and he was led from the cell. The officers helped him step into the open cart and stood on either side to balance him as the driver spurred the horses on through the streets toward the place of execution. As they progressed toward his appointment with the hangman, Erik was paraded through neighborhoods that became more crowded as they approached the main plaza. The public exhibition of the condemned was a favorite treat, a spectacle of the just reward for evil, a morality play in earnest. Although the crowd heckled Erik, accosting him with insults and sneers and derisive laughter at his hideous face and imminent demise, no one dared pelt him with stones or garbage for fear of hitting one of the officers by mistake.

Erik felt his pulse race to a frenetic pitch as the gallows appeared, rising two or more stories above the crowds assembled in the square. The rope hung, a noose already fashioned for his neck. The fall itself would be brutal. He hoped the muscles and tendons in his arms and chest would not be torn from the bone. In the theater, many other supplementary supports would be disguised under the actor's costume to make the stunt as safe as falling out of bed. In this case, such precautions would have been impossible to disguise to those as near as the execution squad would be.

The officers pulled him down from the cart and escorted him to the stairs leading to the platform where the hooded executioner waited. All of a sudden Erik couldn't help himself; he laughed out loud as he saw this stranger masked with a burlap hood waiting for him, the Phantom, whose mask had been confiscated. The formerly masked phantom, unmasked and presented to the masked executioner, who nonetheless lived his life unmasked. What irony that he whose disfigurement cried out to be covered was to be hanged by this strange mirror image in a mask. Leroux, appalled, assumed that Erik had indeed finally lost his mind.

Erik laughed only briefly. Assuming a quiet, dignified stoicism, the condemned man took his first steps up the gallows. Midway he paused to look out toward the crowd. So many people, complete strangers, had amassed in the square to witness and celebrate his death. Surely his mother would not be out there somewhere reassuring herself that her abandonment had been justified. See what a monster her child was?!! But there was no reason for Erik to believe that his mother lived in Paris or even that she still lived. The fair had traveled far and wide, never stopping at the same town twice, it seemed to the young orphan. He didn't even know the name of the settlement where his mother had left him. As he scanned the crowds an odd face here and there struck him as familiar. Then he recognized the old nun, Mother Superior of the Convent of

St. Isidore. Yes, here was one kind face, one sympathetic heart who would cringe at his death and mourn his last agony. She already grieved for his end.

Someone barked for him to continue up the stairs. He delayed too long. Erik bowed his head slightly, just enough that the nun saw he had recognized her among the throng. In that gesture was a plea for her blessing. As if he knelt before her, Mother Superior made the sign of the cross over him.

The crowd suddenly hushed as the executioner roughly pushed the Phantom in place, directly over the trap door. Erik pretended to resist, and in the jostling the executioner made the final adjustments to the contraption, attaching the wire to the harness. Although Erik felt the executioner place the safety wire, all his former doubts and fears came upon him, and he feared he might pass out or cry out for mercy at this moment of truth. To control the trembling he felt imminent, he bit down hard enough to draw blood from his lip. He took several deep calming breaths to steady his nerves. Now the hangman placed a burlap sack over Erik's face. Under the fabric, Eric again laughed at the absurdity. What relief! Masked again!

Someone had been talking. The official crier read the various crimes, even those falsely attributed to him, and the sentence was pronounced yet again for the benefit of the gathered onlookers. As these last words drifted away over the heads of the mob, all became oddly silent. Then Erik heard the mechanism release the trapdoor just before the world disappeared under his feet, and he fell into blackness.

CHAPTER 15

The Phoenix

Something had gone wrong, wrong, terribly wrong. He was wrapped in darkness, surrounded by the smell of his own body. He couldn't move. His arms lay by his side, and then he became aware of a tremendous pain like belts being pulled tightly around his chest and neck. Was he dead? How could he feel his chest and his arms if his neck had broken? A thud. Something had made a hollow wooden sound. Wood. He was surrounded by it. He was in a box, a coffin, and they were burying him. He had died, and this was death! He was aware and felt pain, and they would bury him because he had died!

It took him some effort to calm down and listen. Nothing. Somehow he thought he was still above ground. Then he understood why. He was able to make out the ridges in the wood of the coffin. Some minimal light found its way inside, and his eyes were beginning to adjust to it.

He had to alert someone that he was alive! He pushed up against the wooden lid, but it was nailed down. But he didn't dare cry out. They would take him back to the gallows, and the whole nightmare would be repeated! He couldn't decide which was more terrifying to him.

Erik heard the gravediggers approach with horror. They were complaining that it was nearly sunset, and they still had this grave and another to fill in before they could go off to their families.

Erik stifled his impulse to scream as they dropped shovelful after shovelful of dirt and gravel onto the lid of the coffin. Raoul would come, he told himself.

The gravediggers joked about the price of good kindling and the waste of it on the dead. The sounds of falling dirt on the lid of his coffin gradually became distant and muffled. Dirt trickled in between the imperfectly fit slats, and he swallowed gritty saliva in rising terror. How long would it take to be buried and for them to leave? How long would it take Raoul to find him? How long could he hold out before he suffocated or went mad? What if Raoul never came or came too late?

"Pierre, Roger, hurry! You two dig there. Put your backs into it, for pity's sake. We might yet save him!"

In the glow of the lamp, they worked at the grave. Meg and Christine stood nearby in spite of Raoul's orders that they remain on the road by the carriage. Raoul was still angry that Christine had insisted on coming with them in spite of the child they were expecting. She was in no condition to be here. And it was impossible to keep Meg away. If not for the fact that there was no room for her, she would be clawing the dirt away with her own hands. How would he deal with both of them if they were too late? He worried that neither woman would hold up if they found the unfortunate devil dead, suffocated in his coffin! God, let him be still alive! The only way to end this nightmare was to smuggle him out of the country to freedom. Hopefully, then, this madness would end!

They had dug several feet down when Raoul stopped his valet and driver and bent to listen. An ominous silence was all that met him. "Quick!" He could not give up hope, even though he worried that too much time had already passed to find Erik alive. He knew that Christine and Meg wouldn't rest until they either found him alive or saw him dead in the coffin with their own eyes.

The spade struck a muffled blow against wood. Now Raoul and Roger cleared the loose rubble from the lid and pried it open with the edge of the shovel. The boards cracked in ragged shards, and the lid came free. It was pitch black inside, and there was no sign of movement. He dreaded they had come too late.

"Bring the lamp closer!"

As the light fell across the body, Meg screamed.

"Wait! Wait!" Raoul bent down to Erik's chest and listened. "My God, he's breathing! Help me lift him."

The men hoisted the unconscious man to the edge of the grave. Christine was the first to kneel at Erik's side. Raoul restrained his disapproval as she ran her hands over his neck and chest in what appeared to be an effort to stimulate his breathing. Her touch was so direct, so familiar, almost intimate, that Raoul felt the return of long suppressed pangs of jealousy. Meg had come to Erik's side as well and pressed her face close to his and whispered words too soft for any but him to hear.

"We can't stay here. If he doesn't revive soon, we'll have to carry him to the carriage." His servants nodded in agreement with their master.

Meg saw Erik's eyes flutter and heard a low moan rise in his throat. He was coming to. As he stirred, Christine withdrew, leaving Meg alone with him.

"My love, thank goodness. Things didn't go exactly as planned. But you're safe now."

Erik raised his hand to her face wincing at the soreness under his arms and around his chest where the harness had borne the weight of his fall. "I thought I'd be trapped for eternity in that grave."

"Quick. We need to move on. We need to be at the border by dawn." The men helped Erik rise from his gravesite. Securing him under his arms, in spite of the pain, they managed to rush him to the carriage.

Meg held him braced against her side. All the tension and terror of the last several days melted away as he surrendered to her caring touch. He drifted in and out of consciousness; he had never felt so exhausted.

The moonlight that filtered through the window into the carriage fell across Christine's face. She sat across from him, beside Raoul, and her smile comforted him.

there they sleep, my partners in crime, it's nearly dawn and I've slept fitfully through the night under their protection, I start and wake dreaming I'm buried under miles and miles of dirt, my throat constricts and I can't breathe, mercifully I wake to see Meg still holds me, so small she is by my side and yet clasped in her arms lying against her breast I'm comforted and go back to sleep, now I watch them as they slumber, the carriage sways and rocks us in its womb, Christine sits before me and I want to drink in her face, consume her, to fill myself with her, as I look at her, her lips are parted and sleep smoothes out her face as if she were that child again that I watched and pitied so desperately in the dormitories, I remember that child, it awes me to see that child's face in this woman's, and it fills me with the need to protect her, she reclines ever so gently against Raoul, he sits straight, his head lolls to one side, this the only sign that he, too, sleeps, her hand lies soft and generous in his upturned palm, two lovers, and this simple gesture, this quiet tableaux convinces me more than words ever could that I have lost her, she stirs slightly and nudges closer to him and that's when I notice that she's with child, I've never imagined her thus, but here she is before me, heavy with life, cradling the future she will share with him ... this should make it easier now to imag-

ine my life with Meg, to ask for one last kiss when we stop, when we are about to part, and join my fate to Meg's ... when we go, I will carry this stamp of my beloved always at the back of my eye, an amulet to soothe my soul, to heal my wounds

As the driver pulled into the village, they awoke.

Erik drew his hand to his face to cover himself before Raoul and Christine could look at him. He had no mask. In the early light of morning, they had arrived at a small village on the border. Although the streets were mostly deserted except for one or another man on his way to work—milk and fresh bread deliveries were being made from door to door—it was impossible for Erik to descend from the carriage and walk among these people without some means of hiding his face.

Raoul left the carriage and walked to the stables to make arrangements for the next leg of the journey. Meg stirred by Erik's side and seeing his hand raised to conceal his face, she rummaged around the folds of her skirt until she found her bag. There within she had placed a simple mask that Erik could use as they traveled. Relieved and grateful, he took the mask she offered him. It was simple, featureless, and dark, but at that moment it was to him the most precious possession in the world. Turning from both Meg and Christine, Erik fixed the mask over his face.

Several townspeople stared curiously at the strangers, especially the one who wore a mask, as they entered the inn and asked for some refreshment. The matron was so nervous as she served them tea, darting her eyes back and forth from the masked stranger to his companions, that she spilled the hot liquid on the table. Meg reassured her, dabbing at the water with a napkin.

"I know you mean no harm, but you're staring at my husband. He was badly burned in a fire. He's more comfortable wearing a mask so as not to startle anyone with the scars."

Meg's explanation served to put the matron at ease. "I had a cousin once who was scarred from here to here," she said indicating with her thumb a line that went from the corner of her eye to the corner of her mouth. "Used to scare the young ones who didn't know him well. He'd have liked a mask like that, sir. Sorry to have stared. Your breakfast will be ready soon." She was a kind woman and regretted that such a handsome gentleman should have suffered such a cruel accident and been left disfigured. She returned the kettle to the spit by the fire and went to the kitchen to hurry the cook.

Erik was touched by Meg's invention. It was a role he thought he might be able to play to advantage. The other guests in the inn, having overheard Meg's explanation, returned to their meals. Even so, they couldn't refrain from staring from time to time in Erik's direction, but it was less frequently than before. He wondered if he would be able to disregard strangers' curious stares, their morbid desire to see behind his mask, their cautious revulsion. Had he left one prison only to wall himself up in another in some rural part of the countryside? He worried that such a life would be a prison sentence for Meg as well.

After breakfast, Raoul explained the arrangements he had negotiated with the new driver. This is where their two paths would part. Raoul and Christine would return to Paris. Meg and Erik were to continue on to Italy. Meg and Christine embraced each other in tears and promised to write while the two men eyed each other awkwardly.

Raoul was the first to hold out his hand to Erik. "I wish the two of you luck in your new life."

Hesitant for only a moment, Erik accepted his rival's hand and clasped it. He sensed Raoul's ambivalence. Once upon a time, Raoul had led the search to rid the world of the Opera Ghost. The same man had now risked everything to save that same monster from a just execution. But Erik wasn't fooled into believing that they were now friends. He understood the reasons Raoul had acted to save him from the hangman's noose. It was perhaps Christine's last kindness to her "teacher." Erik wondered what she might have vowed to her husband to exact this momentary alliance between enemies.

"You worry that you've helped a murderer, perhaps even a madman, escape punishment. Or worse, that you allow Christine's Phantom to continue to haunt you both. I know you've done this against your better judgment because Christine wanted you to. When you doubt that you've done well in this matter, you must consider how my execution might have affected her. I say this with no ill meaning, believe me." Then as an afterthought, he addressed Raoul yet again. "I would ask one more favor. I know that you've already granted me several and perhaps think me unworthy even of those, but I do ask one more. Seek out Madeleine, Mme. Giry." Erik seemed suddenly less confident, more tentative than before. "Tell her that her daughter and I are married. She will certainly receive this news badly, but it would be a tremendous favor to my wife and to me if you could commend me to her. At least you might refrain from speaking against me. Tell her that on my part all is forgiven and that she is welcome to come live with us if ever she would wish to do so."

"I shall, most gladly."

Erik bowed his head just slightly at the count in reluctant gratitude and started toward the carriage where Meg was waiting.

As he helped her into the carriage, he looked back over his shoulder toward Christine. They had not yet said their farewells. Meg took his hand in hers, forcing him to look up at her. He quickly looked away and stepped back from the carriage.

He had hoped to avoid this moment, unsure of himself still, unsure of what he was capable of doing. His pupil, his angel of music, his Christine waited for him to come to her. Raoul walked a way up the road to give them a moment alone. She stood in the middle of the path, waiting for him, a smile lightly gracing her lips. Why does she smile? he wondered. Is she happy to see me go? Erik went to her, suddenly drawn irresistibly to her side as before.

"Mme. De Chagny." Erik took Christine's hand and drew her closer to him. All the resolve he had mustered to release Christine, to quell his desire for her, to commit himself body and soul to Meg, crumbled and fell away the moment he touched her hand and looked into her eyes. He knew that it was all for nought. He could never leave Paris, leave Christine. "Christine, must it be?"

Christine's smile was replaced by a worried frown. His hand tightened on hers. She was so near him that she felt his breath warm and moist on her face. For an instant, she softened and leaned in toward him mesmerized by his presence, the power that he would always have over her. His voice wrapped around her, as it had when they lived in the opera house, like the folds of a warm blanket; his eyes bore into hers, two candles lit against the darkness that threatened to consume her. Suddenly, she was aware he had been talking and only then caught his last words.

"Can you truly say that I am to go?" There was a plea hidden in his gruff demand. There was also a dark intensity that frightened her, for she understood that if she were to give him any hope that she could love him, he would take her, he would kill Raoul, and he would drag her back to the bowels of the opera house where he would, most certainly, be hunted down and killed. And even though she was frightened, there was a part of her that wanted to cry for him to take her away from all the world. She must control that part of herself! Part of her wanted desperately to lie in his arms, to sink into the darkness and live in the music with him. And as long as he sensed this desire of hers, he would never be free!

"What? Would you have me tell you to stay?" She must be firm, but kind.

Yes, she saw his eyes confirm her understanding. He wanted her to ask him to stay by her side even though this would certainly mean his death.

"No, Erik. I want you to live. You must live."

"For what must I live? Do you want me to live in hope that …? Is there any hope that …?"

She could feel him struggle to find the words, words that frightened her for she understood what he wished to say.

"Christine, you must tell me. I don't know what to do." Such sadness lay behind those eyes!

She must be cruel to be kind. "You already know, Erik. You've always known since that first day Raoul and I found each other. I love him."

Meg had accused her of enslaving this poor man, and she saw that her friend had been correct to accuse her. She had loved him, even when she knew he had killed, even when she knew his obsession was leading to his own destruction, even when he risked her happiness with Raoul. She had thought Raoul unjustly jealous of the Phantom, and herself misunderstood. She had always loved her Angel, but love could slice the heart, blind the eye, and cripple the soul if it was a love that was always just out of reach. Erik—this powerful, dangerous man—presented himself before her as her most vulnerable victim. As long as he thought she loved him, he would be incapable of relinquishing her, and he would never be able to give his heart to Meg.

"I love Raoul," she repeated. And even though it was true, it was as if she had to rip it from her breast, so reluctant was she to watch that light of passion and desire that burned in Erik's eyes fade. "I love Raoul with all my soul, and I wish to end my days only with him."

The stillness of his body was betrayed by the faintest tremble of his lip as he asked, "You swear to me? Swear to me as angel or demon or monster that will haunt you forever if you lie! Swear it! You will be happy? You will love him and be happy in that love and not regret that you sent your … that you sent me away?" His eyes turned dark and ferocious in the intensity of his request.

He had drawn her so close to him that Raoul, even at a distance from them, became alarmed and had stopped to watch them.

"I swear!"

His eyes narrowed in an indecipherable expression. Was it belief, dejection, pain, incredulity, or anger that assailed him? Christine wasn't sure.

He released her hand abruptly and turned to go when she called him back.

"Wait! Before you go, may I see my friend's, my angel's face once more?"

She saw his hesitation, his resistance. She almost regretted asking it of him. Slowly he edged close to her. In his eyes, she saw a glint of fear.

Reluctantly, never looking away from her, he pushed the mask up and away from his face. He burned with the discomfort of having her look upon his ugliness as she had done in the opera house that night she unmasked him in betrayal. But he saw no loathing, no revulsion on her face.

He was much taller than she, so she had to stand on tiptoe and gently pull his face down toward her to reach his lips. There she placed a chaste kiss. Still holding him close, she whispered, "I'll never forget your kindness to me or what you have taught me."

He didn't answer her, didn't dare respond, but he placed his hand gently on the cradle of her unborn child as if imparting a final blessing. Then quickly he lowered his mask and turned away. He walked purposefully toward the awaiting carriage and stopped by the door. Meg leaned forward. There were tears in her eyes, too, and Erik choked back his own and told her they were ready to go.

Behind him, Erik could hear Raoul giving the last instructions to the driver, and the horses set off at an easy canter. The carriage wheels clacked away at the stones carrying Raoul and Christine back along the road toward Paris. Soon they would be gone.

Meg reached out to Erik before he could turn away. "Are you …?"

He didn't let her finish. Instead he reached inside the carriage and placed his hand tenderly behind her neck drawing her close to his face. He placed his lips softly, yet passionately, on hers. Hardly had he withdrawn his lips from hers than he whispered, "Forgive me, Meg. Forgive me for wanting …"

"Ssshhh. You're here. I'm here." She raised her handkerchief and wiped the lone tear that had escaped his mask.

He cleared his throat and bit his lip until he knew he could control his voice again. "I want to ride above with the driver for a while. We've several days travel before we get home." He pressed her hand quickly to his lips, released it, mounted the coach next to the driver, and took the reins in his own hands. Without a backward glance, he spurred the horses down the road as fast as they would go, away from his beloved Christine.

978-0-595-42966-0
0-595-42966-1